Steam on the Horizon

Book One of the Aether Saga

by

Melissa Ann Conroy

STEAM ON THE HORIZON

Cover art and book design by Brent Schreiber

www.brentschreiber.com

SteamyGirl Publishing

11261 Martin Ave.

Omaha, NE 68164

ISBN 978-0989504317

Printed in the United States of America

Acknowledgments

I dedicate this book to my wonderful oldest brother Seth Conroy who has whole-heartedly supported me every step of the way and has provided a multitude of plot twists, research ideas, and insight. As my current roommate, he has seen every element and stage of this book, and I could not ask for a better companion on this writing journey.

Matt Manning has been an expert source on everything from boiler explosions to 19th century firearms, and his keen insight and enthusiasm for this project has turned it into a far better piece of writing than I could accomplish on my own.

Charles and Kristine Shumway have been an unending fount of ideas, inspiration, and support, and they deserve medals for their boundless generosity.

My father Martin has continued to be an encyclopedia of engineering wisdom, expounding upon such topics as fluid bed boilers, wet-bulb temperature measurements, and other scientific knowledge that an MA in English literature failed to bestow upon me. My mother Marsha is both my greatest cheerleader and my best friend, and she has been a staunch support in all my writing endeavors. Thanks goes to Nathan and Sean, my two other brothers, for their love and support.

Special thanks goes to the members of the Steampunk Society of Nebraska and the Gaslamp Society of Eastern Nebraska for their support.

I extend a particularly warm thanks to a group of wonderful individuals who contributed to my Indiegogo fundraiser during August 2012 which allowed me a six-month absence from the workforce to write the bulk of this book. I heartily thank Mark Arnold, Joe and Miriam B., Jason Burns, Heather Carouth, Barret Dent, Dustin Fickle, Theresa Frankovsky, Molly Ketchum, Scot Klinger, Gary Lange, John LeVan, Matt Manning, Luna Meschiari, Merinda Peterson, Daniel Moreau, Stephen Ormsby, Adam Reiff, Kenneth Robertson, Jenna Tomlin, Thomas Werner, and Dave West for believing in me and providing the funds to follow this wild hare of mine.

Steam on the Horizon

Chapter One

The airship *Lucky Lady* bobbed and swayed in the light breeze, tugging at her mooring lines like a rebellious horse pulling against its halter. From his position on the wharf, first mate Gavin Roberts critically eyed the airship's bloated envelope as he approached the vessel. Tight as a woman's corset, the envelope was straining to contain cubic yards of agitated steam that threatened to split the overstretched airbags as the boiler continued to channel more steam into the overburdened canopy.

It was an early May afternoon in 1854, and the crowded airship wharf was filled with vessels either snugly strapped down in canvas-cushioned berths or firmly tethered on ropes in preparation for takeoff, but they were all sedate and restrained in comparison to the *Lucky Lady's* erratic dance across the sky. She was hissing in impatience, and Roberts' feet quickened, carrying his broad-shouldered frame through the press of crowds roving up and down the length of the chaotic wharf.

Silverman's ignoring the pressure gauge again, Roberts thought darkly as he irritably shoved his way past an airman overloaded with gunnysacks. The airman staggered to the side, barely avoiding a collision as Roberts plowed through the crowd with nary a glance at those surrounding him. *I'm gone a half-hour and it all goes to blazes,* he groused, his gray-green eyes fastened intently on the *Lucky Lady* as he worriedly examined her for any sign of an imminent catastrophe threatening to break loose.

Cursed ship. They all said it about the *Lucky Lady,* too many burst valves and men falling overboard to their deaths to encourage an onslaught of eager volunteers every time there was an opening on the airship's manifest. Her jovial name belied her dark horse reputation, and there were few airmen crowding the massive airship wharf who would welcome a chance to serve on board the *Lucky Lady,* especially not with the idiotic Captain Albert Smothers at the helm.

Roberts knew better; while the *Lucky Lady* was a fussy little bird, apt to sulk or threaten a crash if mishandled, she was as light as a cloud and admirably fast, capable of racing a scant twenty hours from London to Edinburgh on a good run if she had the right crew to baby her. However, Captain Albert was not the type of man to get the most out of an airship like the *Lucky Lady* or any airship, truth be told. When he wasn't boozing it up in his quarters, the captain was apt to be barking out orders that changed by the hour or arguing with the engineers or routinely leaning over the edge of the airship spewing his guts due to chronic airsickness combined with too much alcohol.

It was Roberts who ran the show, had to, otherwise the *Lucky Lady* would be lucky enough to simply get off the ground, much less stay airborne. Their current run was yet another example of Captain Albert's magnificent incompetence: he had demanded a pointless change of course halfway through their flight to London that had added an additional hundred miles to the trek and drained their coal hoppers nearly empty, and he wouldn't keep them at the wharf long enough to refuel. Eying the *Lucky Lady*, Roberts hoped fervently that they had enough fuel to make it to the next coal station and muttered a few curses under his breath. He had been flying under Captain Albert's unskilled leadership (if it could be called that) for nigh on two years now, and it took skillful tact on Roberts' part to mitigate the worse of his captain's decisions and keep crew and airship alive and afloat.

Now, worriedly observing the *Lucky Lady*'s bloated envelope straining to the bursting point, Roberts knew that his brief absence had been long enough for imminent chaos to threaten. With luck, nothing irredeemable had happened and once back on board, he could enact some tactful damage control and get the ship back in the air where she belonged. However, if an airbag or two decided to burst, as they were clearly threatening to do, the *Lucky Lady* was stuck at port for the foreseeable future.

Preoccupied with these thoughts, Roberts stalked forward, mind growling irritably and eyes intent on the bobbing bulk of the *Lucky Lady* dancing impatiently in the stiff wind. Here, further down on the wharf, there was less traffic and fewer barriers to impede his feet except a huge stack of crates piled high in the middle of his path. The boxes were being negligently supervised by a small knot of Chinese dock workers, the tonal chops of Cantonese rising in the air and mixing with the clanging of gears and hisses of steam that enveloped the wharf. Despite his grumbling worries over the *Lucky Lady,* Roberts had to smile thinly to himself as he caught wind of the men's conversation: he knew enough of their tongue to surmise that they were talking about women, as men were wont to do after too many weeks crammed inside an airship with nothing but other men for company.

Roberts' smile was fleeting as he stepped irritably around the traffic jam of crates, impatient to get back on board and discover just how much chaos had been unleashed in his brief absence. Mind thus preoccupied, he was taken completely off guard when an enormous explosion rocked the wharf, shock waves reverberating along the wooden beams as something exceedingly powerful slammed into the heavily-reinforced structure like a battering ram. Knocked off balance, Roberts fell to his knees behind the stack of crates, then rolled out of the way as a crate on top teetered for a moment, then fell to the deck with a crash, spilling open and sending a battalion of paper-wrapped opium logs careening across the planks.

A scream of Cantonese and one of the Chinese dock workers slid helplessly toward the edge of the wharf, slithering down the length of a floor plank that had knocked loose and was acting as a chute to tip the unfortunate man toward the ground two hundred feet below. With a growl, Roberts shot forward on his hands and knees and grabbed the man's ankle, halting the fall as the worker dangled upside down from the lip of the wharf, his thin arms flailing pitifully as terror shook his small frame. But Roberts had a firm grip on the man's bony ankle and pulled him to safety with one swift jerk of his arm before clambering to his feet with a heart-thumping suspicion of what had just happened.

He wasn't mistaken. Rounding the edge of the tower of boxes (which was now a disorganized jumble), Roberts froze at the catastrophe spreading before him. It was worse than he had anticipated, much worse. The *Lucky Lady* was wreathed in angry smoke, a gigantic hole gouged out of her starboard side hull and her engines shrieking in alarm as the airship sagged on her mooring lines, her envelope already deflating before Roberts' eyes. The once taut stretch of canvas was now rapidly collapsing from a sizable hole in the envelope which was loosing steam in angry waves of white: a piece of shrapnel from the explosion must have torn though the envelope and punctured several of the airbags inside. With a jagged wound in her envelope and her airbags rapidly deflating, the *Lucky Lady* was already starting to sink on her mooring lines, floundering helplessly in the sky.

On Captain Albert's orders, they hadn't properly docked the airship, hadn't carefully set her down on an empty berth where she could have rested against the canvas-cushioned supporting beams and waited safely for Roberts' return. The captain had insisted that the crew simply tie the *Lucky Lady* off at the wharf and let her bob in the wind. Now, with nothing underneath her but empty air and her deflating airbags struggling to keep her aloft, the injured airship was tilting backwards, her aft sagging toward the ground as her bowsprit edged upwards into the sun in a ferocious squeal of overheated engines.

Boiler explosion, Roberts thought furiously. *I'll kill that damned Silverman.* Already the wharf alarm was blaring as soldiers and ship workers poured across the deck, racing for the wounded airship, and Roberts' feet joined them at full speed. It was only a few moments before he ran out of walkway and halted at the edge of the wharf, but in that brief gap of time, the *Lucky Lady* had sunk several feet and her main deck was now a good five feet below the wharf. Roberts' feet did the thinking for him and with one heart-stopping leap, he jumped from the wharf and landed on the *Lucky Lady*'s slanted main deck, her forecastle now several feet higher than her poop deck as the airship's rear continued to sag downwards. The explosion had knocked loose random equipment and cargo, and heavy objects were sliding down the angled decks and filling the aft with weight, dragging the airship's back end toward the waiting ground below.

On board the *Lucky Lady,* men were staggering up and down, barking out orders or scattershot bits of information, and Robert's eyes quickly swept the crowd as his feet hit the deck. No sign of the captain, but Roberts wasn't too particularly concerned about that, his attention diverting to Matthew Carter, the bosun, who was staggering across the tilted deck toward him, blood pouring freely from a head wound.

“Sir!” Carter gasped out. “Boiler blew all the...”

“I know!” Roberts bellowed back. The *Lucky Lady* was clearly too injured to keep afloat, and she was doomed for a crash landing if assistance wasn't quickly forthcoming. However, snatching several tons of falling airship out of the sky was a nearly impossible feat, and a lightning-fast assessment of the situation told Roberts that evacuation was the only real option.

"Prepare to abandon ship!" he bellowed into the chaotic air. Crew members began stumbling forward to obey orders, fighting against injury, panic, and the steeply tilted decks of the *Lucky Lady*. As Roberts roared his way towards the men to get them off the sinking airship, the groaning squeal of a crane filled the air, mixing with the screams of the *Lucky Lady*'s engines overheating in their desperate plight to keep the ship from plunging to the ground.

Already the airship had reached the end of her mooring lines, and the thick ropes were wire-taut, creaking with stress. After a minute of valiant effort, one broke under the relentless pressure, the rope snapping with vicious force. The airship jerked in recoil, sending her nose toward the ground as the deck pivoted: loose gear, baggage, and men now sliding toward the bow forward.

A few seconds later, another mooring line broke under the relentless tension, jarring the airship again and starting a nasty seesaw motion as the *Lucky Lady* continued her uncontrolled descent, the ground below looming up to embrace her in its unyielding arms. However, a crane jib was now swinging directly overhead the *Lucky Lady's* rapidly deflating envelope, its thick tow chains dangling around the gondola and Roberts saw one desperate chance to save the floundering airship and the men on board. He knew his odds of evacuating the crew were poor at best: there were now only two intact mooring lines holding the *Lucky Lady* to the wharf and no means of getting off her safely. They were all dead unless luck and desperate action came swiftly to Roberts' aid.

Filling his lungs with air, he roared out, "BELAY THAT ORDER! ALL HANDS TO THE TOP DECK!" his sonorous bellow cutting through the riotous clamor of shouts and metal clashing against metal. The crane squealed as it swung a little closer, the dangling tow chains several feet from Roberts' outstretched arms. By great good luck, there was a long-handled hook by his left boot, and he used it to snag the tow chain and jerk it toward him. The chain was split into two separate lines, one for each mooring ring, and each line ended in a heavy clasp. The clasps were thick with rust, and the chain lines seemed deliberately insubordinate in Roberts' quick fingers as he fought to fasten the clasps on both mooring rings. Time raced past in gigantic gulps, each millisecond precious, until the port side mooring rings were chained and Roberts was racing for starboard.

Reaching the other side of the airship, he nearly crashed into Oboe, the second mate, who had managed to snag the other tow chain just as Roberts reached his side. Oboe wordlessly shoved one of the lines at Roberts who grabbed it and raced for a mooring ring, leaving the second mate to chain the other ring.

However, the *Lucky Lady* was continuing to sag downwards and when Roberts grabbed the closest mooring ring, the clasp refused to meet it by a good three inches. Straining ineffectually at the chain, Roberts darted his eyes over to see that Oboe had one hand clamped on a mooring ring and the other on the chain's clasp and the second mate was valiantly attempting to bridge a gap of nearly four feet: however, even Oboe's strength was not sufficient to force the chain's clasp to meet the mooring ring.

Roberts knew in a heartbeat that unless he could fasten his chain on the mooring ring, the *Lucky Lady* and everyone aboard her was doomed: chained on just one side, the airship would break under the strain and fall to the ground in pieces, killing them all. Bellowing furiously through the chaotic air at the crane operator, he strained with all his might to force the chain's clasp and the mooring ring to meet in the middle, praying for just one more inch of length. His right hand wrapped around the chain and his left on the mooring ring, Roberts willed his hands together, muscles screaming under tension, back rigid as steel, attempting to lift the *Lucky Lady* out of the sky by sheer force of his own strength and will.

Whether it was through muscle or the quick actions of the crane operator, the chain clasp finally closed the distance and slid under the mooring ring, snapping shut and sending the chain rigid. Roberts pushed violently away from the side of the airship, bracing for the jarring shock that would hit the second the chains took on the full weight of the falling airship. A moment or two later, and with a thunderous crash that nearly rent her asunder, the *Lucky Lady* reached the end of the chains' slack and juddered to a halt as the crane plucked the floundering airship from the sky.

The *Lucky Lady* rocked chaotically in place, suspended from the massive crane and liberally shedding broken pieces of futtock, assorted barrels, and shredded ends of rope into the open air. Secured on only three points, the airship was dangerously off-balance and she flailed recklessly in the sky as the crane jib lifted her up and swung her around into an unoccupied berth as gently as a mother placing her child to bed, Roberts shouting for order and counting heads as the *Lucky Lady* was secured. With a final coughing grunt, the airship's belabored engines stopped, sending the airbags sagging as she rested her full weight on the berth with the sound of groaning wood and escaping steam filling the air.

Brown, Richardson, Carter, Smith, Roberts counted quickly as men started to emerge from the rubble, pull themselves shakily to their feet, and stagger toward him. Carter was bleeding even more heavily and Richardson, the day pilot, was being dragged forward by Brown, a gangly airman with only a month of flying under his belt. Richardson had a chunk of wood embedded in his thigh while Brown looked unhurt but about three seconds away from total panic.

"Where's Johnson?" Roberts bellowed to Oboe as the second mate materialized quietly at Roberts' elbow.

Oboe regally bowed his ebony head and intoned solemnly, "Sir, I believe he fell." As he spoke, something crashed heavily below deck and Roberts heard the bellows of Farrington, the quartermaster, coming his direction.

"Sir! The Captain! Captain's dead, sir!" Farrington staggered into view, clutching a bleeding arm and rolling his eyes with pain and barely controlled panic. The quartermaster was a dreadful sight: half his shirt was gone and patches of exposed skin were covered with the angry red wounds of a steam blast. Boiler explosions were no trifling matter: such a disaster could strip the flesh from a man's bones in a heartbeat, and as Roberts thundered down the ladder toward the engine room, he instinctively knew that what awaited him would not be a pretty sight.

He was right. The hold was a chaotic mess, hot steam filling the air with choking clouds and jagged debris littering the floor. The door and much of the bulkheads to the engine room had been blasted outward and the heavy engines in the middle of the wreckage were silent, their cogs stilled. A twisted mess of distorted metal was all that remained of the boiler; shrapnel from the mechanism lay in chunks across the hull as boiling hot water spilled out of the ruined boiler and puddled on the floor. The water hit Roberts' boots, soaking through worn areas in his soles, but he momentarily ignored the hot liquid as he took in the sight before his eyes.

Two, well, *bodies* was perhaps too strong a word for it, lay not far from the mangled boiler, strips of angry pink flesh and shredded bits of clothing loosely arranged around exposed bones. The faces were mutilated, and what looked like an arm was lying against the opposite wall. A sickening odor that faintly reminded Roberts of spoiled meat filled the air and he turned away, choking back the bile. However, the brief glance had been enough: the captain and the day engineer were clearly beyond any hope of recovery.

Poor bastards, Roberts thought grimly. Captain Albert had been a colossal idiot and Silverman little better, but neither man had deserved that kind of death. *At least it was quick,* Roberts thought, shaking his head. Or at least he hoped so; both men had literally cooked to death and such a death would be agonizing if it wasn't instantaneous. Roberts backed away from the grisly picture, his feet already complaining mightily as the hot water soaked into his boots and his lungs beginning to strain against the effort of breathing in the choking, reeking air. Pausing, he caught the sound of footsteps racing toward him and held up a hand to check the onslaught as Brown's thin, anxious face appeared at his right side.

"Sir! I..." Roberts cut him off halfway and steered the youth away from the sight, blocking the view with his frame.

"You don't want to see that lad, trust me," Roberts warned the young airman. Brown gulped audibly and for one moment looked as if he were going to vomit, but he bit back the nausea with a swallow and tried to pull himself upright.

"Right! I...eh...um...sir, we think we lost Johnson," Brown said anxiously. "Mr. Oboe saw him fall out the hole in the side of the ship and...uh..." Brown trailed off as a sickly green pallor crept up over the whiteness of his face.

Roberts nodded grimly. In his head, he counted *Brown, Richardson, Carter, Smith, Oboe. Where's Jenkins?* Footsteps sounded and, as if reading Roberts' mind, the man in question appeared, staggering down the ladder into the hull, fury written on his face.

“Just what have those idiots done to my engines?” Jenkins growled, clutching a dirty cloth to a bloody head wound as he gazed at the interior of the boiler room with barely controlled anger.

Roberts intercepted the engineer and shook his head darkly. “They're dead, Jenkins,” he stated bluntly. “The captain and Silverman both.” Jenkins froze and for one brief moment Roberts saw the engineer's eyes narrow as the two exchanged a meaningful glance. Both men knew without saying that the boiler explosion was no mere accident, that foul play or poor decision-making skills on someone's part had caused the catastrophe spreading out at their feet.

No one said anything for a few moments as the three stood in the ruined hold, water quietly dripping out of the mangled boiler and shouts intensifying on the wharf as more workers rushed to the scene of disaster. Roberts' mind was busy with a hundred thoughts all vying for attention when Jenkins' terse voice broke through his musings and jerked him back to reality. "No offense, sir, but Sir Smothers is going to have your guts for garters, you know.”

Looming reality punched Roberts in the gut, shaking him out of his reverie and actually sending him backwards a step. *Oh dammit,* he thought with heartfelt sincerity as he glanced back at the ruined engine room which currently interred the still-steaming remains of Mr. Albert Smothers, the second son of the shipping tycoon Sir Cornelius Smothers whose iron fist ruled half the airships cruising the skies from London to Canton and everywhere in between.

Without his father, Albert Smothers would have never burdened an airship with his incompetent command and very likely the *Lucky Lady* would not currently be a shattered wreck. The younger bore startlingly little similarity to his sire who had clawed his way out of a childhood of stark poverty and built himself a vast empire encompassing thousands of workers and hundreds of vessels, both marine ships and airships. As part of his grandiose vision, Sir Smothers had fought to build a legacy with his family and had lavished upon his two sons the best education and finest opportunities he could command. Walter, the elder of the sons, had become his own legend in the railroad industry and at age forty was steadily accumulating a fortune to rival his father's and with the elder's blessing.

In marked contrast, Albert Smothers had accomplished little in his thirty-five years of existence except one catastrophic failure after the other. After both Oxford and Cambridge had made it known that Albert was no longer welcome to grace their ancient halls, Sir Cornelius had determined to put his younger son to work in the family business, to the detriment of all parties involved, the elder included. After too many years spent dragging his wastrel son from assorted bawdy houses and opium dens and back to the office, Smothers senior had finally put Albert in command of the *Lucky Lady* in a last-ditch effort to make something out of him. The *Lucky Lady* was considered a black sheep anyway, and Sir Smothers didn't have much expectation for her performance as long as she kept Albert gainfully occupied and out of trouble.

The responsibility of actually running the *Lucky Lady* had been handed to Roberts two years ago when he had accepted the position of first mate on board the airship. After twenty years in the employment of the Smothers' empire, Roberts had worked his way up from a common ship boy to an officer and had built a reputation for being a skilled and reliable employee. A recommendation from the captain of the *African Queen* had landed Roberts a generous salary as the *Lucky Lady's* first mate with the understanding that he would be the one responsible for running the airship and managing Albert's shortcomings as best he could.

It was no small task: after two years, the *Lucky Lady* had escaped crashing, bursting into flames, or running out of coal in the middle of the ocean more times than Roberts cared to think about, thanks to his tactful hand and realization that keeping the captain's rum stores well-stocked meant that Albert would stay holed up in his cabin out of the way, leaving everything to his capable first mate. Under Roberts' leadership, the *Lucky Lady* had actually shaped into a reliable transport ship that contributed to the Smothers empire in more ways than simply providing an occupation for Albert. Roberts took personal pride in knowing that the *Lucky Lady* had become more than simply a glorified babysitter for her incompetent captain, yet it was an inordinately difficult task keeping her functional.

It was at this point, standing with his back to the patch of flooring containing one newly dead captain, that Roberts realized his entire career, not to mention reputation, was in complete shambles. Smothers elder was generous with success and utterly ruthless with failure, and with the still-steaming corpse of Albert Smothers clogging up the ruined boiler room, swift and extravagant retribution from the tycoon would be quickly forthcoming.

Roberts' troubled musings were interrupted by Jenkins. "Ship won't last when the old man gets ahold of her," the engineer stated gruffly, reaching out awkwardly to pat the wall next to him in an oddly affectionate gesture. "Sorry, girl, but he'll have you for firewood in his house, I'd be bound."

Roberts' mind ticked as it recounted an event several years in the past. Sir Smothers' only daughter had died in childbirth barely a year after her wedding, and the doctor who had attended her birth had been quickly sent packing, some said with knives and clubs following after him. Roberts had a distinct feeling that before the day was out, he would be doing some hasty packing himself, but his eyes narrowed at the thought of the *Lucky Lady* bearing the full wrath of Sir Smothers' fury.

"It's not the *Lucky Lady's* fault she was commanded by a fool," Roberts growled to Jenkins but his words were interrupted by the sound of other voices. Something official was being shouted above deck, and it sounded as if Her Royal Majesty's military airmen were on the scene to assess the situation. Boiler explosions on board airships were common enough that sabotage was easy to conceal, hence the uniforms currently crawling all over the *Lucky Lady*. However, Roberts guessed that the soldiers wouldn't prod too far: the *Lucky Lady* was well-known as a tricky vessel and the younger Smothers as a complete disgrace to the captain's hat he wore. Few men would suspect anything of foul play. Sir Smothers, however, would be far less easy to placate. He would want answers and quickly, and if a culprit couldn't be found, he would make one.

Frowning, Roberts turned to Jenkins and Brown. "What was the captain doing down in the boiler room anyway?"

"He was, um, discussing something with Mr. Silverman," Brown ventured timidly. "Um, well, I guess arguing was a better word for it."

The young man flushed, and Roberts put a hand on his shoulder. "It's okay, lad," he rumbled. "Whatever reason he was down here, he's dead all the same." Actually, Roberts had a fairly good premonition of what the topic of discussion had been, and the aftermath was currently lying in pieces across the lower deck. A month ago, Captain Albert had insisted on purchasing a new boiler model, even though the *Lucky Lady*'s old boiler was perfectly serviceable. The new boiler was supposed to reduce their weight load by two hundred pounds and increase their fuel efficiency by five percent, and the captain had demanded its installation.

Roberts had hated the new boiler at first sight; the seams looked dangerously weak and while it was certainly lighter than the one it had replaced, he would have welcomed the extra two hundred pounds if it meant another layer of protection against an explosion. Nevertheless, Captain Albert had brushed aside Roberts' concerns and paid an exorbitant price for the mechanism. Even worse, he had taken an uncharacteristic interest in the boiler's operation and was forever tinkering with it in a way that set everyone's teeth on edge. Although his skills were few, Albert did have a mechanical bent and he occasionally took interest in operations on board the *Lucky Lady*, usually to everyone's detriment. Both Jenkins and Silverman had complained about the captain being underfoot in the engine room, and his endless fiddling with the new device in attempts to coax more efficiency out of it had been the source of more than one heated argument.

None of this, of course, was of any help to Roberts in his current predicament. In the wake of Albert's death, Sir Smothers would be swift to drop vengeance on the nearest handy victim, and Roberts knew without asking that he was first in line as the target of parental wrath. And, just to his cursed luck, they were in home port, the head office of the Smothers' empire not a quarter-mile from where the crippled *Lucky Lady* lay drunkenly in the berth, waiting for the ministrations of the dock workers. Sir Smothers would hear the bad news quickly; in fact, word was probably winging its way to his plush, opulent office right now.

The heavy tread of official footsteps sounded across the top deck and thundered imperiously down the ladder as Roberts swung around to face the newcomers. *Lieutenant Wittam. Of course,* he groaned a little to himself. The poker-straight military officer was so deep in the pockets of Smothers that he was practically welded to Smothers' aged leg. Wittam would tell Smothers what he wanted to hear: that Captain Albert was entirely innocent of fault and the entire fiasco had been completely out of his control. Roberts could practically see the newspapers of London pouring out articles about the tragic death of Captain Albert who had gone down at the engines, sacrificing himself to save his crew.

With hush money and outright threats for anyone who breaths a word different, Roberts snorted inwardly. Not that the crew would mind some extra cash but keeping the secret was a pointless endeavor - no one expected any sort of competence from the youngest Smothers son and before the day was out, the wharf and surrounding shipping communities would be abuzz with news of the idiot rich boy playing at being captain who had gotten himself and two other men killed. Silverman and Johnson had family they were leaving behind, and people would not easily forget nor forgive the incident.

However, Smothers was fiercely protective of his name, and he carried a very big stick in the form of beefy, stone-faced men who thought little of leaving a trail of shattered kneecaps behind them. Roberts had every intention of keeping his knees intact and he was not about to see Smothers lay a hand on the *Lucky Lady*. Although his career and reputation were on the line, Roberts was also seized with a fierce protectiveness for the vessel he had worked so hard to keep afloat and functional. He wasn't going to stand aside and let her be the target of Smothers' wrath.

As Lieutenant Wittam bore down upon Roberts with military briskness, the smell of wax and polish filling the small hallway, Roberts intercepted him with a brisk nod. Both men were acquainted and the situation demanded quick action, so he skipped the pleasantries. "Lieutenant Wittam, there was a boiler explosion on the *Lucky Lady* just now," Roberts stated bluntly. "I wasn't on board when it happened, but I am sorry to report that both Captain Albert Smothers and engineer Gordon Silverman died in the explosion."

The officer halted, and his brows drew together in a dark furrow. "Captain Albert Smothers?" he repeated and Roberts saw the look of dawning horror and outright fear cross his face before Wittam shouldered Roberts out of the way and moved toward the nexus of the disaster. Roberts moved aside to let the lieutenant through, and Wittam stopped abruptly as his eyes fell on the mangled corpses.

"Mother of..." Wittam began, whiteness creeping over his face as he and Roberts stood side by side for a terse moment, both examining the accident scene. However, after a second or two, the lieutenant sprang to life and began barking out orders to his men. "Keep the wharf rats off the ship and tell every man alive to keep his mouth shut!" he snapped out to the quartet of alert soldiers at his back as they scrambled to obey. "Sir Smothers has the right to hear of his son's death in private, and I'll hold each man here personally responsible if word gets out about the accident!"

Roberts fleetingly wished Wittam luck: airmen gossiped worse than fishwives, and the boiler explosion had grabbed the attention of everyone on the wharf. When the incompetent captain of the *Lucky Lady* failed to make an appearance on the main deck, conclusions would be very quickly drawn and Sir Smothers would soon hear of the disaster. The oncoming wrath of the house of Smothers would descend quickly upon the crippled *Lucky Lady*, and Roberts realized that it was time to take the initiative and mitigate some of the damage if he possibly could.

There was a bustle of activity as the men abandoned the gruesome scene below deck and hurried topside. Lieutenant Wittam began snapping out orders with the crisp staccato of a Gatling gun, and Roberts had to shout to make himself heard over the din of commands being given and carried out. "Lieutenant!" he bellowed, just catching Wittam's attention. "I'll report to Mr. Smothers and inform him of the captain's death." Wittam nodded and for one brief moment, military rigidity fell away for a human moment of clear relief. Roberts could practically hear the unspoken words Wittam flashed with his eyes: *Better you than me. Good luck, you poor sod.*

Stifling a groan, Roberts pushed his way across the top deck which was steadily filling up with people: airmen shoving against dock workers as self-important soldiers shouted and pushed in vain attempts at crowd control. The *Lucky Lady's* surviving crew members were clumped together in a huddle, the injured being tended by a few medical workers. Oboe, seemingly unhurt, was supervising the first aid with a careful eye, but he lifted his head to glance at Roberts as he appeared topside. Roberts jerked a head and thumb in the direction of Sir Smothers' massive office complex just visible in the distance, and Oboe nodded in understanding. Roberts returned the nod, then pushed against the flowing tide of men surging into the airship, knowing that he could leave the *Lucky Lady* and her injured crew in Oboe's capable hands while he delivered the bad news to Sir Smothers personally.

The wharf was steadily filling with soldiers, dock workers, and other people who were helping the situation, getting in each other's way, or simply standing around gawking. The Smothers were not well-loved despite their great wealth, and Roberts heard bits of conversation floating around him as he shoved his way forward.

"Knew that idiot younger son couldn't keep an airship afloat to save his life..."

"Hah, too much time in the whorehouse and not enough in the air, that one..."

"Wonder what the daft idiot was up to..."

"Old man Smothers'll be furious. Heard he was threatening to cut the younger son off completely..."

"Where's that fool Albert anyway?"

With his mood and his future growing darker by the moment, Roberts stalked heavily across the thick planks of the air wharf, grimly determined to face down whatever awaited him at the other end of the dock.

Chapter Two

Determined sunlight elbowed its way through the thick haze of London's ever-present pollution and set the vast Smothers headquarters on fire with light as Roberts pushed his way forward. Ahead of him was the gargantuan stretch of activity and industry that Sir Smothers claimed as his own, a bustling hub which commandeered a generous section of the city's footprint and employed thousands of London's workers.

The crowded air wharf and the constant movement of ships spoke eloquently of the commercial might of the Smothers industry. Airships landed and took to the winds again, their gondolas groaning with silks, spices, and affluent passengers who could afford to travel on the aether while marine ships, both steam-powered and sail-driven, filled the Thames with their sleek forms, bearing goods from afar.

Beyond the airship wharf and the marine docks, massive work yards stretched for miles as Smothers' engineers and inventors toiled endlessly in their research labs churning out ways to create better, faster, stronger airships. In vast, chaotic caverns, shipwrights scrambled to bring ideas to life as vessels grew from conception to birth and newly-minted airships poured forth from the sweating work yards to add their strength to the Smothers' empire.

London, Europe, and the world beyond had airships cruising their skies largely due to the indomitable determination and unparalleled innovation of Sir Smothers. It had been scarcely three decades since the world had received its first airship, and Smothers had been at the forefront of development. He had built his wealth off of creating transport airships that roamed across air and water faster than any other method of transporting goods, and while other inventors had scrambled to keep pace, the best transport airships in the world came out of Smothers' work yards. No other country in the world could boast such reliable and quick air transit as England, and Smothers' crushing grip ran a tight monopoly on trade throughout the world. The main headquarters of the Smothers empire was in this London location, but the aggressive Smothers crest was throughout the country and beyond - Smothers ships, both air and water, cruised across the Indies, the Orient, and to the colonists: wherever there was chance of a profit, Smothers was there.

Roberts moved through the chaotic broil of activity that was the airship wharf and the endless stretch of sweating work yards filled with men and machines. His destination was the massive office complex which reared up like a war elephant, looming impressively over the sprawling industrial zone in a magnificent testimony of grandeur, obstinate hard work, and an almost grotesque amount of wealth. Sir Cornelius Smothers, proud possessor of the finest title money could buy, had kicked his way up from a hardscrabble life as the son of a common laborer to this plush, iron-wrought hive of activity and profit. Every one of his airships sailing the sky, bale of cotton on his dock, or gilt finishing lining a picture frame in his office had been bought with dearly-won gold, and Sir Smothers had earned every single farthing through sheer tenacity and a near savant's capacity for business.

At sixty-two, Smothers showed no sign of slowing down and as Roberts picked his way through the work yards, he saw overwhelming evidence that the rigorous, domineering empire was in no danger of stagnating. Barring illness or injury, Smothers would very likely maintain an absolute grip on his empire for the next few decades, but he was already laying down a solid foundation for when he at last yielded to Death's demands and his rule passed onto his kin.

Albert Smothers, however, was not to be a successor and not just because he was currently dead: Smothers elder had possessed enough sense to keep much of his money away from his profligate younger son and had severely limited Albert's role in the family business. Roberts guessed that Sir Smothers did not wish to break up his empire by dividing it among his two sons, especially since passing any sort of control onto Albert would only wreak spectacular disasters on the business the elder had worked so hard to build. Most likely, Walter would have been given the burden of managing Albert after their father died, and likely both Walter and Sir Smothers had been secretly praying that Albert wouldn't outlive his older brother, lest the youngest son become master of the empire.

Problem solved, Roberts thought to himself with grim humor as he crossed the vast expanse of work yards which were noisy with vigorous activity, great cranes lifting massive crates with crunching squeals of their overloaded gears. Hissing steam rose in great puffs of white, and throngs of workers labored mightily to serve the never satiated beast of commerce. Roberts quickly threaded his way through gigantic caverns, past the swarming masses of shouting men wielding heavy tools, past skeletal framework of airships being constructed or refurbished, their ribs devoid of flesh, past great balloons of steam-filled canvas and the thudding clank of boilers.

Ahead of the busy chaos was Sir Smothers' opulent office complex, its luxurious elegance in sharp contrast to the steaming reek of the work yards. Just as Roberts reached the end of the industry zone, he spotted a group of men heading his direction and his stomach tightened. The men were led by a rather portly gentleman with a head of luxuriant white hair that marked him unmistakably as Sir Cornelius Smothers. The great man was surrounded by his normal entourage of well-dressed, rather agitated sycophants alert for the slightest command from their leader.

A little away from the men waited a massive steam-powered automobile snorting in anticipation, and Roberts eyed the vehicle coolly. With a title to his name, Sir Smothers had long abandoned the use of his feet for transport and insisted on the dignity of being regally driven wherever he wished to go. A different sort of man, upon hearing that his son was involved in an accident, would have dropped everything and ran as fast as his feet would take him to the scene of the disaster, but Sir Smothers clung to his dignity with iron fingers and nothing stood in the way of proper form.

Sir Smothers' eyes were sharp and missed nothing; he quickly picked Roberts out from the teeming masses of workers and his stern frown became a hard glare. Roberts squared his shoulders and met the old man's fierce gaze with determination. They locked eyes over the crowded din of the work yards and for a moment, Roberts watched as the elder paused and closed his eyes. It was clear that Smothers had already caught wind of his son's death, and his brief eye contact with Roberts had been sufficient to confirm the truth. The knot of men surrounding Smothers paused as one, each man attuned to the slightest shift in mood from their leader, alert and unified as a school of fish. Both Roberts and Sir Smothers ignored the press of anxiously hovering lackeys, the grim situation consuming both of their attention.

Smothers halted, waiting for Roberts to close the gap between them, pride preventing him from hurrying forward to interrogate the approaching messenger. Finally Roberts was within speaking distance, and Smothers looked no less intimidating and resolute at close quarters than he did at forty paces. Deep-set wrinkles like cracked riverbeds lined his face, and there wasn't a strand of dark in the luxuriant white beard and flowing mane of hair, still thick and lustrous as a young man's. The craggy shoulders were held up and back, a bit burdened by the weight of the generous stomach billowing underneath a finely tailored Savile Row suit, and the scent of cologne mixed incongruously with the metallic reek of the work yards.

Both men faced each other, Smothers tilting his head slightly back to meet Roberts' taller-placed eyes and Roberts watching as the elder clenched his jaw, bushy eyebrows like white-capped hoods over his narrowed pupils. With every word tight as a spring, Smothers pronounced in perfectly controlled yet deeply ominous tones, “In my office, Roberts. *Now.*” Turning his head to the knot of attentive sycophants, Smothers glared at them and they melted as one back into the courtyard surrounding the office complex, leaving Roberts and Smothers alone.

Without a word, Smothers pivoted on his heel and stalked back toward his massive office building, Roberts falling in a step or two behind him. Despite his age, Smothers moved briskly as if channeling his grief into pure, barely controlled rage and Roberts had to quicken his pace to keep up. As the two men entered the building, an army of pale-faced clerks and secretaries lifted their heads, then intently returned to their work as a palpable frisson of fear swept through them. Smothers pointedly ignored the workers as he towed Roberts with him through the elegant hallways and into his opulent private office suite which was rich with ankle-deep carpets, Venetian marble floors, lustrous mahogany, and statues of what Smothers would call art but Roberts saw as an excuse to have images of naked women around the place.

The plush office suite was hushed after the riotous clamor of the work yards, and Roberts was able to hear the faint hissing click of Sir Smothers' construct arm, a finely wrought piece of gears and tiny pistons that moved with precise thrusts through the air. The story was that he had lost the original arm as a young man when he had strayed too close to a fast-moving machine which had removed the limb as cleanly as a surgeon's precise hand. Metal limbs were nothing novel: any amputee with some spare pounds could buy a shoddy construct to replace lost flesh, and plenty of men throughout London sported gears and metal where bone and skin once were. However most of these were fiddly contraptions, all too prone to break or leak oil and with a limited range of use.

In sharp contrast, the mechanical limb attached to

Smothers' stump was an elegant piece of pure science, able to function almost as well as the original arm. The long fingers could grasp a pen and write with a commanding script, and the entire contraption moved as if powered by the force of Smothers' mind. The mechanism's strength was enough to crush a man's windpipe with a single squeeze, and rumor whispered that it had done so before.

Smothers stiffly ordered Roberts into his inner office and shut the door heavily. Roberts paused, feet planted on the elegant Turkish carpet and watched as Smothers crossed the room to the wide bay window that offered a magnificent view of both his work yards and docks. Airships floated through London air accompanied by puffs of steam, their engines churning, while screw-powered marine ships began their journey over the muddy waters of the Thames and wind-driven vessels shook out their canvas sails to catch the stiff breezes.

Smothers stood facing the bay window with his hands clasped behind his back, metal fingers entwined in living flesh, his white hair like a fancy woman's elaborate powder puff, watching the panoply of investment, industry, and commerce sail before him. It suddenly struck Roberts that what he was looking at was not a shipping magnate or a titled lord or even an employer – it was simply an old man grieving the sudden loss of his child. For the first time, Roberts felt a stab of pity for Smothers, even more so when the craggy elder broke the silence with a carefully controlled voice.

"My son is dead," he said with quiet finality, not as one seeking information but simply confirming what is known.

"Yes, sir." Roberts responded as gently as he could. "I'm sorry, sir." Silence fell thick over the room for a moment, and Roberts felt his eyes wandering toward Smothers' luminous mahogany desk, its rich wood as glossy and sleek as the finely groomed coat of a prize racehorse. The desk had been built by Chippendale himself from the finest *swietenia mahogani,* a wood without peer and ruinously expensive: an average middle-class man could buy himself a very nice home for what Smothers had paid for it. The desk was impeccably tidy with a gleaming silver inkstand and meticulously organized papers in mathematically precise stacks, but the careful order was somewhat disrupted by a collection of mechanical clockworks lining the edge of the desk. These strange devices whirled and clicked softly to themselves, and Roberts stared at them curiously. This wasn't his first visit to Smothers' office, and he had always wondered what purpose the odd clockwork devices served.

"Albert made those when he was a boy," Smothers said softly as he turned from the window to see Roberts' eyes fastened on the mechanisms chiming softly on the desk. Something tugged at the corner of Smothers' mouth as he continued. "He had some talent for mechanics and liked tinkering with gears." A rare and feeble smile crossed Smothers' lips, but it faded before it had fully come alive. "I tried to dissuade him. I told him he was the son of a gentleman and he was not to dirty his hands with mechanics, that he was best off using his mind instead." His metal limb lifted, its steel fingers clicking against each other like castanets as Smothers turned his attention to the artificial arm, watching in detached fascination as his metal fingers moved through the air. "I didn't want this happening to my sons, not if I could help it." After a moment, the construct arm dropped heavily at Smothers' side as his eyes turned back to the desk. "Maybe I was wrong."

The words dragged heavily and almost silently from his lips, and Roberts watched him narrowly. Smothers was a man of inordinate pride and fond of boasting that he never apologized for anything he did. Something told Roberts that the admission of possible guilt was costing the man dearly and for a brief moment, Sir Smothers looked as old and careworn as a saddle.

A sentence, almost pleading in its tone, emanated from Smothers. "Albert did not wish to see me?" he questioned, looking dangerously close to helpless as Roberts struggled with what to say next. Truth be, Albert could have properly berthed the *Lucky Lady* and spared ten minutes to drop by the forbidding office complex and pay brief homage to his sire. Had he done so, he would probably still be alive, as would

Silverman and Johnson. However, meetings between father and son had steadily become more volatile and less frequent, and Albert only turned the *Lucky Lady* toward home port when no other options presented themselves.

As best Roberts could recall, the now-dead captain had not spoken with his father for over three months, and the only reason the *Lucky Lady* had made for London that day was to deal with a pile of unavoidable paperwork. Captain Albert had made arrangements, ordering for the *Lucky Lady* to drop her cargo at the wharf in Liverpool before reluctantly proceeding to London. Once at port, he had directed the *Lucky Lady* to the far end of the wharf and had her tied up lightly, ready to spring back into action on his command. It was Roberts who had been dispatched to deal with the paperwork, leaving the captain on board where he could avoid any chance encounter with his father. No, Albert Smothers had no intention of seeing the old man that day, and Roberts merely shrugged his shoulders to answer Sir Smothers' question.

The senior took the answer with quiet dignity and dropped his eyes for a moment in contemplation. Then his metal fist clenched while his obstinate shoulders drew back, and Roberts felt himself being nailed in place by the piercing eyes of Sir Cornelius Smothers, master of an empire and intolerant of any suggestion of error. Roberts' own shoulders tensed as if drawing up for combat as the first volley of words hit him full-force.

"You were hired as the first mate of the *Lucky Lady*, Gavin Roberts," Sir Smothers pronounced ominously, dark anger rising in a crescendo and roaring across the carpet like a tidal wave. Stepping around the desk, Smothers bore down on Roberts who stood his ground, coolly meeting the angry eyes as the older man's voice grew deeper and harsher. "I hold you personally responsible for the death of your captain..."

Roberts cut him off. "No. Meaning no offense, sir, but your son was a bloody fool who got himself and two other men killed." The words burst from his throat, filling the thick air and half-astonishing Roberts that he had dared utter them. If it wasn't for the expression on Sir Smothers' face, Roberts would have sworn than he had only thought the words, but they had echoed from the depths of his soul and taken verbal form and now that they had been voiced, he would stand behind them. He would not be cowed by any man, even a tyrannical superior who had the power to make his life utter misery.

Smothers halted and stared at Roberts with a slightly bewildered, detached look as if he didn't quite believe what he had just heard. Rolling with audacity and growing indignation, Roberts instinctively surged forward. It was too late to back down, and he'd be damned if he'd grovel in front of Smothers. With the initiative firmly in hard, he could possibly, with luck and nerve, seize control of the situation while Smothers was still digesting the novelty of being defied. The old man was absolutely intolerant of any backtalk, but deep in his belligerent soul, he admired tenacity and he grudgingly respected any opponent who had the courage to stand up to him.

Sensing that hesitation would be his undoing, Roberts stalked forward until he was practically touching the older man. "Captain Albert had a piss-poor boiler installed in the *Lucky Lady* and wouldn't listen to anyone telling him different," Roberts stated curtly. "I tried to talk him out of it, but he wouldn't listen, *and* he wouldn't stop fiddling with the damned thing and over-stressing it. It blew to bits just now, killing him and two other men." Roberts coolly returned Smothers' white-hot glare and added firmly, "I'll man up to my mistakes, sir, but I won't accept another man's. Your son was a complete failure as captain and you know it."

"How...dare...you." Smothers' voice was a low hiss, an angry vein throbbing in his temple as his face darkened with growing rage.

"I'm speaking the truth, sir," Roberts growled, refusing to be cowed. It was time the old bastard faced the music, like it or not. "Look, you did your best by your son, but he made his own decisions and there's not a damned thing you could do about it. It sure as hell isn't fair, but no one can say you didn't do everything for your son that you could."

The vein juddered frantically as Smothers' heavy jaw

clamped shut, stressing his teeth as a stormy mix of emotions boiled angrily just under a thin veneer of control. Finally, he spat out, “That...cursed...airship...”

“There's not a damned thing cursed about the *Lucky Lady*,” Roberts stated emphatically, protectiveness rising up in him as he sensed Smothers' anger redirecting itself. While he was glad to get out from the limelight, the *Lucky Lady* was helpless against Sir Smothers' wrath.

“She's an airship, sir, a thing of wood and canvas. She didn't set out to kill your son and she's not at fault," Roberts added, trying to be reasonable, but tension was making his words sharp. "The problem was the man who commanded her, not the ship herself."

Smothers ignored Roberts: he had found a culprit and his fury was honing in on it. Being Smothers, he would seek vengeance against anyone and anything remotely connected to the death of his son, and the vessel that had been the scene of the accident was a natural target. “That ship's been an albatross ever since she was commissioned,” Smothers said with finality. “I'll order her destroyed before she kills again.”

“Sell her to me, sir,” Roberts stated impulsively while common sense screamed for a recount. It was an exceedingly foolish proposition he had just voiced, but his mouth seemed determined to get him into as much trouble as possible that day and he had already sunken so low in Smothers' esteem that there wasn't much further he could go. Roberts didn't have near enough funding saved up to purchase and provision an airship like the *Lucky Lady,* but damned if he was going to see her burn.

Inspiration struck, and Roberts seized upon the one rhetorical stance that might possibly break through Smothers' unchangeable will. "Speaking plainly, sir, if you destroy the *Lucky Lady,* every man jack in the air and water will know that something fishy happened on board. If it was a simple boiler explosion, why destroy a valuable airship that could be patched up and put back to work again? Burn her, and rumors will spread, sir. You know how airmen talk, and the word around London will be that Captain Albert did something stupid and his father got rid of the evidence."

Smothers was flushing with rage, but Roberts could see that his comments had hit home and tendrils of rational thought were creeping around the blind fury welling up in the elder. Pressing forward, Roberts continued, "You sell her to me, sir, and that will put some suspicions at rest. Blown boilers are not uncommon, everyone knows that. No hard feelings for her crew, accidents happen. People will understand. Selling her to me will be a gesture of goodwill, proof that what happened on board was just an accident with no one at fault."

The fiery glow of fury was beginning to cool slightly on Smothers' face, and Roberts felt a tingle of hope prickling in his belly. Without missing a beat, he added, "Besides, who's to say that Captain Albert wasn't in the boiler room trying to right a problem that could have put the whole crew in danger? A good captain always goes down with the airship, you know that, sir. Everyone knows that." It was a stretch of magnanimous generosity to hope that anyone remotely connected with the Smothers empire would believe, for one second, that Albert Smothers was perhaps not at fault for the blown boiler. But Smothers senior wore his pride like a suit of armor and if there was the faintest chance of reducing some tarnish on the family's dearly-bought crest, he would seize it.

Smothers stared curiously at Roberts as if the sheer novelty of defiance was enough to pique his curiosity and set his rage aside for a time. However, his jaw was like flint and Roberts knew he was balancing on a very thin ledge. A single word could easily spell his doom.

Running a quick calculation in his head, Roberts stated, "I'll pay you fifteen thousand pounds for the *Lucky Lady*, sir, if you give me three years to pay her off. I give you my word I will have her paid off in that time." The named price was below what the airship was worth, but she was damaged and it would be a pretty penny fixing her up again. Even so, fifteen thousand pounds was a staggeringly large debt, especially with a scant three years to pay it off. However, Roberts had a strong feeling that asking for more time or a lower selling price would only meet with resistance, and in the brief time he had to mentally calculate the deal, this was the best he could offer. With luck, Smothers might actually consider it.

The old man was almost quivering with anger, red vessels in his eyes throbbing and his luxurious hair shivering with the effect of keeping back so much emotion. However, Roberts could see the cogs working in the elder's head: reason and revenge quarreling before the gods of Mammon and fame whom the Smothers empire bowed down to daily. Roberts waited quietly, forcing himself to stand calmly and meet the old man's eyes with cool ease. Smothers struggled internally for several seconds, the battle in his mind warring furiously, but it was obviously turning due Roberts and after nearly a minute of heavy silence, the elder spoke.

"I will sell you the airship *Lucky Lady,*" Smothers pronounced with perfect, ringing clarity, each vowel as heavy as a lead pipe. "For fifteen thousand pounds. You have three years to this day to pay me this amount."

Roberts nodded firmly, his calm exterior belying the churning riot of excitement, shock, and outright fear clamoring inside his innards. The debt loomed like a mountain, but he shoved worry away, determined to focus on the present, for Smothers clearly was not finished.

The elder continued. "I will extend no interest on this loan, but I will also extend no mercy. You will have the full price of the airship paid to me in three years' time to this day, or I swear upon my son's death I will hunt you down and destroy you and everything you hold dear."

Roberts knew that Smothers meant every single word. He also knew without asking that there would be no legal papers, no notarized statement of their deal, no law to assist Roberts if he was unable to fulfill the terms of the pact. It was a blood agreement between two men with no one else intruding. If Roberts failed, Smothers would not bother to seek legal redress. As far as the air was concerned, the Smothers empire *was* the law.

Roberts set his jaw. "Agreed," he said quietly. Smothers turned from him sharply, leaving Roberts to stare at the back of his head. Silence fell once again, and Roberts sensed that the interview was over. Indeed, there was nothing more to be said: they had reached an agreement, and the onus was on him to fulfill it. Turning, Roberts moved to walk back across the expanse of Turkish carpet toward the high arched doors. As his back turned to the older man, Smothers' voice reached out and halted him in his tracks.

"Do not mistake or underestimate me, Gavin Roberts," Smothers' voice was blade-sharp. "The second you leave my office, your time is ticking down. And do not think that you can hide from me."

Roberts glanced over his shoulder to catch a glimpse of

Smothers' face, which had turned to him with an expression of iron. "If you try to run, I swear that there is no place on this God-cursed world that you can hide from me. You can try to disappear into the deepest jungle on the Black Continent or the most barren desert of Arabia, and I will find you. Pay me what you owe me in three years, or I will devote every last penny in my possession and worker in my employ to hunting down your damned, pox-ridden, whoreson hide."

Pausing, Smothers added with piercing clarity, "Do I make myself abundantly clear?"

Roberts stiffened, but he met the angry eyes with narrow coolness. "Perfectly, sir."

Smothers inhaled sharply, then added, "Then get that damned airship off my wharf *now*. If I ever see her near my wharf again, I will blow her out of the sky."

Roberts paused, ordering his voice into calmness before responding levelly, "Understood, sir."

"Then get out of my office," Smothers enunciated heavily, each syllable as sharp as a blade.

Roberts turned back to the door and opened it, willing himself to move smoothly and betray nothing of his inner turmoil. However, as he closed the door, he caught a faint glimpse of Smothers falling into his chair with something like a cry of pain. The thick oak door slid shut, but even its solid denseness was not enough to wholly muffle the sound of a choked lament echoing from the other side.

Roberts laid a hand on the door, pressing his fingers against the wood in a moment of sympathy for Sir Smothers' loss. His mind was roaring with the events of the past hour, and most of his inner turmoil was circling around the massive debt he had just taken upon his shoulders. The terms Smothers had thrown down at Roberts' feet were as absolute as death, but in that moment of time the brand-new captain of the *Lucky Lady* could not bring himself to hate Sir Smothers, not when the old man was clearly grieving the loss of his son on the other side of the heavy oak door.

For a brief second, Roberts closed his eyes in respect for Albert Smothers' death and in sympathy for his grieving father. Then he lifted his hand from the door, his eyes narrowing and his shoulders squaring up. It was time to return to the airship, *his* airship, and set her to rights again.

Chapter Three

Roberts' heavy feet lead him along the crowded wharf, the chaos of the *Lucky Lady*'s exploded boiler still infecting the air and sending tumbles of clattered voices and frenetic activity surging up and down the heavily reinforced walkway. If the accident had been on any other airship, the excitement would not have been nearly as sharp, but by now, Roberts doubted that there was any man or boy within a five mile radius of the wharf who hadn't heard that Albert Smothers had unfortunately offed himself in a misguided but all too expected stroke of spectacular incompetence.

The *Lucky Lady* was slumped in her berth as if utterly exhausted, the gaping hole in her hull as raw and ragged as a wound, and her envelope and airbags now rolled back to clear the path for repair. A steady stream of men were methodically stripping her down to her beams in preparation for transport and in the distance, Roberts could hear the faint hum of a lift ship trudging its way across the sky. *Smothers doesn't waste a second,* he thought darkly. Come hell or high water, Roberts knew he had to get the wounded airship off the wharf before Sir Smothers decided to renege on their agreement and pour the full weight of his vengeance on the unfortunate *Lucky Lady*.

Lieutenant Wittam was standing stiffly at the gangplank with his men clustered around him, and he saluted Roberts crisply. "First Mate Roberts, my orders are to escort you and the *Lucky Lady* off the wharf..." Wittam began, but Roberts cut him off.

"That's Captain to you," he responded curtly, meeting the officer's eyes darkly. "This airship is mine now." Roberts knew full well that his verbal agreement with Smothers wouldn't stand up in a court of law, but he'd be damned if he was going to take lip from some lieutenant, not after he had just accepted the full weight of the *Lucky Lady* on his shoulders.

Wittam's lips thinned as he continued, "A lift ship is approaching to take the *Lucky Lady* to wherever you wish."

The old man works fast, Roberts growled to himself. He had left Smothers barely five minutes ago; however, the brief span of time was apparently enough to generate swift orders regarding the *Lucky Lady*. Roberts glanced across the deck to exchange glances with Oboe who had assumed the mantle of second-in-command with quiet skill. Oboe was calmly directing traffic as men swarmed about deck, urgency in their actions as if they knew time was against them and the wrath of Sir Smothers would fall upon any man negligent in his duties. By the time the lift ship reached them, the *Lucky Lady* would be unloaded down to her bulkheads, light enough for transport.

"Sir!" a familiar voice rang out in the noise and Roberts turned to see Jenkins limping toward him, anger written on his face and blood dripping from the bandage clumsily wound around his head wound. It was clear the engineer was in great pain, but fury was lending him strength. "They said we've got to get her off the wharf *now* or she's leaving in pieces," Jenkins growled and fixed Roberts with a piercing look that clearly demanded more information.

Roberts ignored the unspoken question, his attention diverting as Oboe began plowing steadily through the chaos to his superior officer. When the towering African reached them both, Roberts rapped out, "The *Lucky Lady* is mine now, and we're getting her off the wharf before Smothers changes his mind. Oboe," he turned his head to the right, "As her new first mate, you'll be getting her ready for travel. She's going to a friend of mine, Jacob Halloway, who can put her to rights. I'll go there now and let him know we're bringing her over."

Jenkins' forehead creased in surprise and even Oboe's normally impassive face shifted, but Roberts didn't have time to explain, not with the lift ship approaching, its oversized engines filling the air with noise. The small, chunky appearance of lift ships belied their enormous power. Their boilers went through coal like fire raging through a dry forest, and one lift ship could transport a much larger airship for several miles, providing the airship was stripped of all unnecessary cargo and furnishings down to its hull. The *Lucky Lady*'s destination was a few miles to the east, and the lift ship would have no problem carrying her that far, especially since she was lighter and smaller than many of the other airships on the wharf.

The real question, however, was if Halloway could be persuaded to put his skills to use setting the *Lucky Lady* right again, especially considering what Roberts could afford to pay. It would take some persuasion, that was putting it lightly, and that persuasion started with Roberts arriving at Halloway's doorstep before the lift ship appeared. He needed to move fast, and with a few instructions to Oboe regarding Halloway's whereabouts so the lift ship could get the *Lucky Lady* to the right destination, Roberts was soon striding off the wharf and toward the closest ground transportation he could find: a half-rusted steam-powered cab commanded by a young man waiting at the end of the wharf for his next passenger.

Roberts pressed an extra coin into the driver's hand to coax as much speed out of the machine as possible, and he wasn't disappointed: barely had he settled into the torn leather seat than the cab was roaring away from the wharf at a breakneck pace, its driver honking vigorously as the vehicle tore through the crowded streets, people and animals fleeing at their approach.

Roberts soon lost track of the cabbie's harrowing maneuvers as his mind became preoccupied with the next set of difficulties, namely convincing the most brilliant and reclusive inventor in Europe to put his prodigious skills to use getting the *Lucky Lady* back on her feet. Jacob Halloway was an innovative wonder and he would have been lauded throughout

England and beyond for his engineering prowess if it were not for his complete dislike of human interaction. Halloway had been a prodigy since birth and in his earlier years had completed several grudging collaborations with other inventors which had lead to a number of technological breakthroughs. However, Halloway was no businessman. He saw little need for patents and his acerbic personality had garnered him a number of enemies. Thus his mechanical discoveries had been snatched, pirated, and patented by more enterprising inventors, and hundreds profited luxuriously from his work while the great man toiled away in obscurity.

Finally in disgust, Halloway had effectively sealed himself off from the world and avoided almost all human interaction during the past several years. His cavernous London workshop was known to few, and he took pains to keep it that way. Roberts was only privy to Halloway's whereabouts thanks to a long-standing friendship of sorts with the reclusive man. The two had been boys together, struggling to survive on the hardscrabble streets of London, and Roberts knew that he was one of few people Halloway reluctantly counted as a friend, if indeed such a word existed in the inventor's vocabulary. Although tenuous, there was a long-standing bond between the two men, and Roberts could only hope it would be enough to convince Halloway to help restore the damaged *Lucky Lady*.

With a final hiss of steam, the cab pulled up to a screeching stop and Roberts gratefully disembarked with only a slight tremor in his legs. No sooner had his feet touched the ground than the cab roared away into the distance, leaving him to gaze upon the exterior of Halloway's cavernous workshop which was sandwiched between two factories in one of London's heavy industrial zones. As far as Roberts could tell, the inventor had rarely left his lair in the past several years and time had only made Halloway more reclusive.

It took luck and persistence to coax Halloway into coming out or letting anyone inside and as Roberts raised a hard fist to pound against the door, he hoped he wouldn't have to force his way inside. Halloway was just as apt to ignore a summons at the door as he was to answer it, and Roberts had pushed his way inside more than once when he knew Halloway was inside and simply declining to respond. However, he wasn't keen on repeating the experience: his old friend was near paranoid about his carefully guarded domain, and any intruder was sure to meet with a battalion of sharp whirring gears, ponderous automatons, and other contraptions that promised swift retribution to those who poked their noses inside unbidden.

To Roberts' relief, after only a minute or two of pounding, a clicking of gears sounded and a small window slid open to loosen a telescoping tube of metal which twitched and moved as it drew itself up level with Roberts' eyes. A lens showed Halloway's face weirdly distorted on its smoky surface as the inventor peered through it to identify his visitor.

"Oh, it's you," Halloway's abrupt voice sounded through a speaker box in a metallic, scratchy quality that did not hide the irritation in his tones. "What do you want, Gavin?"

"Stop being a bloody fool, Jacob," Roberts growled. "Let me in. I want to talk to you."

"I'm busy," Halloway responded. "Go away." The metal tube twitched as if in disapproval and began collapsing inwards, signaling its master's complete disinterest in the conversation at hand.

Roberts was not dissuaded. Maintaining a working relationship with Halloway required persistence and sheer, bloody-minded stubbornness at times. To make his point, he seized the metal tube and gave it a firm tug, pulling it back out to its full length.

Halloway's angry voice boomed loudly in the dirty air. "Careful, you idiot, you'll break it!" he yowled.

Roberts' fingers did not loosen their grip. "You'll build another one, I'll be bound," he commented with a sniff. "Now, are you going to let me in or do I have to keep breaking things until I get your attention?"

"All right, all right!" Halloway huffed irritably. "Come inside for all the good it will do you!" The tube vibrated in

Roberts' hand as if he had Halloway's neck in his palm, but he didn't let go until he heard the click of gears signaling that the great, barred portal was starting to open. He stepped inside, dirty sunlight following him as he entered Halloway's lair.

Inside was a high-ceiling den of gloomy shadows and fitful light that cast weird reflections against strange mechanical protrusions. Everywhere was chaos: piles of rusting metal stacked in haphazard clusters, oil slicks turning the floor treacherous, ropes and chains like snakes hanging from support beams. Pathways through the clutter were narrow and turned the floor into a complex labyrinth that could bewilder an unwary visitor, and sinister apparitions loomed out of the darkness as if armed sentinels were lurking in the shadows.

Roberts picked his way through the mess, wondering, as always, how Halloway got anything done with all the chaos surrounding him. The *Lucky Lady* had always been a tight ship; Roberts saw to that personally, and he did not abide disorder on board. On an airship, every ounce counted, and half the challenge of flying was eradicating all superfluous weight that might drag her down. In sharp contrast, Halloway's lair was a magpie's nest of virtually every tool, mechanical apparatus, and metal known to mankind.

The man himself was seated at a worktable so large and overladen that it needed a dozen legs and a strut in the center to keep it from crashing to the ground. Halloway's gaunt, unkempt frame was hunched over the table, both hands busy with the delicate gears of a mechanical contraption in front of him. Around him, the crowded table was stacked high with assorted tools, glass decanters bubbling and oozing vivid liquids, corroded twists of metal, half-rotting leather straps, and the frenetic click and snap of malfunctioning clockwork devices, pointedly ignored by their creator as they twitched in their efforts to regain life. But Roberts' eyes quickly zeroed in on the tell-tale hypodermic needle lying on the table, a thin crust of white staining the wood where the needle had leaked its contents.

He's injecting again, Roberts thought angrily as he took a closer assessment of Halloway's physical condition, which had never been exactly healthy. Both of their childhoods had been grim and survival had been a constant preoccupation. While Roberts had taken to the air at thirteen to earn a living, Halloway had been driven to machines since he could walk. Even as a boy, if given the choice between food and a bit of metal he could fashion into something, he'd take the metal. Halloway's emaciated frame had been comically stork-like from boyhood to adulthood: bones protruding from his waxy skin, sparse hair coarse and dull-looking, eyes sunken back in his head. Roberts somewhat suspected that Halloway had up and died several years ago, but his internal fire had kept the body going long after mortal flesh had given up the will to live.

Halloway drove himself relentlessly, spurred forward by a madness for anything that could be crafted of steel and gears.

Most unfortunately, along the way Halloway had discovered the marvelously energizing power of the *coca* plant. It had nearly killed him more than once when he had routinely used injections of the drug to stay awake for days on end, pushing himself endlessly without sleep or food in order to turn his ideas into reality. In the murky light of the workshop, Roberts looked carefully at his old friend's vein-lined eyeballs, the waxy tightness of his skin and the manic twitching of every digit, and guessed that Halloway was coming off another tremendous bender. That wasn't going to make Roberts' task any easier, he well knew that.

Halloway was completely ignoring the presence of his visitor, and Roberts had a distinct feeling that his old friend had forgotten about him, so intent was Halloway on the machine in his hands. Smiling a little to himself, Roberts reached out and gave one of the twitching clockwork devices a prod with his forefinger.

Halloway instantly snapped to attention. "Don't touch that!" he snarled, glaring at Roberts darkly. "You'll break it."

"Funny, I thought you *liked* having broken things to repair," Roberts retorted, poking the mechanical device again. It gave an annoyed high-pitched sound, and Halloway irritably snatched it away from Roberts' intruding finger.

Setting the clockwork object down at a safe distance from Roberts' prodding, Halloway's eyes immediately drew back to the mechanism in front of him. "What do you want, Gavin?" he demanded.

"I need your help with a little project," Roberts grunted casually, careful to remain neutral. It took skillful manipulating to present a request to Halloway in a way that inclined him to accept it, and Roberts knew he had to tread carefully.

Halloway snorted, "You and everybody else. And don't be a daft fool, Gavin, I know very well you wouldn't come to me with a 'little project'." As he spoke, his hands were roaming across the table, snatching up tools in crisp, staccato movements, eyes twitching and bulging, every muscle in an orgy of inventiveness. Halloway never held still for more than two seconds and the influence of cocaine only made him more manic and irate.

Roberts smiled thinly. "I think you'll like this one, Jacob," he said, still keeping his voice casual, but as he spoke, the deep, grumbling roar of something heavy and belabored sounded through the walls of Halloway's den. The inventor froze, his white-rimmed eyes twitching upward.

"That sounds like..." Halloway began, then abruptly shot off his chair and strode with a jerky, erratic gait toward a lever handle mounted on the wall. With a firm yank, the groan of gears and screeching metal filled the dark interior as the ceiling split down the center and lifted away, the metal roof opening outward to let in the sun and pollution of London. Both men said nothing for a moment, their ears attuned to the sound of deep engines roaring through the sky, coming closer by the minute.

Halloway's long, twitching frame pivoted sharply and faced Roberts who stood with a look of blank innocence on his face. "That's a lift ship," Halloway barked accusingly, glaring at Roberts. "You great *bastard...*"

"My airship," Roberts cut him off neatly. "As of about an hour ago. Mine, did you hear me, Jacob?" Halloway's look of glassy fury softened a trifle as over twenty years of questionable friendship demanded their due and stopped a barrage of protests just itching to spill forth. The ties between the two men were rather tenuous at times, but when the chips were down, Roberts knew that he could count on Halloway. Granted, sometimes it took outright manipulation and threats to make the count, but there were glimmers of loyalty and fraternal concern buried in Halloway somewhere and considering the circumstances, Roberts was going to do whatever it took to wring out every last one of them.

Halloway was staring intently at the open roof, his expression of fury mixed with a growing interest in what mechanical puzzle was approaching him. Roberts knew his old friend well; give Halloway something interestingly complicated to fix and he'd eventually do it, usually after he finished a bout of irate cussing. Roberts was gratified to see Halloway stride over to a platform about the size of a table and step on board. He followed suit and without a word, Halloway jerked a handle and the platform rose smoothly in the air, lifting the two men up through the building into the open sky.

London's grimy, soot-blackened landscape opened up before them as the lift pushed the two men up through the roof. Halloway's domain was in the factory district where great furnaces belched out clouds of choking smoke into the air and even on a clear day, one was hard-pressed to see more than a half mile in any direction. Something was coming their way, growling angrily through the polluted air, and as the two men waited, the shape of a heavily-laden lift ship appeared, the *Lucky Lady* dangling from its belly just a few dozen feet above the smoky factory chimneys.

As Roberts watched, the *Lucky Lady* barely missed knocking a chimney off a tall building, and his eyes narrowed. His newly-acquired airship already had quite enough damage as it was and if she accumulated more in her journey to Halloway's shop, the lift ship captain would be paying for it; Roberts would see to it personally. All airships were required to follow standard regulations and fly at least three hundred feet when crossing cities, but the pilot of this lift ship didn't seem terribly much concerned about the vessel dangling below its gondola. Looking at the *Lucky Lady,* Roberts could practically hear what the lift ship captain had said to his crew, '*No need to waste coal gaining altitude, lads, just get this damned bird off the wharf and who cares if she gets knocked about a bit while we move her.*'

As the lift ship drew closer, Roberts could just make out the words *Hercules* painted on her side, and he frowned. Her captain, a certain John Gallinger, was a loud-mouthed braggart, and he and Roberts had clashed more than once in the past. Now with the *Lucky Lady* in his grip, it was entirely possible that Captain Gallinger wasn't about to pass up the chance to wreak a little revenge; Roberts could only stand on the rooftop and grimly hope that the *Lucky Lady* would make it inside Halloway's shop without more damage.

However, although the lift ship was moving quickly, she began to slow down as she approached Halloway's open roof. Faces appeared on board and activity burst out afresh as the lift ship dropped to a hover and began carefully shunting herself into position to begin lowering the *Lucky Lady* through the opened roof into Halloway's shop.

Without warning, the lift jerked under Roberts' feet as Halloway abruptly pulled the lever and brought them back to ground level in a quick downward swoop that would have caused heart palpitations in anyone not accustomed to being on board an airship with its manifold altitude changes. Barely had the lift touched ground than Halloway was off the platform and stalking irritably toward a corner, calling over his shoulder, "Gavin! Get your great arse over here and help me unless you want your airship permanently stuck on my roof!"

Roberts moved to obey, ignoring Halloway's irritable growls which were loud enough to be heard over the roar of the lift ship now nearly straight above the roof. "*Not set up as a shipyard, not a proper berth to keep her hoisted up, not even...*" Halloway's complaints trailed off as he made some complicated crashing sounds in a dark corner. After a moment or two, the long metal arm of a crane jib woke to life with a screech of poorly oiled gears and began swinging around underneath the opened roof. Roberts critically scanned the mechanism: it looked far too frail to support the *Lucky Lady*'s weight and he stepped forward to protest, but the lift ship was drowning out all other noises as it prepared to lower its burden directly into Halloway's cavernous den.

A flash of movement, and airmen began rappelling directly from the lift ship on quick drop lines: metal handgrips attached to thick ropes which loosened their vice locks when squeezed. An experienced airman could slide down a quick drop line to the ground below within seconds, and the airmen currently winging their way down from the *Hercules* were clearly deft hands at getting out of an airship in a hurry. With what seemed like utter disregard for their own safety, the airmen slid down the quick drop lines at alarming speeds, stopping just when their feet were about to smash into the oil-slick dirt that made up Halloway's ground floor. No sooner had they touched ground than the airmen abandoned their lines and hurried forward to guide the *Lucky Lady* down safely.

Roberts was half-afraid the lift ship would simply unhook the tow chains midair and send its cargo crashing to the ground, but the crewmen were true to their work and expertly lowered the *Lucky Lady* into the darkened gloom of Halloway's den without a scratch. Six men deployed directly into Halloway's lair, and the inventor was quick to bark out orders in a crisp staccato that was almost drowned out by the whining scream of engines. Roberts himself was not spared Halloway's commands, and he gamely set to work obeying them, knowing full well that Halloway could direct the safe landing and berthing of the *Lucky Lady* far better than anyone else in the immediate vicinity. Working like mad, Halloway and his impromptu crew quickly cleared a landing spot on the dirt floor, then extracted several lengths of timber from a murky corner to hastily construct a crude berth while the lift ship growled impatiently above.

Minutes ticked away as the men scrambled about their tasks, then Halloway irritably gestured for the lift ship to continue lowering the *Lucky Lady* into the shop. As she inched her way downward, Halloway manipulated the crane jib to connect with her mooring rings and take on some of the weight of the suspended vessel. The crane groaned in agony as the lift ship began loosening its hold and the full weight of the *Lucky Lady* gradually slipped onto the elderly-looking crane.

It's going to collapse, Roberts thought with heart-stopping certainty. The chains suspending the *Lucky Lady* from the lift ship were now slack, the entire burden resting on the belabored crane as it lowered the airship into the makeshift berth. The rusty machinery groaned as if mortally wounded, and Roberts had just resigned himself to being the new owner of an expensive pile of shattered timbers when the *Lucky Lady* thumped into her new berth with an echoing crunch. She shuddered into silence still intact and miraculously none the worse for her journey, or at least no more visibly damaged that she was when she left the air wharf.

Without further ado, the airmen of the lift ship quickly undid the tow chains, freeing the *Lucky Lady* from her tethers, then promptly took to their ropes again. Mechanized cranks on board swiftly pulled them back into the gondola as the airmen flew upwards in a matter of a few seconds. Even before her crew was safely on board, the *Hercules* was already swinging her nose toward Smothers' wharf, freed of her unwanted burden and metaphorically shaking the dust off her feet.

Roberts coolly ignored their departure, his eyes fixed on his new airship. As the lift ship departed, her shadow was no longer blocking the dirty sunlight from penetrating the gloomy interior of Halloway's crowded workshop, and fitful sun was beginning to creep sullenly back into the vast expanse of cluttered space. Halloway was banging around somewhere in a corner and soon artificial light woke to life, adding its illumination to the dark interior. It wasn't gas lighting, Roberts knew that: Halloway had somehow captured an internal power source inside a network of glass and metal boxes that were beginning to glow with strong, clear light.

Roberts pulled back the portside docking door of the *Lucky Lady,* and light poured into the ruined interior. As visibility increased and all immediate hazards set themselves aside for a time, he had the leisure to fully examine what damage the exploded boiler had wrought. As bad as the outside of the airship looked, he knew it was worse on the inside, much worse.

He wasn't mistaken. Several hundred pounds of exploding boiler metal had shattered the bulkheads like a hammer against toffee and punched a hole the width of five men into the starboard side of the hull. The blast radius was mostly lateral, but a few smaller holes gaped in other parts of the hull. The main deck also had a sizable gash ripped through it and as Roberts prowled the length of the *Lucky Lady,* he surmised that a chunk of shrapnel from the boiler had slammed through the main deck and torn into the envelope, ripping open some of the airbags as it went. If the *Lucky Lady* had been anywhere else than at port at the time of the accident, she would have crashed to the ground, taking all hands with her. Only decisive action and an enormous amount of luck on Roberts and Oboe's part had gotten her safely into a berth rather than laminated against the rocks two hundred feet below the wharf.

Walking the length of the hull, Roberts surveyed the damage, mentally calculating what repairs were needed and what had escaped ruin. The gaping hole gouged out of the *Lucky Lady*'s gondola was not an insurmountable problem, particularly since an airship didn't need a watertight hull, and a few cracks between the timbers only helped with ventilation. However, a few planks and a handful of nails were not going to repair the hole in the *Lucky Lady*'s side. She needed the attention of a skilled shipwright to close the gap as well as gut and refurbish the entire hull and repair the damage to the main deck. Then there was the trouble and cost of replacing the boiler, and the yet unanswered question of what damage had been done to the airship's three engines.

Once, or more properly *if*, the *Lucky Lady* was put to rights again, Roberts was doubtful he would have enough airmen to manage her properly. Several of her existing crew were injured and all of them had to earn a living. Roberts had barely enough money to pay for repairs and refurbishing, and it would be weeks, if not months, before the *Lucky Lady* was back to earning her keep. If he wanted her surviving crew to stick around until then, he knew he would have to provide wages, something he could ill afford.

And then there was the pressing question of who would be willing to hire the *Lucky Lady* once she was in the air again. The Smothers empire dominated the aether and ruthlessly crushed all competition: practically all air cargo under the authority of the British East India Company and much of its sea cargo was transported on Smothers ships. Independent shipping operations did exist: however, the operating cost of an airship, even a short-flight one, was significant, and independent captains faced stiff competition from the Smothers empire. Long-flight airships were even more costly to maintain, thus why the Smothers empire was the only entity that owned and operated long-flight airships. These massive vessels could hold a hundred people, over a hundred tons of cargo, and enough coal to fly from London to China in under a month with only a few stops for refueling. After all, it had been the endless toil and innovation of Smothers engineers that had made long flight a reality, allowing cargo to race from Europe to Asia in a third of the time of marine ships.

The *Lucky Lady* was a short-flight airship, and Roberts' only real option for breaking into the air shipping industry as an independent captain was by keeping his airship close to England. Even then, competition against the Smothers' industry was brutal and Roberts knew that the odds were stacked heavily against him, particularly considering the black mark against his name. He was also acutely aware that unless Halloway was prepared to work his magic, finding cargo to haul would quickly become secondary to the question of exactly how much Roberts could get in scrap from the *Lucky Lady*. He needed a working airship at his disposal before he could start worrying about how she would earn a living.

Halloway, meanwhile, had entered the airship and was peering darkly around him, a portable lantern giving off steady, glowing light in his long fingers. The *Lucky Lady* had been stripped of all unnecessary accouterments prior to transport, and debris from the explosion had disappeared, save for two dark red stains smeared on the floor. Roberts frowned at the traces of blood and turned his eyes back to Halloway who was squatting on the floor and peering thoughtfully at a network of empty holes and indentations marking where the old boiler had sat. Its remains had been taken away, but Halloway was drawing his finger across the marks on the floor, visualizing the absent mechanism as his body stiffened.

Leaving the inventor to his inner musings, Roberts turned his attention to the engine room; only a bulkhead had separated it from the boiler room, and the wooden partition had shattered like glass. However, the wall must have absorbed some of the impact because although all three engines showed damage, it was less than he expected. Pieces of exploded boiler were lodged here and there in the engines, and one iron pipe was bent in a V-shape thanks to a chunk of flying shrapnel. Aside from that, Roberts didn't see too much that worried him and he knew Halloway would have little trouble repairing what damage had been done.

Roberts' thoughts were interrupted by a growl from Halloway. "What in...?" the emaciated man snarled, his waxy white brow creasing into a multitude of furrows. Glaring darkly at Roberts, he demanded curtly, "Tell me you weren't stupid enough to install a Marks and Hammersmith boiler."

"I wasn't. The prior captain was," Roberts answered but barely had he finished than Halloway sprang to his feet and strode towards Roberts, afroth in fury.

"You great daft fool!" Halloway bellowed, an astonishing amount of noise echoing from his washboard-thin chest. Stabbing a skinny finger into Roberts' sternum, Halloway barked out, "Were you trying to destroy the whole damned ship, you daft bugger?"

Roberts coolly grabbed the finger but kept a lid on his temper. Halloway was becoming increasingly agitated which could be useful or disastrous depending on what responses he received. "I told the former captain that the new boiler was bad news, but he wouldn't listen," Roberts responded evenly. "I'm not surprised the damned thing blew, and I'm only sorry that it killed two men along with the captain."

With a snort, Halloway jerked his finger out of Roberts' grip and stalked angrily out of the airship and toward his work bench. "Marks and Hammersmith are a pair of quack engineers who happen to be great salesmen. You're damned lucky that blasted boiler didn't send the whole airship up in flames," he snapped, loud clashing noises accompanying his words in a cacophonous riot of sound.

Roberts didn't respond. Words historically had little effect on Halloway, but the energetic crashing sounds and the way he was unearthing a battalion of tools were encouraging. The inventor continued to stomp his way through his cluttered workshop as a shaft of sun penetrated the pollution-choked air and shone bravely down into the cavernous den, throwing the *Lucky Lady*'s injuries into sharp relief.

"Where's your crew, *Captain?*" Halloway rapped out, the last word sarcastic on his tongue.

"Getting patched up," Roberts answered. Actually truth be known, he wasn't sure where everyone was and had been surprised that none of the crew had arrived on the lift ship. While some of the men had been a mess, Brown, Smith, and Oboe had been relatively unscathed, and it was uncharacteristic of the *Lucky Lady*'s crew to hang back and not attend the damaged airship. The surviving crew members were men Roberts had selected personally, and he knew they were reliable and conscientious. For a moment, a sharp curl of suspicion ran through his gut. Smothers' ire would be quickly descending on anyone connected with the *Lucky Lady,* and Roberts wouldn't put it past the old bastard to currently be making life difficult for the surviving crew members.

Halloway, overloaded with an armful of tools, stomped toward the great gaping hole in the *Lucky Lady*'s side, then paused, brow furrowing. Some remnants of basic human decency must have clawed their way up to the surface for his manic eyes twitched toward Roberts and his mouth creased in a frown. "How many survivors?" he questioned gruffly.

"We lost three: two cooked, one fallen," Roberts responded darkly.

Halloway's frown creased. "Boiled alive. That's a hell of a way to go for anybody." He paused for a second as both men observed a moment of mutual silence in remembrance of the newly dead. After a few seconds, Halloway broke the solemn quiet. "They didn't suffer, Gavin," he said, some of his customary curtness leaving his voice. "Poor sods didn't know what hit them."

"Two of them didn't," Roberts grunted. "Johnson had about two hundred feet to think about it."

Halloway stepped through the jagged hole and dropped his load inside the hull. "The galley was right next to the boiler room which means your steward wasn't ten feet from the boiler when it blew," he huffed. "Trust me, he was dead before he hit the ground."

It was a small comfort, but not much: Johnson's wife had died two years ago, and his twelve year old son was currently being raised by a grandmother and spinster aunt, both in poor health. Having been orphaned at twelve himself with a younger sister to care for, Roberts felt his heart sinking at the thought of informing young William of his father's death. Silverman's wife too, the poor woman was now a widow with two young children to raise on her own.

Life on board an airship was hazardous, and plenty of airmen fell to their deaths or died in fiery crashes every year, both in England and around the world. Over the past few years, it had been Roberts' unfortunate task as first mate to inform shocked, grieving family members that their husbands and sons had fallen off the airship, died from sickness, or gotten themselves knifed during a wild spree of port leave, and that duty did not grow easier with practice.

Halloway was banging something together and Roberts watched him idly, his mind busy with other thoughts. After a few minutes, he offered, "Need a hand?"

"You can get out of my way," Halloway huffed as he shot abruptly to his feet and stepped through the jagged hole in the hull back into his shop. "Go tend your crew and bring the able-bodied ones back. I could use the extra arms, although if you take my advice, a match and a few gallons of oil would solve your problem nicely. She's pretty well banged up."

"I'd still owe on her," Roberts answered casually.

Halloway kicked something out of his way and stepped forward to gather up another armful of tools. "She's got a big arrogant Smothers crest on her. Just what kind of deal did you strike with the old hard-nose to buy her off him?"

"Gentleman's agreement. I named a price and he gave me three years to pay her off," Roberts responded.

Halloway dropped his armload and turned his skeletal frame to face Roberts, his face incredulous. "You made a bargain with Sir Smothers?" he repeated with a mix of incredulousness and outrage. "You're either stupid or desperate and probably both."

His eyes narrowed as he stared at Roberts suspiciously. "How much are you paying for this heap of timbers?" he demanded sharply.

"I'll get her paid off," Roberts deflected the question with a certainty he did not feel.

"You well better," Halloway grunted. "No one defaults on a Smothers debt, not if he wants to keep upright and breathing." Although Halloway shunned the outside world as much as possible, it was impossible to be a resident of London and not know the might of the Smothers empire. Halloway's superlative confidence in his own abilities and his disdain for mankind in general had left him with bravado instead of a healthy regard for his own skin and if he was worried about Roberts' predicament, the situation was dire indeed.

However, Roberts was determined to stay level-headed. "You just worry about getting her fixed up," he responded calmly. "Let me worry about Smothers."

"Fine," Halloway huffed, his attention already back on the new project that had literally dropped from the sky. Gathering up his discarded tools, he reentered the airship's hull and set to work, ignoring Roberts in favor of the difficult challenge of putting the *Lucky Lady* back together.

It was clear Roberts' presence was not needed, and he had plenty of other demands clamoring for his attention. The *Lucky Lady* was safe in Halloway's hands and now that the inventor had set to work restoring her, Roberts knew that he wouldn't stop until the task was completed. Halloway was far too mulish to give up on anything and once a challenge had grabbed his full attention, an army of automatons couldn't drag him away from it. Feeling a trace of relief, Roberts pulled his shoulders back and called out to Halloway, "I'll go tend my crew and bring the bad news to the families of the ones that died. I'll be back later."

A rapping of metal against metal answered him, and Roberts would not have been terribly surprised if Halloway hadn't completely forgotten about his presence. Human interaction never stood a chance when the inventor had something mechanical in his grasp. Leaving his old friend to perform his ministrations, tender or otherwise, on the broken airship, Roberts stepped through the cluttered shop toward the door. Despite its imposing weight, it swung away at his touch, yet closed with a weighty finality as the latch clicked shut.

Outside, Roberts stood in the dirty sunlight that dribbled down onto the filthy street, his mind churning with thoughts, marshaling everything into orderly ranks. He was tense and exhausted, he had two dead men to bury, and precious hours had already slipped past him, time that could have been spent prepping the *Lucky Lady* for her first run officially under his command. Instead, she was a shattered wreck and half her crew was in little better shape. Two families would soon be learning that they had lost their only providers, and Roberts could already feel his hard-earned savings slip away from him with every ring of Halloway's hammer.

And just to add insult to injury, one of Smothers long-flight airships was sailing majestically overhead, directly above Halloway's shop. At three hundred feet above ground, the airship was still staggeringly big, seeming to cast a long shadow over half of London.

Roberts glowered at it for a long moment, then set off down the grimy street. He had work to do.

Chapter Four

Coughing to cover up a few tears that threatened to leak from his eyes, Roberts gently shut the battered wooden door and stepped back into the dirty street. The sounds of female laments were still echoing in his ears as he tried to push aside his emotions, but his nerves were brittle and his mind was clinging to the two sad interviews he had just concluded.

Silverman's wife had taken the news solemnly and although she was barely twenty and had two young children at her side, she shed not a tear as Roberts gently informed her of her husband's death. She had few questions for him and within a few minutes, he took his leave, but not before placing a small sack of money in her hand. He could barely afford the donation, but he felt duty-bound to offer what help he could; Smothers paid his workers well, but there were no benefits extended to the families of those who died in the line of duty. Even if there were, Roberts knew that the families of the *Lucky Lady*'s crew would never see another farthing from the Smothers empire. Whatever help Roberts could offer to Silverman and Johnson's families was all the financial assistance they would receive, and the money he gave to the young widow would see her and the children back to Stratsford where her parents lived.

In sharp contrast, Johnson's mother and sister had dissolved into a flood of tears at the news: the tiny, white-haired woman trembling from grief and age and her equally diminutive, gaunt daughter with silver shot through her mousy brown hair. Their shabby parlor smelled of age and poverty and the stale air of hopelessness. Roberts knew that Johnson had been left a widower years ago and that both his mother and sister suffered greatly from various ailments. Endless doctor bills had eaten away at Johnson's salary and the rest had gone to schooling for William, whom Johnson doted on and was determined to see educated.

It was William that Roberts sought, now that his painful interview with Johnson's mother and sister had been concluded and the two women were left to grieve in private, a small sack of money as his parting consolation. Roberts had left the money with a sense of hopelessness; it was clear that neither woman was capable of earning a living. William was now the man of the house, not an easy position for a boy of twelve. Roberts knew this personally: when a runaway hansom cab had killed his widowed mother when he was twelve, he had been left to scratch a living for himself and his younger sister. William now had a grave task on his young shoulders, and Roberts was now seeking him out before the boy heard about the explosion on board the *Lucky Lady* and drew his own conclusions.

William hadn't been in the tiny apartment when Roberts had walked grimly up its steps, and the new captain of the *Lucky Lady* had been directed a few streets away to Mrs.

Penny's grammar school where William was supposed to be attending. Although the young lad deserved to hear of his father's death from a sympathetic source, Roberts was dreading the upcoming interview with particular loathing; it was unearthing painful memories from his own childhood that time had not softened.

Johnson's family lived in a poor district; the swarming streets were crowded with bedraggled, anxious faces and the smell of poverty and despair hung thickly in the air. Few steam-powered engines prowled the poorer districts; instead there were gaunt livestock that left behind their droppings, and often their carcasses, in liberal quantities. Despite London's position as a hub of technological innovation, thousands of horses still filled the city, in the place of more expensive steam mechanisms for people too poor to afford mechanical assistance. The city still needed to eat, and its streets were busy with flocks of sheep, herds of cows, feathers from a multitude of chickens, and fragrant reminders everywhere that animals were still a vital part of London's commerce.

Roberts picked his way across the streets, the odorous tides of humanity pressing up around him, until he arrived at the school which proved to be little more than a minute parlor full of a dozen children. A few sat on benches while the rest perched on a dirty rug, their eyes on a plump woman with sagging pink flesh and a tired but resolutely cheerful smile.

Alert young eyes swiveled to Roberts as he entered the room, and he quietly noted the few that had a speculative look to them, likely assessing the potential valuables he might be carrying. Roberts drilled them in place with a hard look, daring them to pick his pocket, while keeping a smile hidden away. *I know you, my lads,* he thought to himself. *I was one of you once.* In his youth, Roberts had displayed quite a knack for discreetly riffling through pockets and helping himself to their contents, a skill he had honed with practice over the starving years of his childhood. The adult Roberts was not proud of those memories, much as he knew that his light-fingered ways had kept himself and his young sister from starving more than once before he had finally landed a job on board his first airship.

Mrs. Penny was pleasant but apologetic. "Young William's been missing school as of late," she said quietly as she steered Roberts away from young, inquisitive ears and back into the street where the two could talk without being overhead. "You'll forgive my speaking plainly, Captain, but, well, living with two sick women and his father gone for weeks at a time, the poor lad needs a man to set him straight," Mrs. Penny commented with a helpless shrug.

"His father died this morning in a boiler explosion on board the *Lucky Lady,*" Roberts pronounced quietly.

Mrs. Penny's plump hands flew to her mouth as her eyes widened in shock. "Oh! The poor boy!" she gasped.

"Where can I find him?" Roberts questioned.

Mrs. Penny blinked several times as the beginning of a tear welled up in the corner of her eye. She wiped her hand across her lips in thought. "Word is, he's been running with the Cockle Alley Boys," she ventured, a trifle apologetically.

Roberts nodded. "Thank you, Ma'am. I'll find him, don't you worry. Good day to you." With a nod of courtesy, he turned on his heel and headed back into the filthy street. *Gang*. Every poor street in London had one, and the slums were fair to bursting with them, babies barely past the walking stage on up to crafty old men who had survived long enough to lose all their teeth. Gang membership meant identity and purpose and some semblance of security in what was a brutal, hardscrabble world. Young William had been stuck with two frail, weak-minded women for company while his father was gone for weeks at a time on board the *Lucky Lady*. In that sort of situation, a boy would instinctively turn to a street gang out of sheer self-preservation before he drowned under suffocating layers of femininity.

In the street, Roberts surveyed the massed throngs of filthy, poverty-weary people slogging tiredly across the muck-laden cobblestones. His eyes searched for a lad much like he had once been. There were plenty to choose from on the crowded street and he soon locked onto a likely target. Like a kingfisher darting after a plump trout, Roberts dipped his hand into the crowd and pulled up a writhing mass of something loosely clothed in rags.

"'Ey! Let go, there!" the boy bellowed, kicking out at Roberts who ignored the cries and brought his prey around to face him fully. A flash of coin twinkled in the afternoon sun, and the boy's movements stilled in a heartbeat, his glassy eyes fixed greedily on the halfpenny in Roberts' fingers. Roberts raised and lowered the coin in front of the boy dangling from his hand; the lad's body odor was almost visible and he was so skinny he practically floated in the air like a windsock. Ignoring the stench, Roberts rumbled, "I want to find young William Johnson. He runs with the Cockle Alley crew."

"Will?" the boy questioned. "Aye, I know him." Now that it was clear that a financial transaction was forthcoming, the boy was all alert and made no further protest about being held two feet off the ground.

"Good," Roberts set the boy down but did not loosen his grasp on the mud-stiffed rags the lad called his clothing. "There will be a shilling for you if you bring him to me. Tell him it is about his father and it's important." Roberts set the coin in the lad's grubby palm. "I'll be at the Broken Spar on Haymarket. Step lively.

"Broken Spar. Righto!" With a flutter of dirty fabric, the boy spun on his naked heel and disappeared into the crowd. Watching the street urchin depart, Roberts automatically reached down and felt for the money sack carefully hidden inside his leather waistcoat to ascertain that its contents had not mysteriously transported themselves elsewhere. Nobody is as suspicious as a former thief, and he wasn't about to give the kid any more than he had already bargained for. Satisfied that his meager sack of coins was undisturbed, Roberts left the desperate street behind him to see if there was any word of his crew at the Broken Spar.

As he trod across the broken cobblestones, Roberts turned his thoughts to his crew and wondered how many of them could be persuaded to stick with the *Lucky Lady*. Skilled airmen were in high demand, and the surviving crewmen of the *Lucky Lady* could easily find work elsewhere. With nothing to his name but Smothers' wrath and a crippled airship with a bad reputation, Roberts knew that filling the *Lucky Lady*'s crew manifest would be a difficult challenge, especially considering the wages he could offer.

However, he had a strong feeling Oboe would stay with the *Lucky Lady*. The two men had served together on and off different airships for nearly a decade, and Roberts could offer Oboe a position as first mate of the *Lucky Lady,* something that few men of African heritage had a chance at achieving on a Smothers airship. Roberts had a feeling Carter and Jenkins could be persuaded to stay on board as well, and he tentatively added them to his list.

The pilots were another story: Richardson and Smith had nine children between them and weren't likely to risk their families' well-being on such a shaky venture. Besides, the last time Roberts had seen Richardson, the man had a sizable piece of wood embedded in his thigh. McFadden was nursing a broken arm and Farrington had been a mess of steam burns. Both men had families to support, though they wouldn't be able to work for weeks. Brown was just seventeen and newly married, and he would likely try his luck somewhere else.

Depending on what Halloway would demand for repair work and supplies, Roberts estimated that he had just enough saved away to pay wages for the next few months, but he could not offer near what the men had earned prior to the explosion. If his luck held, the *Lucky Lady* would get back into the air quickly and start earning her keep. If not, Roberts' options were severely limited. A loan was out of the question: the banks of London were too far embedded in Smothers' pockets for any banker to extend Roberts credit, particularly since he had no proof that the *Lucky Lady* was his. There was no title or deed in his name, and he could not thus claim the airship as collateral. His agreement with Sir Smothers had been ruthlessly quick and its stipulations brutal, and Roberts had no choice but to continue the game he had willingly accepted.

Such thoughts consumed him as he strode through London's streets and arrived at the Broken Spar, a foreboding pile of rotting timbers with a tattered section of canvas airbag flapping dejectedly from a faded sign. The tavern was a favorite haunt of many who made the aether their home, offering cheap beer and a useful place to eavesdrop on helpful gossip. Pushing back the tough oak door, which was dented and scored from age and the occasional bar brawl, Roberts stepped into the dank, dark gloom of the interior and scanned the room carefully. It was late afternoon, but airmen worked odd hours and the tavern was nearly full.

Something tinny and cacophonous chimed in the corner; the owner must have gotten his hands on an automaton piano, but this one was so poorly constructed that the noise pouring out of it sounded like someone repeatedly hitting a cat with a hammer. Given the normal clientele of the Broken Spar, Roberts was surprised that someone hadn't got fed up with the garbled attempt at music and smashed the mechanism to shut it up, but he ignored the din and bellied up to the bar.

Something tall and dark materialized at his side: tall himself, Roberts had to tilt his head upwards past glistening ebony skin to two brown pupils set in startlingly white orbs. "Captain," a deep mahogany voice spoke calmly, its tones undergirded by the slightest of accents which identified the speaker as one born in another country.

"Oboe," Roberts replied, relieved to see the new first mate of the *Lucky Lady,* now filling the position that Roberts had given up for the captain's chair. "Report," he commanded. "Where is the crew?"

"They are safe," Oboe responded solemnly. "Mr. Smith suffered a head concussion but was well enough to be escorted home by Mr. Brown. Mr. Carter, Mr. Jenkins, and Mr. Farrington are being treated upstairs by the surgeon Mr. Harding." As always, Oboe enunciated each syllable with perfect clarity and gave each man a title with his accustomed scrupulous courtesy. While some of the crewmen sniggered at Oboe's polished eloquence and referred to him as "Professor" behind his back, Roberts had always found the elegant politeness rather refreshing.

Oboe paused, then continued carefully, "Mr. Richardson and Mr. McFadden are being treated at the Lady Abigail Hospital."

Roberts' brow darkened. "That's a Smothers hospital. Why are..." The words drained away from his lips as sudden clarity hit him with the force of a cannonball.

Divide and conquer: that is how the Smothers empire ran. Roberts could easily picture what had taken place after he had left the wharf to seek out Halloway: an offer of free medical care to the surviving crew members, then a new position on another airship in exchange for never breathing a word about what had actually happened on board the *Lucky Lady*. A man would be a fool to turn down an offer like that, especially with fresh injuries and no better prospects. Richardson and Smith had families and McFadden a badly broken arm that needed expert setting. Roberts didn't think poorly of them for abandoning the *Lucky Lady*, not with what Smothers could offer them for their loyalty and silence.

Oboe watched his new captain keenly and after a moment he said quietly, "After you left us, Captain, there were...offers made. Mr. Richardson, Mr. McFadden, Mr. Smith, and Mr. Brown decided it was in their best interest to accept."

"Brown too?" Roberts repeated. Well, he wasn't surprised: the young man had been an airman barely for a month, and good jobs were scarce in London for men with little experience. Brown would go where the money was, especially since gossip stated he was a newly married man thanks to an unexpected pregnancy and an irate father who insisted on the hasty nuptials. Brown had responsibilities, same as Richardson and Smith, and even less room for risk. *Five men left out of twelve*, Roberts thought, adding himself to the mix. *Can't run an airship with just five*, logic pointed out practically.

Oboe was speaking again. "After you left, Captain, we were barred from entering the lift ship. Captain Gallinger demanded the location of Mr. Halloway's residence. I had no choice but to tell him." In the darkened interior of the tavern, Roberts could see the tribal scarring on Oboe's face rising slightly as he tilted his head in inquiry.

"It's alright, Oboe," Roberts grunted. Halloway closely guarded his privacy, which would partly explain his fury at the unexpected arrival of the lift ship at his doorstep. It would have come to it anyway: there was no way of getting the *Lucky Lady* to Halloway without the assistance of a lift ship. Halloway was simply going to have to deal with the presence of visitors until the *Lucky Lady* was operational again.

"Mr. Jenkins, Mr. Carter, and Mr. Farrington needed a doctor's care," Oboe continued. "I determined that the Broken Spar would be a good meeting point for us to await your return while they were being treated. I sent a runner to Halloway with a message for you."

Roberts didn't bother commenting that Halloway had probably chased the messenger away from his doorstep and merely replied, "Good work." Oboe nodded his head as Roberts continued, darkness in his tones, "I spoke with Silverman's widow and Johnson's mother and sister."

"And his son, Captain?" Oboe questioned.

"I sent a boy to find him and bring him here," Roberts responded. It wouldn't be long, he reckoned. Most street boys could traverse the city faster than a stone sinking through water, especially if there was money to be found at the other end. In fact, it wasn't more than five minutes later when the scarred oak door swung back and two figures stepped inside. The smaller of the two was the grubby urchin Roberts had dispatched on the mission, and his filthy hand was outstretched in confident expectation. The other boy was wary, his eyes anxious and the set of his mouth and chin an eerie replica of his father.

Roberts intercepted the duo and dropped a shilling in the messenger's waiting fingers. "Well done. Now scarper," he rumbled. The coin disappeared in a twinkling, and the boy gave him what looked like a sarcastic salute before sprinting out the door, leaving William alone in a little puddle of light. With a sigh, Roberts stepped forward and placed a kind hand on the boy's shoulder. "Come with me, lad," he said gently. William stiffened, and Roberts could sense the anticipation, sick with dread, riding on the boy's frame.

Nodding curtly to Tom, the landlord, Roberts steered William into a small parlor fitfully lit by dirty sunlight leaking in through a half-opened window. A scarred wooden table and four decrepit chairs were the only furnishing, and the room offered about as much privacy as Roberts could reasonably expect. No sooner had the door closed than William wrenched his shoulder away from Roberts' hand and demanded sharply, "What happened to my father?"

"Sit down, lad," Roberts said tiredly, seating himself in the sturdiest-looking chair available. William swallowed visibly and hesitantly perched himself on the chair opposite Roberts, his face white and tense.

Taking a deep breath, Roberts began heavily, "William, son, I have some bad news."

"Is it about my father?" William asked fearfully. "Is he all right? Is he hurt? He isn't..." the boy swallowed again. "He isn't dead...is he?"

Roberts sighed and William's eyes blared in alarm. Leaping off his chair so fast that he knocked it over, the boy shot to his feet. "No! He isn't dead! Tell me he isn't dead!" he ordered in a high-pitched shriek of alarm.

"I'm so sorry, son," Roberts said with tired kindness. "There was a boiler explosion on board the *Lucky Lady* a few hours ago and your father..."

"*NO*!" the boy screamed, agony clearly etching the truth on his soul as much as he struggled to deny reality. "It's not true! Tell me the truth!" he half-ordered, half-pleaded, backing away from Roberts as if threatened with a knife.

"Easy, lad," Roberts said, reaching a hand out to him, but William backed sharply into the door and flung it open with surprising force.

"It's not true!" Tears were coursing freely down the boy's cheeks. "Go back to the airship! Find my father! He's not dead, I tell you!" Patrons of the Broken Spar were turning their heads to see the commotion, and sympathetic frowns were crossing some of their faces as they realized what was taking place in the room.

Through his tears, William turned his head to see eyes watching him, the room frozen as in a tableau and he the center focus. With a cry intermingled with a sob, the boy raced for the door but in his tears, he could not see the burly fellow who was entering the tavern. William ricocheted off a pendulous midsection as its owner looked down with a frown, but the lad was already stumbling toward the open door as fast as his legs would carry him.

"William!" Roberts bellowed ineffectively, his muscles tensing for pursuit, but a decisive hand quietly restrained him.

"I think it is best to let the boy go, Captain," Oboe said solemnly. "He must accept it in his own way and time."

Oboe was right, but Roberts' feet still demanded forward motion. It was as if for a moment he was a boy again and grieving the loss of a parent: first his father and then his mother. But there was little he could do for William, and as Roberts turned regretfully from the door, men returned to their drinks and the automaton piano sprang to life with a new song that raked painfully along the metal keys.

Oboe's voice rose out of the dim light. "The men will want to see you, Captain," he said, and Roberts' thoughts turned from the grieving William to his three wounded crew members. Silently, he followed his first mate up a dark stairwell to the second story of the tavern which hosted a collection of small, poorly ventilated rooms. All were empty save one which was stuffed with the three patients, a narrow bed, a chair, and a stout fellow ministering to the wounded.

Jenkins' wiry frame was sitting in the chair, a bloodstained cloth pressed to his head and a grim look on his face. Carter, a slender young man of twenty-three, was asleep in the bed, bandages wrapped around his head. Next to him was an unmoving mass of bandages and puffy pink flesh that was Farrington. Roberts paused, observing the men silently, his gut tightening. Jenkins was clearly alive and defiant through his pain but the two silent figures on the bed were as still as corpses, and Farrington's injuries were obviously extensive.

“Sir!” Jenkins bolted to his feet, then jerked in pain and collapsed back into his seat. The fourth man turned around, revealing the stout, puffy-faced John Harding who had been a rising surgeon at the Lady Abigail Hospital until a long-standing habit of speaking his mind had forced him into private practice. From the surgeon's shabby coat and the second-hand bag of surgical gear that lay open on the bed, Roberts surmised that the switch had not been a lucrative one for Harding.

The surgeon gave Roberts a curt nod. “Well, you've certainly made a mess of your crew, Gavin,” he stated by way of greeting.

"Captain Roberts," Oboe quietly corrected but with a weighty sincerity that stated the title was not up for debate.

Harding's face twitched. "Captain Roberts, then," he amended his statement, then turned his head back to Farrington's wounds. "Carter will be fine in a few weeks and Jenkins, if he ever lets me look at his head..."

"Shove it where the sun doesn't shine, Harding," Jenkins muttered loudly under his breath. Airship engineers inevitably ended their careers with varying levels of deafness thanks to long hours spent every day around the squealing roar of engines, and Jenkins was already hard of hearing although he was just under forty. As a result, his muttered words echoed clearly around the crowded room.

Harding ignored the interjection. "...should be back to blowing up boilers in no time at all."

Jenkins gave him a furious look which Harding neatly sidestepped. "This one here, however..." He waved a fleshy hand at the mound of swaddled cloth and angry red wounds that was Farrington.

Roberts stepped forward and gazed intently at the quartermaster. "Will he live?" he questioned tightly.

"Live? Oh, he'll live alright," Harding grunted, as if personally offended by the idea. "But he's a mess, that's no lie, and it's going to be a hard recovery. I've sedated him with morphine and he'll sleep peacefully for awhile. But he's got quite a bit of skin to regrow and he'll be lucky if he regains full use of that arm."

Roberts said nothing for a long moment, silently observing his two wounded crew members on the bed. The pair had shown up at the *Lucky Lady* not long after Roberts had accepted the position of first mate, and he had hired them both. Just three years apart in age, the two men were as close as brothers and nearly inseparable: as Roberts bent down to more carefully examine Farrington's injuries, he noticed that Carter's fingers were wrapped firmly around his friend's left hand. The sight hit Roberts like a physical blow and moisture rose to his eyes as he straightened up hastily.

“Captain,” Jenkins' voice cut through the air. “How is she?” The engineer's voice was tight, biting back the pain with every syllable, and his eyes were aflame with anger and worry.

Roberts suddenly felt as if he had been dipped in lead, but he pushed aside the sensation. This was no time for weakness, not with so much at stake. “I left her with Halloway,” he replied briefly. "He'll put her to rights."

Stepping around the bed, Roberts tried to get a better look at Jenkins' injuries but an impatient arm shoved him out of the way. “You, move,” Harding ordered, swinging his bulk around to face the engineer as Roberts stepped back a pace. The room had barely enough space for three men, and five were filling it out considerably. Oboe was standing at the door watching the proceedings, otherwise there would have been no room for anyone to move. From Harding's impatient gestures, it was clear that he regarded Roberts as nothing more than a nuisance. "You, quit pretending that's going to heal up on its own," Harding snapped at Jenkins. "My God, man," he sucked his breath in as he pried the blood-soaked bandages away from the engineer's head. "I can see your skull through the wound, you daft fool. You're lucky to be alive."

Jenkins' furious glower dimmed considerably when a long needle appeared in Harding's hand and the surgeon began threading it with a length of catgut. With economical, yet careful movements, Harding began stitching up the long strip of flesh that had peeled away from Jenkins' skull while Roberts observed quietly. From the looks of it, all three men faced a long and slow healing period, and Farrington gave every impression that he would carry permanent damages.

As the surgeon was putting his equipment away, Roberts rumbled, "Come by later, John, and I'll pay you what I owe you." To his first mate, he commanded, "Oboe, you're with me. We're going back to Halloway's."

"I'm with you too, Captain," Jenkins said firmly but Harding's meaty hand clamped down on the engineer's shoulder and held him in place.

"Stay put, you idiot," he commanded in a voice that brooked no disobedience. "I'm not wasting all that catgut to see you busting your wound open again. Catgut's a shilling a yard, man. Sit still."

"Jenkins, I need you here to watch over Farrington and Carter," Roberts ordered. "Oboe and I will be back soon."

Harding grunted as he closed the well-worn snaps of his medical bag with a creak of poorly-oiled metal. "You need to wake Carter up every hour or so to make sure he's still with us," the surgeon ordered. "He's got a bad concussion with that head wound, and he could easily slip into a coma. Farrington has had enough morphine, I don't think he'd wake for Judgment Day. I'll be back later this evening to check on all three of you." Sternly, he prodded a finger against Jenkins' chest and admonished, "Do be a good boy and don't move from that chair until I return."

Jenkins glowered freely but said nothing as Harding shuffled out of the room. On the heels of the departing surgeon, Roberts and Oboe picked their way down the rickety stairs and out into the dirty sunlight. With a curt farewell, Harding excused himself and swung his pudgy frame into the crowd in search of his next patient while Oboe followed his new captain in the opposite direction.

The two men rolled forward, each pondering his own thoughts until Roberts broke the silence. "We'll go to Halloway's and see what help we can offer. I'll want you to stay with him. He could use another pair of arms." A regal nod of Oboe's head signaled his acquiescence as Roberts continued, "I'll be dividing my time between Halloway's and the Broken

Spar. As soon as Jenkins and Carter are on their feet, they'll be working with Halloway too. Farrington, well, we'll just have to see how he heals."

"He will recover, sir," Oboe responded calmly. "The *Lucky Lady* too."

Roberts responded with a sniff, his eyes swinging upward to the slowly darkening sky. Although the early parts of the day had been full of sunshine, London was a popular destination for every raincloud that formed across Europe. As the men stalked forward, fat droplets began falling from the sky and turning the streets dark with mud.

Chapter Five

Halloway let Roberts and Oboe into his shop with a minimum amount of fuss and assessed Oboe with a critical eye as the newly minted first mate stepped into the anemic light of the building's interior. Oboe merely smiled beatifically as Halloway completed his frank scrutiny and exclaimed, “You're a whopper, boy.” To Roberts, he frowned and commented, “You didn't tell me you had darkies working for you."

“Halloway, this is Odhiambo Alamieyeseigha, the first mate of the *Lucky Lady,*” Roberts responded evenly, letting a skim of warning cross the surface of his words and emphasizing “first mate” with firmness. Halloway's attitude was typical of most Londoners who encountered someone not of their color, but Roberts was not going to allow disrespect toward his crew. However, Halloway was not likely to present further problems: the inventor wasted little on human interaction, and maintaining a good steam of racism took away valuable time from machines.

“If you don't care to memorize that pronunciation, he also answers to Oboe,” Roberts continued. It had taken him weeks of practice and careful tutelage under Oboe's patient instructions until he could correctly pronounce all eleven syllables of the man's native name without verbally stumbling. The lessons had been an educational endeavor and had helped pass the time: when an airman is stuck on board an airship with nothing to look at but sky for hours on end, any diversion is heartily welcome.

Halloway didn't respond as he continued to eyeball Oboe with the look of someone assessing a plow horse for its prowess. Well over six feet fall, Oboe's broad-shouldered frame was sculpted like a Greek god, and his worn shirt and faded trousers hung on him with the dignity of royal garments. A galaxy of tribal scarring patterned Oboe's face and a cluster of thick braids hung nearly to his waist and was held back with a strip of leather.

After a few more seconds of scrutiny, Halloway snorted and shot a look at Roberts as he commented, "I told you to bring me any extra pairs of arms you had. I reckon this one here counts as at least two. Come on." With that, the gaunt inventor spun on his heel and marched back into the chaotic mess that was his workshop.

The *Lucky Lady* was sitting in the middle of a morass of equipment, hastily-assembled scaffolding creeping up her sides and the ringing of a hammer echoing in the cavernous den. Roberts frowned in surprise at the noise: Halloway lived like a monk in a cloister, shunning human company for steel mechanisms. He must have been desperate to turn to an assistant. Roberts was frankly surprised that the inventor had accepted someone else into his workshop which was normally locked down tighter than an asylum.

Knowing Halloway as he did, Roberts should have guessed that it wasn't living hands that were wielding the hammer. As he stepped around the *Lucky Lady*'s gondola, light fell upon a gigantic, fantastical humanoid-shaped mechanism methodically pounding away at the airship's hull. Steam hissed in short blasts of white as a massive mechanical arm swung a hammer in its metal fist, driving iron into wood. Two sturdy legs sprouted under a thick torso and steel-plated shoulders were hunched upwards to support two enormous arms and a proportionally tiny head. A quick assessment, and Roberts estimated the contraption to be at least eight feet tall and easily a ton in weight, if not more.

As he watched in stupefied amazement, a mechanical arm moved to a table at its side and, with exquisite delicacy, picked up a nail with fingers as thick as a sausage. The nail was lifted to the wooden hull as the other arm swung around to carefully lift a board and maneuver it over the yawning hole in the *Lucky Lady*'s side. As Roberts watched, the mechanism lifted the hammer and slammed it down on the nail, driving the nail, its hand, and part of its arm through the board, in the process considerably widening the already gaping hole in the gondola by several inches.

Halloway gave a grunt of exasperation and thundered toward the contraption as it pulled its hand loose with a heart-rending crunch of shattering wood, taking a few more inches of gondola with it. Undaunted, the mecha selected another nail from the table at its side and lifted it up to position. Halloway jerked back a cover on the mechanism's back, revealing a relay of valves, levers, and pressure gauges inside. Two levers snapped downward under Halloway's expert hand, and the golem froze in place, one hand still gripping the nail delicately between its monstrous fingers.

As the last echoes of shattering wood died away, Roberts felt his heart climb down his throat and settle back into his chest where it belonged. For a few frenzied moments, he had envisioned the enormous mechanical aberration methodically tearing through his airship until he had nothing left but a splintered pile of wood and canvas to claim as his own. But the thing, whatever it was, had stopped, and not a single hiss of valves called out a warning that it was about to move again.

When he could trust his voice to sound without an embarrassing squeak, Roberts demanded heavily, "What the hell is that?"

"This? Experiment I'm working on," Halloway said abruptly, eyes busy with the relay of gauges and intake pipes that made up the device's innards. He made several adjustments as Roberts and Oboe watched the humanoid construct with extreme wariness, both wondering precisely what they would do if it suddenly decided to rise up and revolt against its creator and any bystanders. Roberts had seen similar devices before, automaton constructs that toiled alongside human workers in the factories, shipyards, and docks of the Smothers' empire. These highly valued devices were put to work lifting great loads and performing heavy manual labor that humans could not do as efficiently or safely. However, these were clunky prototypes compared to the humanoid-shaped object currently frozen in position as Halloway impatiently fiddled with its innards. Roberts had never seen an automaton capable of such fine motor movements, and he knew that many keen-eyed businessmen would sell their souls to own the construct's schematics.

Halloway gave the controls several more prods and the mecha stirred to life again. A shovel-sized hand lowered as it placed the nail and hammer back on the table, then took five slow steps toward the far wall, Roberts and Oboe moving out of the way in a casual sidle that belied how much they were quelling an innate desire to run for safety. No construct Roberts had ever seen was capable of independent locomotion: the devices that lifted and carried under Smothers' rule had a fixed base or moved on a track. In sharp contrast, Halloway's creation had two legs that lifted and stepped in the manner of a human. Granted, it was an exceedingly heavy, unwieldy tread that shook the earth with every step, but the two thick legs carefully balanced the massive upper body without a wobble.

At a wall, the construct paused and lifted a heavy beam in its gargantuan arms. With a clang of metal, the upper torso rotated cleanly at the waist as it began retracing its steps, its thick jointed legs stepping backwards with the same precision as its forward movements.

"Hey, Tuba, or Piano, or whatever your name is," Halloway stated irritably as he began ascending the scaffolding, turning his attention back to the *Lucky Lady.* "I need your arms. We have work to do. You too, Roberts."

"First, tell me what that thing is I am supposed to be working with," Roberts responded evenly, trying to cover up his wariness. The mechanical contraption carefully set the massive beam alongside the hull of the *Lucky Lady* and stopped as if patiently awaiting orders, but Roberts wasn't convinced that it was completely under Halloway's control. It wouldn't take a very creative imagination to envision what sort of harm the construct could wreak if a few parts fizzled in its head. Next to it, the damaged *Lucky Lady* seemed appallingly fragile and she was already carrying fresh damage the mecha had just created on her hull. For all its appearance, an airship was a surprisingly delicate and highly-tuned contraption, and Roberts could easily see the automaton causing more damage than Halloway was trying to fix.

"New automaton model," Halloway called from somewhere inside the *Lucky Lady*'s belly. "Been working on it for several years, but I've only recently been able to put it to use. It's more useful than a human assistant and a lot stronger."

Roberts examined the mecha closely. "Anyone else know about it?" he questioned carefully. That was the problem with Halloway: he never fully considered the far-ranging possibilities of his many inventions, particularly the widespread devastation they could cause in the hands of the wrong men. Roberts had a fleeting but vivid image of automaton armies treading through the streets of London under the direction of a totalitarian maniac. Or take Smothers - give his engineers a crack at figuring out Halloway's automaton and six months to build a fleet and the collective monarchs of Europe might as well hand over their crowns to who was now their new dictator.

"No," Halloway replied. "It's just for me to use." *Typical,* Roberts thought to himself. It was a different world in Halloway's brain, one that stopped not far beyond the doors of his immensely complex workshop. Roberts thought about commenting on Halloway's complete disregard for the complexities of Europe's political structure or, come to that, basic human behavior patterns, but the *Lucky Lady* was clamoring for his attention.

Ignoring the automaton for now, or as much as one could ignore an eight foot mechanism capable of independent motion, Roberts joined Halloway inside the *Lucky Lady*'s hull and halted in surprise. Halloway had been busy in the few hours Roberts had been gone. Complex diagrams and schematics were scribbled on the floor in chalk, and off to the side was a crude work bench Halloway had constructed out of several planks and two sawhorses. It was already covered with assorted tools and a stack of drafting paper, and Halloway was bent over the work bench, a thick pencil in his fingers and his forehead creased in a frown.

Leaving Halloway to his own devices, Roberts walked the inside of the *Lucky Lady*'s hull, noting the chalk scribbles Halloway had etched on the floor and trying to make sense of what they indicated. He was mulling over a particularly baffling chalk scribble when Halloway's voice broke through his thoughts.

"Still speak that Chinese lingo?" Halloway questioned, apropos of nothing.

"Enough to get by," Roberts grunted in surprise, wondering at the question. Unlike many of the poor children he and Halloway had grown up with, Roberts had managed four years of formal schooling, courtesy of a mother who had worked her fingers to the bone to afford it. He had brought away with him a basic competence in Latin and Greek and a realization that he possessed a natural knack for languages, which had come in handy. An airship was often an ethnic soup with more than English words filling the air, and Roberts still recalled quite a bit of the Cantonese that old Dao Suen on board the *Gallant* had taught him all those years ago. The *Gallant* had flown to China more than once, giving Roberts opportunity to put his language lessons into practice, although his grasp of Chinese was beginning to fade a bit with time.

"What about Indian?" Halloway demanded. "Hindo or whatever they call that heathen tongue?"

"Hindi," Roberts answered. There had been another long-flight airship with Ashkor on board, a lanky young Indian who had drilled Roberts in his native language. Roberts still couldn't make heads or tails of written Hindi, but he'd grasped the basics of spoken Hindi and could get around on the streets of Bombay with more or less success.

Halloway grunted, almost as if in disapproval. "You'd better remember those lingos. You're going to need them."

Roberts let several seconds pass before responding. "Why?" he questioned. suspiciously, his forehead wrinkling in dark puzzlement. Halloway was being uncharacteristically obtuse, and Roberts didn't see where he was heading with all this talk about language: the inventor barely acknowledged people of his own race and color, let alone anyone who wasn't white and didn't speak English.

"Because you'll be flying to places where they're spoken," Halloway said impatiently as if his statement was obvious and Roberts was being willfully dense.

"Flying where? To the Orient? On the *Lucky Lady*?" Roberts' incredulous bark filled the airship's hull. "Jacob, you're a damned fine inventor, but don't try fooling me that this airship of mine is going to make it anywhere more than four hundred miles beyond London. She's a short-flight ship. Domestic only."

"When I'm done with her, she'll fly to Canton and back," Halloway said with precise finality.

Roberts stared at him for a long second. "That's impossible," he pronounced flatly. Halloway's grasp on reality had always been tenuous at best, but the inventor had never been mistaken when it came to machines. However, his last statement was so completely absurd that Roberts almost laughed in Halloway's face. "It's completely out of the question, not with a little bird like the *Lucky Lady,*" he continued, watching as Halloway bristled under his words. "Do you know just how much coal a long-flight ship burns through on average to get from London to Canton? The *Gallant* carried twenty tons in her at one go, and we stopped to refuel five times. The *Lucky Lady* doesn't have room for anything like twenty tons of fuel, and even if you could cram all that inside her, she'd have no room or weight left for cargo..."

"That's because the *Gallant,* like all airships has a standard water tube boiler," Halloway snapped impatiently. "Inefficient and fuel-hungry and takes so much coal it's a wonder the ships ever make it off the ground, let alone fly to the Orient."

Halloway drummed his fingers impatiently on the table. "A water tube boiler wastes two thirds of the fuel you put in and gives you damn little in return. Fuel bed boilers are what was first considered back in the early airship days, but no one could make one that actually worked, so they ended up using water tube boilers instead." He slammed his hand down on the table impatiently. "I can."

Roberts considered his words carefully. Halloway took offense easily and did not graciously accept a challenge to his intelligence and skills. After several seconds, Roberts stated levelly, "You do realize it was a new boiler that's the reason she's got a bloody great hole in her side, don't you?"

Halloway's shoulders stiffened. "Yes, you were daft enough to let a Marks and Hammersmith boiler on board," he responded icily.

"Not my decision," Roberts replied coolly.

Halloway inhaled sharply, the beginning clamors of battle rising to life in his eyes. "Do you want me to fix your airship or do you want to hang around griping, Roberts?" he demanded harshly. "I've got plenty of other things to do than putting this heap of wood back together, you know."

Before Roberts could respond, the sound of metal waking to life roared ominously, and they both turned their heads to see the automaton beginning to move as if obeying an invisible command. Before either man could move, a gigantic metal arm moved in a wide arc, accompanied by a cacophony of crashing noises signaling that many metallic objects had just hit the floor.

Halloway was on his feet in a second and racing for the automaton before it destroyed something valuable. Roberts watched him go, heavily weighing his options, of which there was a regrettable paucity. Despite his many eccentricities, Halloway was a savant with anything mechanical and no invention of his ever failed. Granted, his mechanical construct had just knocked over an entire shelf's worth of equipment, but Roberts knew that the device simply needed some fine-tuning to perfect it. He had absolute trust in Halloway's skills, and that trust had never been tested, not up until now with the inventor's madcap proclamations ringing in Roberts' ears.

The absurdity of the *Lucky Lady* flying from London to China was so out of touch with reality that Roberts could not begin to wrap his head around the idea. It was the ever-present paradox of an airship: more altitude and distance meant more coal, more coal meant more weight, more weight meant less altitude and distance. Smothers hadn't made his millions on airships alone: even with the most meticulous of engineering, airships couldn't carry nearly the cargo of marine ships, and water-going vessels still filled the world's oceans, particularly when the cargo in question had thousands of miles to cross and its owners were more interested in low shipping costs than speedy delivery.

Although every year brought with it new airship developments, particularly from Smothers' overworked inventors, there were still only a handful of airships that could span the distance between Europe and the Orient. Those that could were massive beasts which filled the sky like thunderclouds, their hulls positively abristle with weaponry and enough equipment to cope with the hazards that awaited any airship crossing a distance of thousands of miles. The thought of a short-flight airship making it around the world was ludicrous. It wasn't just fuel and distance that a long-flight airship had to cope with but also mountains, violent air streams, ferocious storms that could blow the airbags off a ship, hostile vessels, massive patches of empty land below where a crash would go unnoticed for months, the possibilities were endless. Flying wasn't just about boiler efficiency and weight ratios but also lightning bolts, erratic air currents, and a host of other catastrophes that could besiege any human who took a hankering to travel on air.

For the first time in his life, Roberts felt his confidence in Halloway's skills disintegrating. A small part of him was beginning to wonder if he could tactfully remove the *Lucky Lady* from her current location and bring her somewhere else where she could be attended by someone with a better grip on reality. There were skilled airshipwrights across London, and not all of them labored under Smothers' reign. It would not be a terribly difficult matter to find someone who could patch up the *Lucky Lady*'s hull, install a used but serviceable boiler, and hammer out the dents in her engines, enough to make her airworthy again. Roberts had just about enough money saved away to get her put right again, maybe not as pretty as she once was, but useable. Once she was repaired, he wouldn't trust her flying beyond England's shores, but there was work to be found domestically if he dropped his prices low enough to compete with Smothers.

However, a hack repair job and cut-rate shipping fees weren't going to repay the debt Roberts owed on the *Lucky Lady*, nor would flying her within England's shores earn him the income he needed. If he grew desperate, there was the possibility of selling *Lucky Lady* if no other options presented themselves. That was not a promising option: the *Lucky Lady* was six years old, and there was little demand for older airships, particularly since new models and modifications were churned out yearly. Not to mention that few people would be tempted to purchase an airship with a reputation like the one carried by the *Lucky Lady*.

The sound of Halloway stomping back inside the wounded airship interrupted Roberts' musing. "You can't *still* be thinking this over, Gavin," he growled irritably.

Picking his words carefully, Roberts responded slowly "Jacob, you know you're the best damned inventor and engineer this side of Europe and beyond. I just...well, *look* at her. She's a little bird and it's a hell of a long way from here to China. Even with the right engine power to get her there, what's to keep her from getting blasted off course by a storm or shot out of the sky by pirates or..."

"I said she'll fly," Halloway interrupted curtly. "Airship pirates and storms, that's your problem. You're the airship captain. What you do with your ship once she's back in the air is your lot, not mine. Now," he snapped out sarcastically, "are you planning on doing something useful anytime soon or are you going to stand around bellyaching? I've got better things to do with my time than listening to you whining."

Further protest seemed pointless. Although Halloway's proclamation was ludicrous at best, Roberts knew that he didn't have many other options. He'd simply have to trust Halloway blindly and hope that he'd end up with a working airship once the inventor was finished with her. He severely doubted the *Lucky Lady* could fly as far as Halloway promised, but if Roberts was lucky, he'd end up with a fast, agile vessel that would give him an edge in the cutthroat competition. That alone would be more than he hoped for and far more than he could afford elsewhere.

For now, thoughts of his wounded men tugged at Roberts' attention; if he wanted to check up on them back at the Broken Spar, now was the time to leave. Many parts of London were to be traversed after dark only by the brave or foolish, and Roberts didn't want to tempt fate by risking the chance of being robbed. Making his decision, he stifled a yawn and said to Halloway, "I'll leave Oboe here with you and go back to check on the wounded crew. I'll be back first thing in the morning."

"Fine. I'll have a list of what I need when you get back," Halloway responded shortly. "It'll be a cost rebuilding her, you understand," he warned.

"I'll get you the money," Roberts promised but with some trepidation. Halloway could easily blow through everything Roberts had saved in order to outfit the *Lucky Lady* in the latest in technical wonders; however, the inventor was unlikely to ask compensation for his time and labor. Halloway seemed curiously immune to the charms of money except as a medium of exchange for tools and gadgets, and as long as Roberts could keep a check on Halloway's spending, he might just walk away with some of his carefully-saved money still in his pocket.

The sun was dropping low on the horizon of the city, and a few fitful gaslights were beginning to glow in the oncoming darkness as Roberts stepped out into the street, his eyes sweeping ahead of him watchfully despite the press of demands on his thoughts. Rain pattered sullenly on his shoulders and ran down the back of his collar, but he irritably ignored the discomfort. The streets he stalked were rough for a man who walked by himself, but tall ones with broad shoulders tended to discourage would-be attackers, and Roberts ended his journey at the Broken Spar unmolested.

The tavern was crowded and noisy, but someone at least had mercifully turned off the cursed automated piano or simply broken its innards to shut it up. Airmen of assorted sizes, ages, and nationalities filled the tables and bar, English mixing with a handful of other tongues. As Roberts pushed his way through the crowd, he noticed several eyes staring at him, then carefully looking away when he met their gaze evenly. He wasn't precisely surprised: word spread fast, and wise Smothers employees already knew that it was a bad career move to be seen speaking to Roberts.

In contrast, Tom, the landlord of the Broken Spar, caught Roberts' eye and nodded as he approached the bar. "Harding's up with them," Tom shouted over the noise. Roberts nodded a thanks and clumped heavily up the stairs to the room where his wounded men lay.

Carter and Farrington were in the narrow bed and Jenkins rested on a rough cot that took up almost all available floor space. Harding was just putting his equipment away, and he nodded briefly as Roberts entered the room. "Oh, there you are, Captain," he commented shortly. "I just gave Farrington another injection to keep him happy. I'll leave you salve for his wounds, and he'll need his dressings changed twice a day. I'll also leave morphine to give him if the pain grows unbearable. And..." the surgeon dusted his hands off, "That will be five pounds from you, Captain."

Roberts handed the money over and questioned gruffly, "How are they?"

"Jenkins and Carter will need those sutures out in ten days, so send them back to me then. Do try to keep them in bed at least until tomorrow, but I imagine they will be clamoring to be back to work in a day or two. At least make sure they don't rip their stitches out."

"And Farrington?"

The surgeon sighed. "Well, his arm's a piece of work, no doubt, but I've seen worse. I want to see him every day and after a week or so, I'll have a more accurate prognosis. Best you can do is keep the dressing changed and the bandages fresh. If it goes gangrenous..."

The thought trailed away into silence as both men considered the alternative. Up until a few years ago, a rotten limb had meant an excruciating removal involving bone saws and long minutes of total agony, until the British Medical

Academy had patented a steam-powered cutting device that could remove a gangrenous limb in a matter of a few seconds. That and a decent construct limb could get a man back to work in a reasonable amount of time, but Roberts was determined that Farrington would not have to face that option.

Harding picked up his bag with a grunt, his sagging frame heavy on his relatively small feet. "Keep an eye on your men, Captain," he cautioned. "And get some sleep and something to eat. You look half-dead."

With that, Harding departed, leaving Roberts with three slumbering men to monitor. He seated himself heavily in the vacant chair and listened to the thrumming of rain which mixed with the sounds of men making merry at the bar below. The night spun on its way as he watched and waited, dark worry fighting against sleep until unconsciousness at last claimed mastery.

Chapter Six

Fitful edges of the dawn crept through cracks in the battered shutters and crawled across the dusty floorboards to where Roberts was propped uncomfortably in the chair, his head against the wall. Instinct opened his eyes for him as various knots in his shoulders and neck began griping about the uncomfortable night he had just spent sleeping upright. Roberts ignored the complaints: life on board an airship meant long and arduous hours, and it was common for airmen to work until they dropped asleep where they fell, hopefully on something reasonably soft. The chair hadn't been the most uncomfortable thing Roberts had ever rested against in pursuit of slumber.

Farrington, Carter, and Jenkins were all still breathing, and no fresh blood seeped through their bandages. Deciding against waking them, Roberts limped down the uneven steps and into the deserted bar, the sounds of the streets drawing him forward to see what sort of day was dawning. Outside the cobblestones were sticky with mud, but a hopeful-looking sun peeked over the edge of the taller buildings, and the streets were already busy with early morning traffic.

In search of a privy, Roberts stalked into the alleyway leading off behind the Broken Spar and in the dim shadows of the passage, he didn't see the jumble of barrels and pieces of wood piled up inside the alley until he had stubbed his toe on a board. With a string of low curses, Roberts angrily kicked a barrel, sending a small figure scurrying frantically out from the middle of the pile of wood.

"William? Lad, what are you doing here?" Roberts asked gruffly as the boy shot to his feet. A ray of pale morning light fell across William's face, illuminating his mud-streaked features and the red-rimmed eyes that had clearly spent the night crying.

The boy sniffed and angrily wiped his sleeve across his face, then drew his shoulders back and gave Roberts a belligerent look that did not quite disguise his sorrow. "Wanted to talk to you, Mr. Roberts," William muttered, one foot drawing a squiggle on the filthy cobblestones.

"I'll listen to what you have to say, lad, but it's Captain now," Roberts said, striving for kindness. "The *Lucky Lady* is mine now." William's face registered dull surprise, and Roberts nodded him forward. "Go on inside, lad. I'll be in shortly." When he returned, William was standing uncomfortably in the middle of the empty bar, mud from his clothes dripping slowly onto the dirty rushes covering the floorboards. Tom was visible as an irritated grumble and balding head sticking out of the basement doorway as he bellowed at his wife about something, but the tables were empty of customers.

Roberts wearily towed William back into the small, still-dirty parlor they had conferenced in last evening and shut the door behind them. He didn't want to be curt with the lad, but he had quite enough on his plate as it was, so he dropped heavily onto a chair and looked at the boy expectantly.

William was drawing himself up, his thin chest defiantly pushing forward as his jaw tightened with determination. Swallowing as if gulping in courage, the boy said in a rush, "I reckon, Captain Roberts, you need a steward for the *Lucky Lady*, right? Now that my father is..."

He paused and for one second, Roberts thought William was going to burst into tears. But the boy stoically clamped down on his emotions and pushed resolutely forward, "...my father is...dead." William swallowed again, but Roberts, sensing where the conversation was headed, tactfully cut him off.

"William, lad, a steward's a man's job on an airship," he stated kindly, but William's eyes blazed angrily.

"I can do it!" the boy snapped out. "My father taught me a lot of things and...I can do it!" he repeated belligerently.

Roberts ran an appraising eye up and down the boy's small frame and shook his head slightly. "How old are you, son?" he questioned. At that moment in time, he couldn't quite remember William's exact age.

"Fourteen," William stated quickly, but his eye barely held Roberts' gaze for a second before darting away.

Roberts rumbled a short bark. "If you're going to lie,

boy, you're going to have to do better than that." He rose to his feet and added, "And I don't abide liars on my airship."

"I'll be thirteen in two months!" William quickly amended, almost frantically.

Roberts sighed. "Will, the *Lucky Lady*'s a wreck: her boiler blew and chewed a big hole out of her side. She won't fly for weeks, if not months. Three of my men have already gotten jobs elsewhere and three more are upstairs with stitches and bandages. If the ship flies again, we'll be gone months at a time. She needs men to fly her, not boys." Pausing, he added, "Your father wanted you in school, lad. That's what he talked about all the time."

"And let Granny and Auntie Mae starve?" the boy spat out angrily. "I'm all they've got left! It's my job to take care of them!" By now, tears were beginning to roll down the boy's face despite his best efforts to keep them sealed away, and Roberts could not help but see his younger self mirrored in the lad's defiant, desperate expression. Unbidden his mind swept away to a long-ago memory when he had begged a job off the *Gallant*'s quartermaster so that his sister would have food to eat and a roof over her head.

William was swiping angrily at his tears. "I'm done with school," he declared firmly. "I've got responsibilities now. Who else is going to care for Granny and Auntie Mae except me?" An audible sniff of restrained grief followed his words.

Roberts considered this and finally sighed. "Alright, William," he said heavily. "I'll pay proper wages for a man's job, but I expect a man's work out of you." William's eyes flashed with triumph through his grief and fear, but he forced himself to nod firmly. "You'll work directly under Mr. Farrington, the quartermaster," Roberts continued. "Right now, he's upstairs with a mess of steam burns and a shredded arm. Your first duties are getting him back on his feet. You'll change his bandages, learn how to give him morphine injections, and take care of his needs."

Roberts was already turning toward the stairs and William scrambled to keep up with him. "Mr. Jenkins, the night engineer, and Mr. Carter, the bosun, have head wounds. You'll be getting them what they need until they are up and moving on their own." Shooting a look at William, Roberts growled, "Are you hearing me, boy?"

"Yes," William answered.

Roberts stopped dead and fixed the boy with a steely eye. "Yes, *Captain*," he growled.

"Yes sir, I mean, Captain," William stuttered hastily, but Roberts had already turned his attention back to the room where his men were resting. He pushed open the door to find Jenkins carefully unwrapping the bandages encircling Farrington's arm. The engineer stiffened to attention as Roberts entered the room.

“Meet the new steward, Jenkins,” Roberts rumbled as he pushed William forward. “This is William Johnson.”

Jenkins frowned at the name, his eyes sweeping the boy and noting the features of the father present in his son's thin, slightly bewildered face. “Steward, Captain?” Jenkins repeated.

“Nurse boy for now,” Roberts grunted. “Young William here is in charge of getting the three of you back on your feet.” Turning to the boy, he ordered, “Change Mr. Farrington's bandages. You need to keep his wounds clean or he will lose that arm to gangrene."

William swallowed but obediently moved to the side of the bed and began carefully unwrapping the bandages. As the white cloth fell away to reveal the terrible wounds underneath, his face whitened and he looked close to vomiting. Farrington shifted and a low moan escaped from his lips.

William froze, but Roberts glared at him. “Change the bandages, boy! He's got to keep that arm,” he ordered. The words shook the lad from his reverie, and he continued to pull away the sticky wrappings, dropping them to the floor with a shudder of revulsion. Timidly, he took the tin Roberts shoved into his hand and carefully began daubing a noxious yellow concoction on the quartermaster's wounds.

Roberts watched closely, then grunted, “If Mr. Farrington is in major pain, he'll need an injection of morphine. You know how to give one, William?” he questioned.

William mutely shook his head. "You'll learn," Roberts grunted. "Mr. Jenkins can show you." The boy looked entirely displeased with the idea but he stuck to his work and carefully daubed the dressing on Farrington's wounds.

After a few minutes of watching to make sure William was sticking to his task, Roberts stated, "I'm going to Halloway's to check on the *Lucky Lady*. I'll be there most of the day. William, you're in charge of keeping Mr. Farrington's bandages clean. Mr. Jenkins and Mr. Carter are to stay put in bed. Don't let them walk around."

"I'm *fine*, Captain," Jenkins growled. "It's just a few stitches and I..."

"You keep yourself in bed for one more day of rest, Jenkins," Roberts commanded. "Doctor's orders. And your captain's as well." Jenkins shot him a resentful look, but Roberts let it pass. "I'll be back later," he announced, then stomped out of the room, leaving William to tend to the men.

The air outside was thick with moisture and the ever-present stench of London, and Roberts tried to keep his breaths short as he stepped across the mucky road toward Halloway's. After a boyhood growing up in the contaminated, soot-laden air of the city, life on board an airship flying through clean skies had been a new beginning for his belabored lungs. Even now, Roberts hadn't quite given up wishing that he could simply stop breathing whenever he walked through London.

An airship roared in the distance as Roberts' mind circled around the events of the past twenty-four hours. *A crew of six, well, five men and a boy,* he mused to himself. If the *Lucky Lady* got back on her feet again, six crew members would be just barely enough to keep her in the air for short flights. Roberts could pilot her, and Oboe could also take his turn at the helm. Jenkins, once he was recovered, would keep her engine room running, although he really needed an assistant. Farrington and Carter would return to their duties, as well as take their turn on the airbags and the myriad of other tasks that needed attention. They needed at least one able airman, if not two, particularly a skilled catwalk man to keep her airbags tight and leak-free.

If Halloway was somehow right and the *Lucky Lady* could fly internationally, she would need several more crew members to keep her aloft: two or three pilots, a well-trained steward, a day and night engineer, and a handful of skilled airmen, particularly ones capable of wielding weapons in defense of the airship. Safety was always a pressing issue once an airship ventured out of English air, and long-flight airships were massive beasts that plowed sedately through the clouds, their gargantuan frames daring any airship to attack them. If their size was not enough of a deterrent, the cannons mounted on their sides were usually enough to convince pirates to try their luck elsewhere.

In sharp contrast, the small *Lucky Lady* would be a tempting target for any enterprising attacker. Flying her through foreign skies was a reckless venture, and all Roberts had to offer potential crew members was a pitiful salary and a madcap story about a short-flight airship flying all the way to China and back. Only the crazy or very desperate would take him up on the offer.

Such thoughts consumed Roberts' mind as he stalked moodily through the muddy streets, stopping once to buy three hot pies from a plump, cheerful lady with a tray around her neck. The pies could have contained beef or alligator for all the attention Roberts paid to them as one disappeared untasted down his throat and the other two found their way inside a handkerchief. Halloway could run for days without food, kept alive by sheer adrenaline and the occasional assistance of chemical stimulants, but Roberts wanted the best work out of the mad scientist and was determined to keep shoving food down Halloway's gullet before the man starved to death.

The door to Halloway's shop swung open when Roberts banged on it, the normal battalion of locks quickly unfastened as if awaiting his return. As he stepped inside, he noticed that the divided ceiling was flung wide open to take advantage of every last drop of sunlight the morning sun had to offer. In the middle of the cluttered shop was a heart-stopping sight: Halloway's automaton was standing directly under the belly of the *Lucky Lady*, hoisting the airship aloft in its massive arms, the entire weight of the vessel cradled in its grasp as it balanced the airship in its splayed fingers.

Roberts froze, eyes gaping in surprise and his whole frame seized with a premonition that the slightest wrong-doing on his part would send the *Lucky Lady* crashing to the ground. The mechanical automaton had looked unbelievably powerful the other day but now, perched under the airship and supporting her entire weight in its arms, it seemed pitifully frail, despite its height and bulk. The *Lucky Lady*'s makeshift berth had disappeared, replaced with a complex cat's cradle of wires and chains dangling from the reinforced beams of the building, and Roberts realized that Halloway intended to suspend the airship from the roof. He sincerely hoped that the building's structure could take the *Lucky Lady*'s weight and not collapse around their ears.

A screeching of the elderly crane told Roberts that Halloway was busy at work, and he shifted slightly as Halloway called out, "About time. I've already got a list of parts and equipment I need." The engineer was busy at the controls of the crane as he carefully manipulated it inside the crowded building, making good use of what little space was available.

When the crane hissed to a stop, Roberts tossed one of the hot pies up to Halloway who caught it inquisitively. Examining the offering for a moment, Halloway took a large bite as if eating were a strict necessity to be dealt with as quickly as possible.

A slight noise, and Oboe appeared at Roberts' elbow. His face was calm as usual; but Roberts suspected that Oboe had gone with little sleep or food the entire night. Handing over the last of the pies, Roberts commanded, "Go get some rest, Oboe. I'll take over for now." Oboe nodded, then disappeared into the depths of the shop to find a pile of gunny sacks or a soft-looking patch of ground to serve as a makeshift bed and catch some well-earned sleep.

Halloway cranked the crane's controls and waved a long arm at Roberts. "Here, guide these cables underneath her belly, Gavin," he ordered. Several thick cables dangled from the ceiling, and Roberts hesitantly took hold of one as he stared critically at the automaton still holding the *Lucky Lady* off the ground. He was less than thrilled about standing directly under several tons of suspended wood, but Halloway was in no mood for cowardice.

"Get under there, you great baby!" Halloway barked impatiently. "The construct'll hold her. Stop being a pansy." Hoping deeply that his old friend was right, Roberts stepped directly underneath the belly of the airship, guiding the canvas-wrapped cable underneath to support her as a long day of work noisily commenced.

Chapter Seven

Halloway was a brutal slave driver, and no one was exempt from his non-stop orders and the ferocious demands of his vision. With complete disregard for rank or privilege, Halloway freely bullied everyone he allowed to step foot into his workshop, and the *Lucky Lady*'s crew wearily obeyed, but not without plenty of grumbling and muttered threats directed towards the incorrigible inventor.

Jenkins and Carter were back to work within three days, against Roberts' better judgment: he knew the men needed more time to recover, but he direly needed all hands to assist with rebuilding the *Lucky Lady*. Farrington was equally determined to add his contribution and within a week he was clamoring to return to the airship, but the tangled network of steam burns and the mangled flesh of his right arm had taken their toll. Mottled scars, shiny and pink, were slowly closing the wounds together as new tissue grew over the damage, but the fresh skin was tight and painful, even with the regular morphine injections that were leaving their needle marks on Farrington's arms.

Halloway kept his own injections quiet, but Roberts knew that there was no way his old friend could sustain his days-long work marathons without the stimulating influence of cocaine. As much as Roberts disliked having a drug addict directing the rebuilding of his airship, he had to admit that

Halloway's productivity was exemplary. The rest of the crew seemed determined to outpace the inventor, to no avail. William too plunged into the work with grim resolution: the lad did his best to keep pace with the other men, refusing to leave the shop to sleep at home, and it was clear that he was drowning his grief in constant preoccupation.

There was plenty of work for all parties concerned, but the lynchpin of all their activities was the massive automaton that lifted and turned as it obeyed the commands of Halloway. At first, the crew had been edgy around the construct, half-convinced it would malfunction and squash them all underneath its metal feet, but after it became apparent that the automaton harbored no malicious intent, they gradually accepted it into their midst. Before a week had passed, Carter had christened the thing "Mary" and the rest of the crew quickly adopted the moniker with barely an eyeblink.

For the most part, Roberts kept his mouth shut and let Halloway play drill sergeant with the crew: though it was out of line for Halloway to bully around a captain on his own airship, said captain well knew that humoring Halloway was the best path toward getting the *Lucky Lady* back into the air. Roberts had never allowed insubordination among his men and it was no easy task choking down Halloway's careless insults and relentless demands, but it was either that or find someone else to patch up the *Lucky Lady*. If a regular crew member showed a fraction of the attitude Halloway generously dished up, he would have found himself booted off the ship midair, but until the *Lucky Lady* was operational again, Roberts had few options but to bear up gamely and hope the crew wouldn't revolt and string Halloway up by his toes.

In the endless boil of activity, the *Lucky Lady*'s hull was scoured and refurbished, her engines stripped down to their base components, then springing to life again, nearly double their original size and promisingly powerful. The new boiler of Halloway's design, a sizable but surprisingly light mechanism heavily festooned with valves, struts, and a bewildering network of piping, grew to life inside the rebuilt boiler room. Jenkins practically lived in the room, he and Halloway in a constant froth of innovation and frequent, full-blooded arguments that shook the distant rafters of the high ceiling until Roberts bellowed at them both to stop. But as a whole, the short-tempered engineer and the half-mad inventor worked side-by-side in grudging but tolerable cooperation, feverishly renovating the crippled airship from the inside out.

As the days stretched into weeks, the mood around Halloway's shop was somber, the men attending their tasks with grim determination, every crew member doing the work of three and all of them bearing up wearily under the inventor's incessant demands. Life on board the *Lucky Lady* had never been easy, not when it had taken all of Roberts' skill and energy to keep her running despite Captain Albert's failures, but he had always seen to it that the men were well-fed and paid, and crew morale had normally run fairly high. Farrington and Carter had kept the airship lively with a running string of pranks they had played against Smith and McFadden, and several of the men had musical instruments on board to keep everyone's spirits up. However, with a broken airship, their own injuries, back-breaking work, and no clear picture of what the future held, the remaining crewmen were uncharacteristically subdue as the weeks passed.

Roberts' carefully hoarded savings rapidly diminished under the constant demands of equipment, food, parts, and other items for the rebuild, as well as food and wages for the crew. He counted every groat, constantly worried, and he was not at all pleased when Halloway insisted on purchasing a load of anthracite coal for the *Lucky Lady*'s fuel boiler. The shiny black chunks of anthracite had cost nearly three times as much as the standard bituminous coal that customarily fueled airships, and Roberts had handed the money over with exceeding reluctance. Without a qualm, Halloway had promptly converted the entire load of anthracite into an enormous vat of finely pulverized coal dust without explaining why, and at that point Roberts had demanded answers.

While Halloway did his best to explain the mechanisms of the new boiler he had constructed, it took Roberts and the rest of the crew long sessions of patiently untangling the inventor's words to arrive at any sense of understanding. As best Roberts could tell, what happened inside the boiler was that the powdered anthracite burnt while suspended in the air, giving the coal the property of a boiling liquid that required a lower temperature to stay ignited and also spat out prodigious amounts of heat. Beyond that, Roberts failed to grasp much more of what Halloway was saying: the inventor did not have a teacher's gift for breaking down complex topics into manageable chunks. Even Jenkins had difficulty keeping up with the immensely complicated world that populated the inside of Halloway's skull. Roberts knew that he had little choice but to trust that Halloway knew what he was doing, but until he saw the *Lucky Lady* airborne again, that trust was somewhat shaky.

A month passed, and a second one was threatening to come to a close as the work reached its final stages. July was nearly finished, and the summer had been unseasonably warm in London; Halloway's shop had been a Turkish bath for weeks on end, particularly when he was running the boiler and filling the building with clouds of steam. The men were exhausted, grim, and heartily sick of Halloway and his demands, but with the airship almost ready to take to the skies again, there was a definite sense of excitement among the crew as they neared the final stages of the rebuild.

When the airship flew again, it would be under a different name. Roberts had taken particular satisfaction in removing the ornate Smothers' crest from his airship's side and had done so as quickly as he could, but it had been Oboe who suggested a new name for her.

"Have you thought of renaming her, Captain?" Oboe had questioned one day. He and Roberts were sitting with their backs against a barrel as another hot day drew to a close, both men close to collapsing from exhaustion. Halloway was mercifully, miraculously asleep and in the absence of his constant, demanding presence, everyone else enjoyed a much-needed break.

Roberts grunted as he wiped a filthy hand across his forehead, rearranging some of the dirt on his face into an interesting pattern of streaks. "Not really," he replied shortly.

Setting a water flask down, Oboe continued. "She is almost being born anew with the work being done to her. A new name could be a good omen for the future."

Roberts thoughtfully considered the suggestion. Changing a ship's name when she was transferred to a new owner was not uncommon and with the reputation the *Lucky Lady* had earned for herself, a brand new name could be the fresh start she needed for a better future. After a few minutes of pondering, he ventured, as if testing to see how the word sounded on his tongue, "*Horizon* might not be a bad name."

Oboe was silent for a moment, then repeated the word, "*Horizon*. It suits her, Captain." A few other heads swung their direction, and Roberts watched as Carter and Farrington nodded in agreement. With that, it was decided. The next day, Roberts carefully painted *Horizon* on the airship's sides in clear, bold lettering, and from then on, not one of the men referred to the vessel as the *Lucky Lady* again. Under a new name and with a crew determinedly pushing forward despite their weariness, the airship took her final form until that long-awaited day when she was ready for a test flight.

The morning of the first flight dawned sullen and tired with little indication that the sun was going to grace them with her presence that day, and the prior night had ended far too late. Nevertheless, Halloway drove them all to their feet before dawn and although the crew was nearly stumbling with fatigue, excitement soon overtook weariness as the men set to their tasks, anticipation building in their movements.

Despite Halloway's enthusiasm and the barking commands that he liberally bestowed on all and sundry, it was nearing evening before the *Horizon* was ready to lift from her earthly housing and take to the skies once more. The sun was beginning to tilt toward the ground when Roberts stood at the wheel of his airship, feeling her engines waking to life and the wooden planks under his feet trembling with anticipation. The ship's airbags could not fully inflate inside the building, so the men had hoisted her upwards through the opened roof on a complicated system of wires and chains attached to pulleys biting into the reinforced roof. Eager to fly, the *Horizon* was still suspended from the rigging system, all but a few feet of the lower part of her gondola still inside the building as the bulk of the airship reared out into the open air, rigging wires on the roof of the building restraining her as her airbags inflated in preparation for flight.

In the boiler room, Halloway and Jenkins were shouting robustly at each other over the steadily growing roar of the engines. Steam hissed liberally as the tough canvas envelope steadily tightened under the pressure of the inflating airbags rippling in the light breeze. Oboe, Carter, and William were clambering inside the envelope checking for leaks while Farrington kept a careful eye on the mooring lines. Information and status reports continually poured along the complex communication system Halloway had installed in the airship as the crew relayed pertinent data to each other.

At the wheel, Roberts listened to the words emanating from the com device and nodded in approval. Most airships had a rudimentary speaking tube between the engine room and main deck, but Halloway had worked a complicated network of speakers throughout all important areas of the airship that allowed information to be transmitted from stern to bow and keel to birdsnest in an instant. Already Roberts could see that the com device was a marked improvement on traditional means of on-board communication, which namely involved yelling over the roaring crash of engines.

At the moment, Carter was passing along the latest set of temperature readings from the inside of the envelope. Roberts compared them to the outside air temperature, his forehead frowning over the calculations. The summer had been broiling, and hot weather made for poor lift; airships could not carry nearly as much cargo during the hot summer weeks. As a result, there had been a noticeable decrease in airships sailing over London in the past few months. The Smothers empire and other merchant ventures were leaning more heavily on their marine ships as they rode out the steamy hot weather, and anyone wanting to fly cargo via airship would pay dearly for the privilege. On this particular day, however, a merciful cool front had moved in, sweeping across the grateful city and bringing with it much-needed relief. With evening approaching, the warmth of sunlight was fading away and the lower temperature was better for the *Horizon* as she stepped forwards on her first flight since her rebirth.

The *Horizon* shifted, then hissed in anticipation as her steadily inflating airbags began lifting her fully out of Halloway's workshop, her keel rising above the opened roof. She rose in the air until her progress upwards was halted by the bow lines tethering her to the building which held her in place until she was fully prepped to take to the air under her own power. Carter and Farrington positioned themselves by the tow rings connecting the airship to her tethers, awaiting their captain's orders to set her free. As his hands gripped the wheel and his ears tilted toward the com device, Roberts could hear Halloway shouting about something and the deafening roar of the engines crackling on the line until finally the madcap inventor bellowed through the speaker, "All set, Captain! Turn this blasted airship of yours loose!"

Roberts grinned in triumph and filled his lungs with air. "Carter! Farrington!" he ordered. "Cast her loose! We're taking off!" The men scrambled to obey the shouted command, throwing off the mooring lines with quick skill. Barely had the ropes loosened their hold than the *Horizon* rose up in the air like a penned horse turned out to pasture. As if on cue, a glorious shaft of sunlight pierced through the dirty clouds, setting the air to golden and shining off the airship's fresh paint as she soared upwards. Roberts' flight goggles were perched on his forehead in anticipation of eventual use but for now he kept them away from his eyes: he wanted nothing obstructing his view of the events.

At the wheel, Roberts guided the *Horizon* into the heavens, tilting her controls back just slightly to ease her up into the clear blue sky. To his surprise, she responded enthusiastically, clawing through the air and sending her decks slanting sharply downwards. Carefully, he edged her nose slightly downward, but again the airship responded to his light touch and swiveled alarmingly, jerking the decks in the opposite direction with a liquid fluidity that set Roberts' heart racing. She had been a fast vessel as the *Lucky Lady,* but Halloway's expert ministrations had apparently made her uncannily agile and sensitive.

"EASY!" Halloway bellowed impatiently through the com device. "Take it easy, you idiot!" A bead of sweat ran down Roberts' face as he delicately maneuvered the wheel to steady his airship in the aether and hold her level. During his two years as first mate of the *Lucky Lady,* the airship had been steered by two experienced pilots, and Roberts had spent little time behind the wheel: he'd be the first to admit that his piloting skills had grown rusty. The airship dancing under his rather clumsy guidance seemed a different vessel altogether from the one that had arrived at Halloway's shop a broken wreck. She had always been sensitive to the touch and demanded a gentle hand to keep her moving smoothly, but her rebuild seemed to have left her highly tuned to the most subtle movement of the wheel.

Slowly, carefully, Roberts delicately balanced the wheel between his fingers, gently wrangling the *Horizon* into place until she leveled out, the compass bubble embedded in the heart of the airship's wheel showing her orientation true and level at last. Breathing outwards in relief, Roberts shot a look at the altitude meter and saw, to his surprise, that they were nearly eight hundred feet above the ground and rising fast. With a yell down the com device, Roberts slowly pulled the lever which regulated steam to the airbags, partially closing off the main steam valve to hold the airship steady at her current height. The *Horizon* quivered in the air, but a hesitant flutter of the rudder and she was already sailing forward, eating up the ground underneath her keel while holding steady at just under eight hundred feet.

Feeling his shoulders lose a little of their tension, Roberts kept his fingers firmly but lightly on the wheel, gently directing the *Horizon* forward as she soared through the late afternoon sky. Patches of glorious setting sun broke through the grumpy clouds and set the tip of her bowsprit on fire as the glossy wood reflected the sun's radiance. After a few minutes, a gust of wind pushed up against the *Horizon* and Roberts felt her respond, swaying slightly and veering a bit to starboard. "Easy, my lady," he crooned, more to himself than the airship as, with exquisite care, he gently directed her back on her original path. She hummed to him as another hearty gust tugged the bow forward, but Roberts was getting a feel for how his airship liked to dance across the sky and he anticipated it, gently nudging the *Horizon* through the occasional gust of wind and keeping her from veering or rocking unpleasantly.

Shooting a glance at the speed meter, Roberts noted that that the *Horizon* was chugging along at a steady fifteen knots and seemed eager to go faster. He called out through the com device, "We're at fifteen knots! How's she looking?"

"Beautiful, Captain!" Jenkins' voice sailed over the speaker. "She's flying like a bird!"

Halloway's abrupt voice cut in. "She can go faster, Gavin. I'm sending you more steam. Stand by."

"Easy now, man," Roberts cautioned. "Don't burn her engines out, not when you just overhauled..."

Halloway's voice interrupted him. "Stop babying her, Gavin," he ordered. "She's a tough little bird. Let her show you what she can do."

"You bust her up, and you're fixing her," Roberts warned, but a clanging below told him that Halloway and Jenkins were already shoveling more scoopfuls of pulverized anthracite coal into the boiler. Hoping he would not sincerely regret his actions, Roberts seized the handle of the engine divert valve and slowly pulled it backwards, routing more steam to the engines and increasing their power. The *Horizon* responded enthusiastically, charging forward in a way that set Roberts' blood thrumming with excitement.

Wind begin whipping across the deck of the *Horizon* as her increased speed pushed her through the sky, sending ropes flapping and canvas rippling. Roberts jammed his goggles down over his eyes, glad for the leather and glass protecting his eyes from the steadily increasing wind. His hair spun, flapping against his goggles as he kept the *Horizon* on course. She was practically dancing with joy at the faster pace, and he watched carefully as the needle of the airspeed gauge inched forward.

"Twenty knots!" Roberts bellowed into the com device. A cheer erupted to his right as he saw Carter and Farrington exchange a hand slap of congratulations. William was clinging to the side of the airship with a slightly worried expression on his face, but something like excitement breaking through the stress of being eight hundred feet above ground for the first time in his life.

"We're giving her more!" Halloway barked into the com device, and Roberts frowned before pushing concern aside. The *Horizon* seemed more than able to cope with higher speeds, and he was seized with curiosity to know how fast she was capable of flying.

"Keep it coming! Steady on!" Roberts shouted back, his excitement increasing as more steam roared out of the boiler and shot along the complex network of tubes that kept the airbags taut. The engines growled in response, churning louder as the *Horizon* quickly increased her speed. Seconds raced past. The airship flew like a dream, every cog and gear moving in perfect syncopation as the airship roared forward, eating up the distance and cutting a path across the sky.

"Twenty-five knots!" Roberts barked out in jubilation as his eyes dropped down to the speed meter. They were rapidly approaching twenty-eight knots, the fastest speed an airship had ever flown on record, but Roberts had a strong premonition that the *Horizon* was capable of more.

In the distance was a long-flight airship blundering slowly across the sky, and a strange recklessness seized Roberts as he honed in on the other vessel. Turning to the com device, he barked out, "Can she go any faster?"

"Of course she can, Gavin!" Halloway answered, unaccustomed mirth in his voice. "I built her to do so!"

"Then give it all you got!" Roberts' laughter was like the bellows of a furnace. The noise of his voice rolled across the airship, rising with the avalanche of steam pouring out of the boiler and filling the airship with heat and energy.

Seconds passed, each one increasing the activity on board the *Horizon* to a fever pitch as the needle of the speed gauge inched upwards. "Thirty-three knots!" Roberts finally roared out in jubilation. No airship in existence had ever flown that fast, certainly not the lumbering vessel just ahead of the *Horizon*. The long-flight airship was growing closer by the second as the *Horizon* streaked toward it like a sparrow about to pester a hawk. His fingers anticipating every twitch and shudder of the racing vessel under his command, Roberts steered her forward, eyes lacquered on the airship just ahead.

Its decks were stirring to life as men began noticing the small bundle of wood and canvas charging toward them at the speed of a falcon. Faces appeared on the slower airship's poop deck, arms pointing and voices rising in shock and excitement.

The *Horizon* blew past the other airship about a hundred yards off starboard, her engines whirring and steam hissing in triumph. Seized with recklessness, Roberts had deliberately made a tight pass, bringing the *Horizon* startlingly close to the other airship in an uncharacteristic display of braggadocio. From his position at the wheel, he glimpsed a brief view of astonished faces and not a few looks of envy on board the other airship as the *Horizon* rounded its aft, raced along its hull towards the foredeck, and shot past the slower vessel, leaving it behind her in a trail of steam.

Jubilant, Roberts shot a look at the speed gauge and sucked in a lungful of air before screaming into the com device, "Forty knots! Did you hear me, Halloway? *Forty knots!*" Joyful bellows of celebration poured out of com speaker as in the hot engine room, Jenkins screamed in exaltation, pounding Halloway's gaunt back with a hard fist.

Up on deck, the wind was batting about too strongly to permit much celebration, but Carter was delightedly rubbing his knuckles into William's scalp and Farrington was waving his arms in the air as best his still-healing wounds allowed, the livid scar on his face flashing red with triumph and excitement.

The sounds of excitement were largely drowned out by the whooshing of wind and the growl of the engines, but nothing could dampen the crew's elation.

Roberts, every muscle alert for the slightest change from the *Horizon,* had to keep his jubilation restrained: the smallest of oversights could quickly become fatal at these high speeds. The airship could wheel on a farthing, and the slightest mistake could result in a wreck. Roberts wasn't about to see her crash because his men were too busy celebrating to attend to their duties. However, his spirits were too high to worry overmuch and he kept his gaze ahead, watching as the airship, *his* airship, ate up the miles as she charged across the open country.

Miles and minutes dropped away under their feet as the *Horizon* sailed through the glorious riot of colors that signaled sunset. Finally the com device squawked. "She's getting a bit overheated, Captain!" Jenkins yelled. "Best drop her speed!"

Roberts agreed and manipulated the necessary valves as the engines responded and the *Horizon* began slowing. The pressure of wind beating over the main deck started to drop as she slid back to twenty knots and settled into a respectable cruising speed. With a slower pace to contend with, Roberts relaxed a trifle and thoroughly enjoyed directing his airship across the English countryside, at ease and carefully observing his men as they moved about their tasks, the excitement of the flight wiping away their weariness.

It wasn't long before Halloway began to fuss. "Best head her back, Gavin," the inventor advised over the com device. "She needs some recalibration." Roberts would have happily kept the *Horizon* up in the air for several more hours, but it was a huge stretch of optimism to assume that she was now fully operational. It would take several test flights and more of Halloway's tinkering before the *Horizon* was at her full strength, and with some reluctance, Roberts turned her around and pointed her back toward London.

It was with joyful triumph that the captain and crew of the *Horizon* brought their airship back to her roost and lowered her carefully into the belly of Halloway's workshop, anchoring her in place as her engines stilled and her airbags slowly deflated. Roberts kept his men on task, dispensing orders and holding back the elation that threatened to overtake them all until the *Horizon* had been properly docked and all necessary tasks had been completed. Only then did he let the excitement and triumph spill over the crew like water over a broken dam.

Voices rose in shouts of elation as the crew broke into a merry scrum of celebration, pounding fists against backs and tackling each other with rough embraces. In the midst of their jubilation, Halloway emerged from the engine room, covered in coal dust and showing what passed for him as a smile. "Sixty-three pounds of coal for forty-three minutes of flight!" he barked at the crew. "Yes, you heard me right, *sixty-three pounds!*" The crew stopped, ears twisting in disbelief. As the *Lucky Lady*, the airship had easily eaten through a hundred pounds of coal an hour when she was running at high speeds, and Roberts' mind churned with numbers as he ran a quick estimate in his head. He had been dreading refueling the *Horizon*, especially considering how much anthracite cost, but if they were to expect this type of efficiency from the new boiler system, then he might actually save some on fuel.

This information from Halloway only brought more jubilation and Roberts finally interrupted the noise with a pleased rumble. "Alright lads, you've earned a celebration," he announced while his nearly empty money pouch shrieked in protest. He ignored it: the men had been working themselves senseless and deserved a reward.

Deafening roars of approval filled the air as the crew shouted in excitement. Darkness was brewing outside, but taverns were waiting and them men spilled out into the street in search of others who would join them in merrymaking. Holloway flatly refused to accompany the crew, ignoring their hearty insistence and Roberts' threats that he was going to drag the inventor along with them, protesting or not. It was only after Halloway stomped back into the belly of the *Horizon*, barking out that he'd set Mary on them all if they didn't leave him alone that the crew abandoned the gaunt misanthrope to his beloved machines and poured out into the sticky night.

William was sent home with a coin in his hand and slap on the back. "You're a bit young yet to be out for a night of drinking, lad," Roberts said as he took the boy by his shoulders and towed him along, William grasping the half crown eagerly as his feet scrambled to keep up with Roberts' long strides. "We'll drop you off on our way, but you go along to your granny and auntie. They've barely seen you the past two months." The boy looked flustered and slightly upset to be left out of the celebrations, but he obeyed his captain and glumly parted ways with the crew, his shoulders hunched downwards as he shuffled back home. Now relieved of their junior member, the men stomped loudly through the streets, eyes bent on the Broken Spar with Roberts hoping that his meager funds were greater than the sum total of his men's thirst.

Within minutes of entering the tavern, Oboe was calmly facing an enormous elephant of a drinking opponent, a man nearly as wide as he was tall who was knocking back beer in enormous gulps, empty mugs slamming down on the table like the pistons of an engine. Although Oboe could drink any man under the table and walk away with nary a wobble in his steps, his opponent seemed determined to win as he guzzled down mug after mug in huge, burping swills.

After his sixth mug, Oboe's opponent belched an enormous, sickly blast of air that rattled the windows as he glared blearily at the *Horizon*'s first mate through red-rimmed eyes. His mouth opened as an incomprehensible jumble of speech poured out of it, the slurring consonants drowned out by the noise of the bar. One meaty paw reached out for his seventh mug and managed to grasp its handle on the third attempt. The brim-full mug juddered alarmingly in his hand, beer cascading across his fingers as he brought the container shakily to his lips and missed by several inches. The foamy brew poured across the man's chest as he tried again, this time marginally connecting the vessel to his lips. He was halfway through his seventh mug when Oboe set his eighth one down with a decisive thump on the sticky table.

But his opponent was not giving up without a fight. A thick finger wiggled in the air and made an effort to direct itself at Oboe who sat upright and steady, a gentle smile on his face as he calmly ignored the criticism his competitor was trying to voice through uncooperative lips. Oboe did not break off eye contact as he steadily lifted his ninth mug from the table and drained it in one long, steady pull, the other man watching him through a haze of alcohol fumes. When the mug was dry, Oboe carefully set it back down on the table, nudging it just so slightly so that it was perfectly aligned with the other eight.

"Like I shaid..." the other man began with a brave attempt to continue his incomprehensible tirade but seven drinks were beginning to claim their toll. As onlookers cheered in encouragement, the man's eyes crossed and his head tipped back, pulling his enormous bulk backwards until the overburdened chair snapped under his weight and sent him tumbling into three men behind him, knocking them over.

"Oboe!" Carter roared as bets thumped on the table in a rain of coins. Looking across the room, Oboe caught his captain's eye and grinned, his surprisingly white teeth a flash of contrast against his ebony skin. Elbowing his way up to the table, Roberts jovially slapped Oboe across the back. It was like hitting his hand on a rock.

"I'll buy you a drink if you've still got a thirst after that!" Roberts bellowed over the sounds of celebration, song, and what sounded like a fight starting in a corner of the room.

"Thank you, Captain," Oboe's deep voice cut effortlessly through the cacophony. "A draught of rum after the beer would be a welcome change." Like a mountain shifting, Oboe pushed his chair back and stood slowly to his feet, his long frame unbending and only a slight uncertainty in his movements betraying any effect that nine mugs of beer had wreaked on his liver.

It was more beer and rum and drunken singalongs and a fight to break up when a small, skinny man, infused with the confidence that only alcohol can impart, decided to pick a fight with Oboe. Calmly, Oboe wrapped his long fingers around the man's head and held him at arm's length but the man's friends flew in with teeth and fists bared. In defense of his first mate,

Roberts waded into the mess and banged a few heads together until the excitement settled down. Eventually the warring factions were pacified with more beer, and the crew of the *Horizon* returned to their noisy celebrations.

Somewhere past midnight and floating happily in an alcoholic haze of relief, jubilation, and rum-induced goodwill towards all mankind, Roberts was clumping unsteadily toward the bar when a passing whiff of conversation caught his ear and managed to divert his attention from thoughts of another drink.

"...shot past us like a damned cannonball!" a grizzled old air veteran was rattling out to a huddled knot of listeners. "I swear to God, I've never seen an airship move that fast, not in all my years of flight."

"She flew past us so fast we barely saw her coming!" a downy-faced youth piped up. "Captain about dropped his teeth when he saw that. He ordered a cannon drawn on her, but she was so fast we didn't have time to get the muzzle around and she was out of range in a heartbeat."

A thin smile crossed Roberts' face as the words sailed over him and managed to penetrate the parts of his brain that alcohol had yet failed to drown. Casually, he stepped forward toward the group, ears alert for news but keeping his body posture relaxed as to not betray his interest.

"Wouldn't have believed it unless I saw it with my own eyes," stated an airman with a hideous steam burn scar marring half his face and three missing fingers on his left hand. His grizzled beard wagged along with his finger as he spoke.

"What was she?" an onlooker demanded. "Military?"

The original speaker shrugged. "I don't think so. She didn't fly the colors. Plain paint job. She looked like a transporter: short-flight is my guess. Beats me to hell where she came from."

"How fast was she going?" another airman stepped forward, the hissing of pistons in his poorly made construct leg just audible above the noise of the tavern.

The scarred airman wiped his mutilated hand across his mouth in thought. "Couldn't say for sure, but she was easily going thirty-five knots, maybe even more."

The knot of men rolled with noise as incredulous snorts of disbelief and wonder bounced around their midst. "That's a load of bollocks," huffed the airman with the mechanical leg. "The *Albert* is the fastest airship in the sky, always has been. She broke twenty-eight knots two years ago and no one's been able to touch her since."

Stifling a hiccup, Roberts tried to marshal his alcohol-soaked thoughts into some semblance of order, and a few stray bits of knowledge floated up to the surface. The *Albert* was the crown of Her Imperial Majesty's fleet of military airships and the pride of England. Military airships had speed to spare: with no cargo to haul save for armor and weapons, their hulls were stuffed with massive boilers and high-powered engines that could churn out the power needed for speed. In contrast, transport airships rarely flew past twenty knots, and most of them clocked in anywhere from ten to fifteen knots depending on air conditions. A transport airship racing through the aether would not go unnoticed for long, and the *Horizon*'s maiden voyage had clearly garnered attention.

The elder airman slammed his mug down and barked, "Well, call me a lying bastard, but I'll swear on my granny's grave that the *Albert*'s no longer the fastest bird in the air. Whoever this ship is, she'd beat any airship in the sky in a race. You've got good money on that."

"Who do you think owns her?" a newly arrived participant in the conversation huddle pushed forward as word began spreading and other men swung their boozy attention to what was being discussed.

"She's not a Smothers ship," the young airman volunteered. "I didn't see his crest on her."

"Hah! Well, she will be soon, mark my words," the scarred airman laughed. "The old man hears that someone figured out how to coax that much speed out of an airship, he'll have her in his wharf faster than you can blink."

The mug in Roberts' clenched hand froze as the words slapped against his eardrums, pushing him out of the warm cocoon of alcohol and into something resembling sobriety. His mouth opened to respond, but common sense still had some semblance of control and shut his teeth for him before he could utter something irremediable. Dimly, Roberts began to realize that pledging his crew to silence before their grand night out would have been a wise decision, as well as finding another tavern where they weren't generally known. The last thing he needed was Sir Smothers catching wind that the former *Lucky Lady* was now the fastest ship in the air. Roberts' little trick of buzzing the other airship that evening had been a foolish gesture of pride and bravado that apparently was coming back to haunt him, and he strained his ears for the next words.

"You're right there, mate!" another man exclaimed in agreement. "No way the old hardnose will allow another transport airship to outrun his fleet. Captain of that airship better get his little bird out of English air before Smothers sniffs her out."

"Yeah, but where's she going to go?" an airman with a twitching construct arm added his two bits to the conversation. "Smothers' ships cruise every damned air stream from here to Beijing and back. There's not much hiding to be found."

"Send her to the colonists!" someone at the bar called out. "God knows there's enough skies over that cursed patch of dirt to hide her."

At that, growing roars from a rowdy game of chance off in the corner distracted the men, and Roberts watched as they turned their attention to a conspicuously sober airman running an impressive sleight of hand game against a bundle of rum-soaked comrades who were close to losing their shirts. Groggily relieved that the *Horizon* had been dropped from the topic of conversation, he stepped quietly away from the group, keeping the men in his sights but slowly extricating himself from their vicinity, cold concern pushing out the warm happiness that alcohol and merry-making had generated.

I should have known, Roberts silently berated himself, trying to shake himself back into soberness. The *Horizon* had made a historic flight that day, and he had witnesses to prove it. The other airship couldn't have clocked the *Horizon*'s exact speed, but it would have been transparently clear that she had been tearing along at an unprecedented clip, faster than a military vessel. Word like that would get out fast, and the last thing Roberts needed was notoriety. He doubted his agreement with Smothers would stand in its original form if the draconian tycoon caught wind of how fast the former *Lucky Lady* had managed to fly.

Silently pledging to keep his head as clear as possible and to be alert for indications that the *Horizon* or the *Lucky Lady* were further topics of conversation, Roberts uneasily rejoined his crew as the festivities of the evening claimed him once again.

***   ***   ***   ***

All in all, not a bad evening, Roberts grinned unsteadily to himself as the crew of the *Horizon* lurched their inebriated way back to Halloway's, collectively nursing a few wounds and the last remains of several bottles of rum. Jenkins was an alcohol-soaked rag dangling limply from Oboe's shoulder while Carter had a black eye, not from a bar fight but from a solid post that had discourteously failed to move itself out of his way in time. Roberts was sporting a set of roughly abraded knuckles, courtesy of a few punches he had thrown in defense of his crew, and Farrington's steam scars were flush with booze and vivid red. Regardless, everyone would arrive back at Halloway's more or less in one piece and although hangovers would be very much in evidence tomorrow, the evening's festivities had obviously been a success.

And informative too, the part of Roberts' brain not currently marinated in cheap rum pointed out. He was now aware that the *Horizon*'s first flight after her rebirth had not gone unnoticed. Word would spread, he knew that for an absolute fact. Clearly, even more caution was called for, especially if Roberts did not wish to garner more of Sir Smothers' hatred.

Growing worry was poking through the rum as overheard voices prodded the inside of Roberts' skull. *"The old man hears that someone figured out how to coax that much speed out of an airship, he'll have her in his wharf faster than you can blink."*

Roberts grunted at the memory and tried to push the words away. The *Horizon* had a fresh paint job, her canopy had been altered, and her steam piping network rerouted. She was a different airship from the one that had been carried away in pieces from the wharf, and looked it. Her first flight had been in the early evening with few other airships in the sky, and no other airships had been within eyesight when they docked her at Halloway's place. It would be a job identifying the *Horizon* and tracking her down, and there wasn't too much worry that someone would find out where she made berth.

Still...

"No way the old hardnose will allow another transport airship to outrun his fleet. Captain of that airship better get his little bird out of English air before Smothers sniffs her out."

"You try taking her out of my hands," Roberts muttered to no one in particular. His men were too occupied with song or drink or merely trying to walk without falling over to listen to their captain's mumbles. Although the odds were stacked heavily against him, Roberts wasn't going to be intimidated by a bully: while Sir Cornelius Smothers had half of London under his thumb and ruled the air of Europe and beyond, the old man couldn't hang onto power forever. The *Horizon* would earn her keep, and Roberts would pay off what he owed on her. Then, he could walk away from the tentacles of the Smothers empire his own man at last.

Carter and Farrington were drunkenly staggering

forward, arms over each other's shoulders and passing the same bottle back and forth. Even Oboe was visibly struggling to keep up under the influence of drink and the weight of his comrade slung over his shoulder. Suspended upside down from Oboe's back, Jenkins suddenly jerked himself into semi-consciousness and began caterwauling a muffled ditty.

Roberts blearily ordered his feet forward, his mind hazily determined to set a good example for his men by not falling asleep in the gutter as the rest of his body clearly wanted to do. *Stop your worrying, man,* he ordered himself as the crew staggered forward into the night, their footsteps tracing an unsteady path back to base where their airship awaited.

Chapter Eight

It was August 1st, three days after the rousing celebration of the *Horizon*'s maiden voyage, when Roberts strode decisively into a noisy grain mill and elbowed his way into the foreman's office. The interior of the small, cluttered office was generously coated with flour on every surface, including the red-faced, balding man sitting behind a desk heaped high with assorted papers. He shot Roberts a black look as the broad-shouldered captain strode into the room as if he had every right to be there and, uninvited, collapsed firmly on the spare chair.

“Who the hell are you?” the foreman growled, his flour-flecked cheeks quivering in indignation.

“Captain Gavin Roberts of the airship *Horizon*,” Roberts answered calmly and cut to the chase. “I can offer you a deal: my airship can take twenty tons of flour to Larne in a ten-hour flight. Guaranteed or you don't pay a penny.”

Paper slid from the foreman's fingers as he stared at Roberts with complete disbelief. "Are you out of your damned mind, man?" he growled. "No airship could make that time."

“The *Horizon* could," Roberts insisted calmly. "She'll make the flight in ten hours, and I'll do it for twenty pounds a ton,” Roberts pronounced, naming a price significantly below the current average rate for short-flight transport. The price he had just presented would barely pay for fuel and wages during the run, but if the *Horizon* didn't start earning money quickly, any money, her captain would soon find himself without a crew. Although his men had loyally stuck by him for this long, there were limits to dedication.

The foreman merely blinked at the offer, and Roberts added calmly, "My airship's ready to fly now. You sign for it and I'll bring her here within two hours to load, and we're on our way. Ten hours' guaranteed flight time or you won't pay for it. That's an offer you can't refuse."

He'd better not, Roberts added grimly to himself. He had been scouring London since yesterday looking for a shipping job, but most companies in need of air transit already had long-standing contracts with Smothers airships. Dawn had brought a lucky break: news that the much-contested Corn Law had been repealed and hungry Ireland was now eagerly welcoming any food coming its way. The Corn Law had imposed steep import taxes on all grains coming into Ireland, driving prices sky-high in a country that was only two years out of the Great Famine. When Roberts had seized an early morning edition of the *Times* and seen the Corn Law repeal gracing the front page, he knew that London's skies would soon be full of airships racing to Ireland loaded down with grains. He'd have to act quickly if he wanted the *Horizon* to get a jump on competition.

Roberts had picked this mill deliberately; it was on the outskirts of the sprawling city and had the look of a business struggling to keep up with other grain mills with superior operations. If the *Horizon* could make good on her captain's promise, it would be a start at building her reputation as well as a fine promotion for this mill. The foreman, however, wasn't exactly welcoming Roberts' proposal with enthusiasm, and it was several seconds before he spoke again.

"We're contracted with the *Wind Runner...*" the foreman began, but Roberts interrupted him.

"Which is a Smothers' ship. I don't need to remind you, sir, that his lineup of short-flight airships run just under twenty hours from London to Larne and you know you'll be waiting at least a day before one shows up at your dock," Roberts stated evenly. "Meaning no offense, but Smothers will prioritize the larger mills before you. And I'm betting he charges at least twenty-five pounds a ton, am I right?" Airship transportation costs increased significantly during summer months when airships couldn't get much lift in the hot air, and Roberts knew that Smothers' current fees were steep to compensate for the unbearably hot weather.

The foreman nodded in agreement and Roberts pressed forward, "I'm offering you twenty pounds a ton and a ten-hour guarantee on delivery. You won't find a better deal anywhere."

The foreman wiped a floury hand across his face, thinking hard. After a moment, he shrugged his shoulders, then said, "Captain Roberts, speaking plain, I think you're a daft fool, but...well, why not?" He grinned, the smile cracking the flour caked on his face, then narrowed his eyes in suspicion. "Guaranteed?" he questioned with emphasis.

"Guaranteed," Roberts responded firmly. "No payment unless I deliver on my promise. I'll get my airship and we'll be here within two hours to load."

A few more thoughts skipped across the foreman's face, but it was clear Roberts had won. "Agreed," the foreman pronounced and thrust a floury hand at Roberts. "Name's Goldson by the way. Gerard Goldson."

"Nice to meet you, Mr. Goldson," Roberts accepted the hand in a hearty grip as both men rose to their feet.

The agreement reached, Goldson escorted Roberts out of his office with the pleased steps of someone who knows he will be getting a good deal regardless of how future events unfolded. "I'll look forward to seeing this airship of yours, Captain," Goldson grinned by way of farewell and slapped a hand on Roberts' back, leaving a floury print behind as the captain of the *Horizon* exited the mill and out into the open air.

William was waiting outside in the teeming yard and in the minutes Roberts had been inside, the young steward had already accumulated a fine, powdery layer of flour. Spotting his captain, he anxiously hurried to Roberts' side, dodging relays of white-streaked men. The second William was within speaking distance, Roberts commanded, "Boy, run as fast as your feet can carry you and tell the crew to get the *Horizon* ready. We've got to be back here in two hours." While Halloway's modifications had greatly reduced the *Horizon*'s lift time, getting an airship into the aether was a time-consuming process and two hours was cutting it close. The sooner Will could get back to the shop, the better.

Will nodded and took to his heels, leaving tracks across the floury dirt, as Roberts turned to stride quickly out of the yard. London was choked with morning traffic, and taking a cab would have been slower than walking, so he hurried across the vast, twisting streets of London at a ground-eating stride that tore past slower moving traffic and fetched him up at Halloway's panting and streaked with sweat. However, William must have possessed the wings of a bird for the *Horizon* was already being raised to the roof of Halloway's workshop, steaming extravagantly while the crew swiftly prepped her for liftoff.

Still panting, Roberts stumbled into the workshop and sharply assessed everything with a critical eye. Every man was attending his duties with well-practiced skill, and the *Horizon*'s airbags were inflating in the morning air, her expanding canvas envelope already accumulating soot stains from the belching factory chimneys surrounding her. Halloway was in fine form, barking commands to all and sundry with no regard for rank, and as Roberts caught his breath, he realized that he had blankly assumed Halloway would be accompanying the *Horizon* on her first transport flight. So far, Halloway had been the center point of everything that happened regarding the airship, but it was a stretch of misguided optimism on Roberts' part to assume that current arrangements would continue indefinitely. At best, he hoped he could convince his recalcitrant old friend to fly with them to Ireland and back, and it would probably take some coaxing to pull off even that.

With as much casualness as he could generate, Roberts stepped up to Halloway and said quietly, "Until I find a second engineer, I could use you on board."

The inventor made an impatient gesture, too consumed with his own mental landscape to spare much talk for what he clearly considered nonsense. "Don't be daft, Gavin, I'm going with you," he barked. "Someone's got to keep Jenkins from blowing this bird apart. You haven't hauled anything on her yet, and I'm not letting you have her to yourselves until I know you're not going to overload her."

Halloway shoved a decrepit crate out of his way as he continued impatiently, "I don't want to see her back in my shop in pieces and you with some story about how you blew her to bits again."

Above them, the *Horizon* vibrated as if irritated with all the bickering going on underneath her belly. She was nearly ready to take to the air again and since Halloway was obviously coming along for the ride, Roberts turned his attention to last minute-preparations. Well within her time frame, the airship was soon lifting out of the opened ceiling and into the morning air.

She flew, oh she flew like a bird, soaring across London and gleefully darting around larger or slower airships in her path before arriving at the mill with thirty minutes to spare. Roberts set her down carefully in the mill's docking bay where stacks of flour and grains were being hustled around by teams of flour-coated men, anonymous under thick coats of gritty powder that clung to them like garments. Carter and Farrington pulled back the *Horizon*'s hull doors, opening her innards to receive twenty tons of flour and grains into her cargo bay. The mill workers began carrying the sacks into the airship with Carter directing traffic and Oboe carefully supervising, both men ensuring that weight ratios were evenly distributed and the cargo secure. However, since sacks of flour did little but sit there heavily, even with strong winds batting an airship around, Roberts knew that he wouldn't have to worry about loose cargo rolling around inside the hull as long as everything was stacked properly.

He watched carefully as the flour and grain made its way aboard the *Horizon*, wondering if she could take on more without undue stress. Calculating how much cargo an airship could carry while flying at certain speeds was part math, part intuition: Roberts knew that it would take several full runs before he had a fairly precise understanding of just how much weight he could safely load onto the *Horizon*. Once colder weather hit, she'd be able to take on more, but for this initial run, he had settled on twenty tons as a safe maximum. Halloway had helped Roberts make initial calculations, but even Halloway's brilliance could only go so far: the inventor had little practical knowledge of cargo transportation, and Roberts placed more faith in Oboe and Carter's input.

While the *Horizon* steadily filled, Goldson moved up to Roberts with a stack of floury paperwork in his grip. "Well, Captain, I don't know about this bird of yours, but that's your problem, not mine," he said cheerfully, thrusting the paperwork at Roberts. "Sign here, Captain. It says you are leaving at 10:17 a.m. on August the first and you've got until 8:17 p.m. to land at Larne or this shipment is on you."

"I'll be back to collect payment in a few days, Mr. Goldson," Roberts responded confidently, his calm exterior hiding the dark worry niggling at his insides. If he couldn't make good on the agreement, the entire trip would be nothing but a waste of fuel and time, two things he possessed in short supply. But it was the start of a fine morning and his natural optimism was riding high. Roberts had faith in his airship and his crew, and the chances of the *Horizon* fulfilling her captain's promise were strong.

"I'll believe it when I see it," Goldson responded with a chuckle, his grin deepening as Roberts took the paperwork and added his signature where needed. Noisy loading continued with admirable swiftness as the mill workers moved back and forth under their heavy loads. The second the *Horizon*'s hull doors shut, she roared away from the loading dock, dead set for Ireland with clear skies ahead.

The airship climbed into the sky and flew like an arrow away from London, English ground disappearing under her keel with her captain at the wheel and smoke plumes wafting in her wake. With Halloway and Jenkins below deck tending the boilers and engines, she quickly settled into a cruising speed of twenty-five knots and the crew prepared for what hopefully would be a smooth run.

It was a fine day for flying, the air steady as an old draft horse and a few puffy clouds decorating the blue sky as the *Horizon* put London's filthy air well behind her. Lush green English fields spread out under the airship, and the sun beat down steadily on her well-scrubbed decks. There was a brisk cheerfulness to the crew: the lovely day and high excitement over the *Horizon*'s first official run kept morale running high. More than one crew member was whistling contentedly as he set about his duties. At the wheel, Roberts kept the airship on course and pondered what was ahead of them all when the *Horizon* reached her destination.

Ireland presented a strange and heart-wrenching paradox in regards to food. The country was just beginning to recover from the worst famine in its history, a blight that had devastated the potato crop upon which the country was dependent, with a million or more dying in the process. Yet during the very worst of the famine, Roberts had seen numerous airships and marine ships traveling from Ireland to England overloaded with grain, bacon, and vegetables, all taken from the mouths of impoverished Irish and brought across the water to fill English stomachs. The *Lucky Lady* had flown one such mission in Roberts' early days as her first mate, and when the airship landed on the Irish air wharf, he had seen battalions of armed guards holding back an unruly crowd of starving people who watched helplessly as precious food was flown away. It had sickened him to witness the sight, and Roberts had seen to it that the *Lucky Lady* had never flown to Ireland again.

The crisis of a few years ago hadn't been precisely a famine, for Ireland grew plenty of food. Instead, it was greedy landowners and heartless policies that kept moving food out of the country instead of into the stomachs of those dying of hunger. Bitter opposition, rebellion, and national outrage had finally worked to change policies and with the hated Corn Law finally repealed, hopefully the hungry people of Ireland would quickly find some relief from starvation.

Roberts knew that the cargo filling the *Horizon*'s hull was cheaper fare, and he guessed that mills and farmers around England were currently jumping at the chance to offload poorer-quality food on the starving Irish who were eager for any affordable edibles. However, with only a few coins left to his name, Roberts could ill afford to be choosy. The *Horizon* was full of decent food, it was bound for a place where it would be eagerly accepted, and he would deliver the shipment with pride.

The *Horizon* approached Liverpool a little before four in the afternoon, on course and running well within her schedule. It was only then that Roberts called for a bowl of whatever it was William had been cooking in the tiny galley. There had been little time and even less money for outfitting the *Horizon* with all that her crew needed, and William had few supplies at his disposal. It mattered less on a short flight like this: a meal or two would tide the men over until they landed in Ireland.

William hesitantly approached Roberts with a brimming bowl, thin white broth slopping down the sides of it onto the clean deck. Roberts rescued the bowl before a major spill happened and gazed down at its contents with resigned weariness. So far, the boy had shown little evidence that he had inherited his father's culinary prowess, although in his defense, he'd had little time to practice. Halloway's cavernous lair was ill-suited for culinary pursuits and every hand was needed for work on the *Horizon*, William's included. The men had made an attempt to rotate kitchen duties, a common practice on an airship with a skeleton crew, but putting the *Horizon* back together had taken priority over food. More often than not, William had been dispatched to hunt down one of the numerous hot-cart vendors prowling the streets of London selling sausages, hot pies, baked potatoes, and other items of dubious edibility. So far, no one had suffered any ill effects from eating too much street food, but with the *Horizon* back in the air, it was time for her captain to start demanding that proper procedures be followed, including decent meals for everyone on board.

Tonight's offering appeared to be undercooked potatoes floating in a semitransparent white broth with chunks of dried beef added to the mix. Too hungry to care much, Roberts nodded at William and said, “Here, lad, take the wheel.”

William's face whitened with shock. “Sir?” he questioned incredulously.

“I can't fly her and eat at the same time and all good airmen need to know how the ship steers,” Roberts responded. “Skies are calm and she won't give you much fuss. Take the wheel.” With visible trepidation, William stepped forward and placed his trembling fingers on the well-worn wood. The *Horizon* vibrated as if not liking the change in pilots, and William gulped as he hesitantly moved the wheel to the right.

The airship veered sharply in that direction and the boy, panicking slightly, jerked the wheel other way, trying to right her. That only started a fishtail effect until Roberts' big hand clamped down on the wheel and steadied the *Horizon* again.

"*Easy*," he rumbled. "Light, slow movement's the trick, no jerking. She's a sensitive little bird and just a touch is all she needs to stay on course." William breathed out shakily as Roberts continued the impromptu piloting lesson. "And ease up, lad. If you're tense, she'll feel it. No sudden movements, ease into your turns, and don't panic."

William swallowed again, and Roberts set the bowl down to place both his hands on the wheel. "Like this," he said, slowly manipulating the wheel and letting William get a sense for how the *Horizon* ran. She bobbed a little and danced an impudent shimmy in the sky but with her captain's help, William gained a little more confidence and was soon able to keep the airship on course. After a few disaster-free minutes, Roberts lifted his hands off the wheel, leaving the airship in William's control. The *Horizon* trembled a little but kept her prow pointing forward as the boy stood at the wheel, directing the airship through the late afternoon air.

Roberts watched his new pilot carefully for a few moments, then reluctantly picked up the bowl of cooling stew and brought a spoonful to his mouth. It tasted like it looked, and he half-suspected William had used up all their salt stores on it. The meat was full of gristle and fat, but the insipid glop was the first thing Roberts had eaten that day and he wasn't inclined to be picky. With a grunt, he lowered himself to the deck, his back propped against the side of the hull and his entire frame welcoming the break. It was taxing work piloting an airship, both mentally and physically, and higher speeds meant constant winds beating across the deck as a continuous, thudding force against anyone standing topside. With the *Horizon* moving forward at a steady twenty-five knots, Roberts was more wind-fatigued than he cared to admit after six hours of piloting.

Grateful for the brief rest, if less so for the slop William had handed him, Roberts downed the contents of the bowl, leaned his head back and closed his eyes. William was frozen at the wheel, his white knuckles visible, but so far the *Horizon* had stayed aloft and Roberts was enjoying a few minutes of rest before he took the wheel back again. They were just at the edge of the Irish Sea, and winds were unpredictable over water, too dangerous to trust William's inexpert skills.

The boy's hesitant voice broke into Roberts' thoughts. "Did...did my father sail her, sir?" he questioned timidly.

Roberts didn't open his eyes as he smiled ruefully. "We all had a turn at the wheel. Your father did his bit as well." He cracked his knuckles, feeling the strain in his fingers reluctantly leave his hands.

"Oh." The wind whipping at them made it difficult for Roberts to hear the boy's words. On an airship, conversations had to be carried out at a shout, and airmen grew quickly accustomed to having to bellow over the sound of engines and roaring wind. It was a rare airman that reached his older years without significant hearing damage, and most of them eventually forgot how to carry out a conversation at anything less than a throaty bellow.

William hadn't quite gotten the knack for speaking aboard an airship, for his next words were lost on Roberts. "Speak up, boy," he commanded as he rose to his feet and stepped forward to reclaim the wheel. William's fingers dropped away when Roberts' calloused hands closed down on the wheel. William took a step back, his eyes not quite meeting his captain's face.

"Did...did he suffer any?" the boy asked. The oversized goggles on William's face obscured the tears that were surfacing, but Roberts could read his expression plainly. He'd known William would have a breakdown eventually, would have to properly grieve his loss. But there hadn't been time: he had kept the boy on the run with scarcely time to breathe in order to channel William's grief into something productive and keep him from giving into sorrow. Grief, however, demands its due, and it would eventually present its bill to William, one way or the other.

Choosing his words carefully, Roberts responded, "He didn't suffer, son. Your father likely didn't know what hit him." During his father's small funeral, William had held his chin high, tears leaking down his face as his grandmother and aunt sobbed beside him. There hadn't been much to put in Johnson's coffin: the blast had shredded his body and his fall from the *Lucky Lady* had caused more damage. It wouldn't be long before the worms had picked his bones clean, ready for the charnal house.

William sniffed audibly as Roberts handed back the empty bowl. "Go make some tea, lad. Strong," he said genially.

William sniffed again, and Roberts could practically hear the words begging to pour from his lips. "Go on now," he commanded, firmly but kindly. The boy had to learn that there was a proper time for mourning and now was not it, not when they had just under four hours to reach Larne. With engines roaring under their feet, and a guarantee to make, there wasn't cargo space for emotions.

A third sniff, and William was stumbling away obediently, his small body staggering in the stiff winds that blew across the airship from prow to stern. Roberts frowned as he watched William pick his way across the deck toward the galley: the boy was awfully light, and a particularly strong blast could easily lift him right out of the *Horizon* if she was charging along at high speeds. Falls were an occupational hazard on board an airship, and those who fell seldom survived the experience. Lighter airmen were preferred over heavier ones since every pound of weight counted against an airship's fuel consumption, but smaller men were easier to blow off the decks. William, light as he was, would need to take extra precautions, lest Roberts have the unfortunate task of informing the boy's grandmother and aunt that their last remaining male relative had just fallen to his death.

Roberts turned his eyes to the chronometer and frowned. He dug in his pocket and checked the chronometer against the expensive pocket watch that Captain Albert Smothers had bestowed upon him last year in a fit of alcohol-infused magnanimity. Both the watch and the chronometer checked at 4:29 p.m. Leaving one hand on the wheel, Roberts turned his attention to the series of maps clipped to a small table at his elbow. He had been charting their path the entire flight, switching his attention from the wheel to the maps in front of him, and it had been a difficult juggling act. The wind tore at the pages, threatening to rip them from their clips, and the papers flapped irritably. Trying to chart in high winds while piloting was foolish, but the *Horizon* was running on a skeleton crew. Her captain had no choice but to serve as both the navigator and pilot. Oboe would normally have stepped in to help, but his supervision was needed below as Roberts had no time for anything but flying. Normally, he would be working out their path in the comfort of his own cabin, but necessity called for this awkward juggle.

As they soared out over the Irish Sea, Roberts sounded down the com device to the boiler room, "How's our coal stores looking?" The *Horizon* hadn't burned much coal during her first test flight, but she had been carrying nothing but her crew. Holding twenty tons of grain and flour several hundred feet off the ground demanded great stores of energy that took a significant toll on the coal hoppers.

"She's eating like a bird, Captain," Jenkins' voice cut in over the com device. "Even with all this weight in her belly, she's not taking in near the coal I'd have thought." Roberts nodded his head at the news, although neither Halloway nor Jenkins could see him. Fuel had been a pressing concern: anthracite coal was astonishingly expensive, and English mines could only offer low-grade quality. Superior anthracite had to be shipped in from Wales or transported even further from the Americas and China at even greater costs. Considering the price of fuel in her hoppers, Roberts was deeply grateful his airship had a light appetite.

Another blessing was clear skies, nearly empty of air traffic once the *Horizon* left Liverpool behind and sailed out over the Irish Sea. Liverpool was home to a bustling air and marine port, but as far as Roberts could tell, there weren't many airships currently sailing from Ireland to England and the few he spotted were well in the distance. Larne was an important shipping port, but Roberts knew that the *Horizon* would drop her load and be safely berthed hours before the first Smothers airships responding to the Corn Law repeal touched down in port. The thought lifted some of the fatigue off his shoulders, and he stood a little taller in pride.

Roberts' musings were interrupted by the appearance of William, silently bearing a large mug that he had covered carefully with a plate. Roberts accepted the drink with a nod of thanks. The tea was steaming hot and ferociously strong, a thick sludge of leaves coating the bottom of the mug as if the boy was entirely unacquainted with the use of a strainer. Roberts gratefully downed the liquid anyway and felt its energy creeping into his weary frame.

William stood uncomfortably at his captain's side until Roberts lifted an eyebrow in his direction. "Did everyone eat?" he questioned.

"Yes, sir," the boy responded, digging his foot into the deck. "They...um...I don't think they liked the stew very much," he muttered apologetically.

"You'll learn to cook better, boy," Roberts rumbled firmly. "You told me you could do it and I aim to hold you to that promise."

A blush rose under William's goggles and his head dipped down. Roberts downed another gulp of tea and added,

"We're running a skeleton crew, and Mr. Farrington is more useful as an airman than a quartermaster now. But we'll be taking on more crew and you'll be working with him to better learn your duties as a steward." William's feet shuffled as Roberts continued, "A steward's an important position on an airship. Crew members will take sick or leave the ship if they're not fed properly."

William said nothing. Roberts downed the last drops of tea, spat some leaves out of his teeth, and handed the mug back to his youthful steward.

The lad reclaimed the vessel reluctantly, and Roberts gave him a sharp look. "You having second thoughts about this job, boy?" he questioned in a rumble.

"No," William mumbled back, the beginnings of a sulk on his face.

"Stand up straight and look me in the eye when you talk to me!" Roberts barked.

William's back shot straight up. His chin tilted and his eyes flashed with angry determination. "No, sir!" he repeated.

"Good lad," Roberts permitted himself a tiny smile. "That's what I want to hear." William breathed in deeply, inflating his thin chest and sticking his jaw out determinedly. "Go down below and see if Mr. Oboe has any chores for you," Roberts ordered in a kinder tone, and William nodded obediently before disappearing below deck.

However, it was Oboe who appeared on deck next. "Captain," Oboe's deep vibrato thrummed in the evening air. "I can fly for a few minutes if you would like a rest."

Since this was the *Horizon*'s first official job after her rebirth, Roberts was loath to abandon the helm, but he needed a privy and a few minutes to work out a cramp in his right calf. Oboe took the wheel as delicately as he would a china teacup and the airship didn't seem to protest the change in hands. Roberts left his first mate at the wheel while he sought out the tiny closet the crew used for sanitation purposes. It wasn't uncommon for airmen to urinate and defecate off the side of the ship, but Roberts had never allowed the practice on board the *Lucky Lady* and he certainly wouldn't on the *Horizon.* It was a filthy surprise for anyone on the ground and dangerous too; over the years, plenty of airmen had tumbled to their deaths with their trousers around their ankles after relieving themselves overboard. Besides, the *Horizon*'s hull was still gleaming with fresh paint, and Roberts had no intention of sullying it because his men were too lazy to walk twenty steps to the head. Any crew member who decided to take a quick pee off the *Horizon* would find himself scrubbing down the hull next time they were in port while the other men were enjoying ground leave.

When Roberts reclaimed the wheel, Oboe disappeared into the envelope's complicated innards to assist Carter and

Farrington with checking valves and pipes for leaks, a neverending job. Roberts tried to roll some of the stress out of his shoulders, but tension was riding in his muscles, more so as the time ticked past. As they sailed over the Irish Sea, the winds became brisker, and the *Horizon* bounced and jerked friskily in the air, her captain alert for her every whim and fighting to keep her on course.

As evening set in, the minutes skipped along faster than Roberts liked. Finally he sighed and reached for the com device. It was just after 5:30 p.m. and he had no intention of cutting it too close. "Halloway, Jenkins," Roberts commanded, eying the speed gauge. "We're running low on time. Increase her to thirty knots." He didn't want to run the *Horizon* at maximum speed lest he burn out her engines on her first official run, but she needed to push forward a little faster. The load in her belly was considerable, but she was flying easily and Roberts was confident his airship could increase her pace without undue strain.

"About time you asked," Halloway's sarcasm was apparent through the speaking tube. "Stand by at the engine divert valve." Clanging sounds echoed from the com device as Halloway and Jenkins shoveled more powdered coal into the boiler and adjusted the necessary dials and valves with much shouting between the two. On his best days, Halloway was not the most tractable of coworkers, and Roberts knew that he needed to find another skilled engineer as soon as possible. Even if by some miracle Halloway was interested in the job, the crew would object mightily, Roberts included. For all Halloway's brilliance, he had no respect for authority and he could easily throw a well-run airship into chaos. The *Horizon* needed a functioning crew that obeyed orders if she had any chance at helping her captain pay back the debt he owed.

A few minutes passed, then Jenkins called through the com device, "All clear, Captain, release more steam!" Roberts tugged the handle to the engine divert valve and listened carefully as the engines growled in anticipation. They took on the extra energy and pushed the airship forward while he kept his eyes on the speed gauge.

The needle climbed upwards until Roberts barked down to the engine room, "Thirty-two knots! Hold her steady. We've got a little under three hours left." The increased speed only accelerated Roberts' weariness, but there was no time for weakness, not with Ireland still in the distance ahead. Time passed, the air chronometer beating out a tempo as the *Horizon* roared forward. The sun began dropping to the skyline in a brilliant blaze of color, and night was crouched on the edge of the horizon, waiting for its turn in the sky. The sound of wind thudded endlessly against Roberts' ears, mixing with the rhythmic thrusting of the engines and the hisses of steam. Every minute seemed to race past like a second while he kept his eyes fixed on the chronometer. His muscles cramped with tension as fatigue slipped like poison through his veins and tugged determinedly at his eyelids, but he kept his back straight and his eyes resolutely open.

Six o'clock. They were passing the Isle of Man with Ireland dead ahead and skies as clear as glass. The setting sun blazed with splendor, but even its magnificence couldn't ease Roberts' worrying. He knew that the *Horizon* was moving forward quickly, that only a significant problem would hinder her from reaching her destination in time, but there were a thousand ways an airship could flounder in the sky: a blown valve or twisted cog could easily throw her off course.

Seven o'clock. A series of loud chimes sounded from the chronometer, and Roberts checked it against his pocket watch. Both were still in perfect sync, right down to the second. *An hour and seventeen minutes.* The charts flapping under their paperweights showed the airship's position as just over Ireland's coast with Larne approximately thirty miles away. There was no reason why they wouldn't make it into port with time to spare. Even so, Roberts reached for the com device and called down into the engine room. “We need to increase speed, Jacob,” he ordered.

“What, are you worried about her missing her time?” Halloway called back. "How far out are we, anyway?"

"About thirty miles," Roberts relayed back.

"You fuss like an old woman, *Captain*," Halloway barked sarcastically. "She's got all the time in the world."

"I don't want to risk it," Roberts responded.

Halloway's snort was audible through the com device. "Oh, for the love of God, she's got over an hour to go thirty miles. You could *walk* faster than that."

"You said she could take it," barked Roberts in a dark growl. Halloway wasn't an official crew member, but Roberts wasn't going to put up with any further backtalk from his old friend, lest he set a bad example for the rest of the crew. "I want her pushed up to thirty-five knots. Stand by on my mark."

Something that sounded like complaining emanated from the com device, but Roberts ignored it as the boiler steamed to life afresh. He put his hand on the engine divert valve, ready for Halloway's clearance.

"Pull her, Captain!" Jenkins bellowed and Roberts opened the valve, carefully working the *Horizon* up to thirty-five knots. The airship had been running for seven hours, but she showed no sign of fatigue as her speed increased, her engines at full roar and steam pouring from her vents as they raced forward into the falling night.

Time ticked, each minute like the beating of a heart. Roberts' eyes did not leave the vast expanse of growing blackness in front of him. As darkness fell, the *Horizon*'s relay system of lights flickered to life and filled the airship and surrounding air with brightness. Halloway had captured the same lighting source he used in his shop to power the *Horizon*'s lights, and Roberts was astonished at how brightly they illuminated the airship. Flying at night, even with clear skies, was hazardous and proper lighting on board was crucial. Most airships made do with oil lamps which were dangerous and ineffective. In sharp contrast, the *Horizon*'s lighting system illuminated the darkness like a bonfire and had the extra benefit of being flameless, a bonus when wood and canvas were brought into the equation.

Roberts had switched over to the green-tinted night goggles that all pilots wore when darkness fell. His had received a few extra touches, courtesy of Halloway's endless innovation, which enhanced their efficiency. With the new night goggles and Halloway's lighting system blazing throughout the *Horizon,* Roberts felt confident that he could keep the airship racing forward at high speeds without accidentally smashing her against some unseen object.

The darkness ahead was softened to gray under the full moon, and visibility was excellent. Roberts could see pricks of light that signaled cities ahead and felt both relief and worry at the sight of their destination. *Forty-five minutes left*, he thought, glancing down at the watch in his hand.

It was a few minutes before 8:00 p.m. when the *Horizon* sailed into the port at Larne, her envelope glowing in the light of the full moon and her engines churning rhythmically. There was nary an airship at the port. Roberts carefully nudged the *Horizon* into a berth as the port master and his workers began hurrying down the dock toward them.

The second he could safely take his hands off the wheel, Roberts quickly disembarked and strode forward to meet the port master. "Captain Gavin Roberts of the airship *Horizon,*" he said in greeting, thrusting the still-floury paperwork at him. "Please note, we landed at 8:00 p.m. exactly. I need the time documented for my records."

The port master grabbed the paperwork and blinked at it owlishly, his eyes trawling the sentences until an oath slid from his lips. "Sweet mother..." he said reverently, then gave Roberts an amazed look. "You don't mean to tell me this ship of yours sailed from London in under ten hours?"

Roberts' grin was broad. "She did." They had made it with seventeen minutes to spare, and Roberts' pulse had not slowed down for the last hour. He watched narrowly as the port master gamely worked through the sheaf of shipping forms and other paperwork, then relieved Roberts of a docking fee before calling for a small squadron of dock workers to began unloading the sacks of flour and grains from the belly of the *Horizon*.

The airship seemed no worse for the journey and neither did her crew. Ten hours in the air was long, but most airmen were accustomed to long shifts, and there was no more than the usual amount of yawning. William was a different matter: the boy had not quite built up the endurance he needed as an airman, but he did his stumbling best to attend his duties as the crew hurried to secure the *Horizon* for the night.

Roberts toyed briefly with the idea of turning the *Horizon* around and heading back to London that night, but he abandoned the thought. With the time needed to unload her and fly back, this could easily stretch to a twenty-four hour shift without a rest period for anyone on board, and that was a dangerous situation. Fatigue made for careless mistakes, and as fast and sensitive as the *Horizon* was, the last thing she needed was a crew of sleep-deprived men stumbling around inside her.

It was nearing ten o'clock before the airship was properly put to bed for the evening and her crew freed to find their hammocks. William managed to put together another round of insipid stew, this version slightly more edible. After grudgingly drowning it, most of the men headed for the berthing area, letting the salty Irish air soothe them to sleep.

Chapter Nine

Morning rose in a glorious expanse of sunlight glinting off blue waters as white clouds drifted in the warm summer air. On board the *Horizon*, Roberts breathed in the salty tang of the ocean and appreciatively surveyed the grassy green expanse that was Ireland, a living emerald nestled in the aquamarine waters surrounding it. Even in August, Ireland was cooler than London had become that summer, and Roberts gratefully welcomed the more temperate climate surrounding him. And, to only add to his gratification, there were two airships settling into berths and three more in the air, all bearing a Smothers' crest. The five airships were some of Smothers' swifter vessels, but the *Horizon* had beaten them all by several hours.

Out on deck, William was dishing out thin gruel and ferociously strong, over-steeped tea for breakfast, which Roberts eyed with some reluctance. He had long preferred coffee to tea, especially after his first pot of fragrant, full-bodied *qahwa kahla* in Morocco many years ago, and he gladly spurned the reheated swill sold in London's many coffeehouses for his private stock of Arabic beans. Johnson had known how to brew a perfect cup of coffee, but until young William could make a decent pot of tea, he was not getting his hands on the bag of coffee beans tucked away on board the *Horizon*.

Roberts accepted a mug of inexpertly strained tea and allowed himself a few minutes to contemplate Ireland's beauties before barking for order, the crew hastening to obey. The stilled airship began waking to life as her boiler was stoked and her airbags began inflating in the warm sunlight. As steam began pouring into the airbags, the *Horizon* was a buzz of activity, her crew preparing for departure, but not before her captain had found cargo to transport back to London. An empty airship would fly faster and burn through less fuel than a full one, but the *Horizon* had to earn her keep. Bringing her home without cargo was a waste of time and energy.

Potential work came to the airship in the form of a tall man in a tailored suit. "Pardon me, sir, are you the captain of this vessel?" a crisp and unmistakably English voice cut through the babble of noise on the dock.

Roberts turned to face the voice. The speaker was faultlessly attired, bowler hat on his head, cane at his side, and a thin mustache lining his top lip. English to the core, the tall man stood on the edge of the dock facing Roberts and close enough to hear each other over the noise of dozens of workers rushing around.

Roberts gave the visitor a once-over. "I am," he rumbled. "Captain Roberts of the *Horizon*."

"I have a business prospect for you, Captain," the man called. "Might I come aboard?"

Pleased to see work seeking him out, Roberts motioned toward the gangplank. "You're welcome aboard, sir," he said genially. The man fastidiously stepped his way onto the *Horizon,* his glossy shoes reflecting the sun's rays and his hair shining with pomade. Reaching the captain, he extended a thin, rather soft hand to Roberts who took it in his callused paw.

"Rodger Wakefield," the visitor introduced himself, presenting Roberts with a card. Roberts peered at the white rectangle and his brow furrowed as he read the words. "Wakefield & Wakefield Grain and Greengrocery Wholesale" was etched across the card in elegant lettering, followed by addresses in both Ireland and England.

Wakefield gave a slight bow. "I was told that your fine vessel flew from London to Larne in just ten hours. Indeed, I believe all of Larne has heard about this by now." He scanned the *Horizon,* nodding his head in admiration before turning back to her captain.

Roberts said nothing, but his fingers tightened, bending the card under his grip. Not noticing the gesture, Wakefield continued, "This is simply a marvelous accomplishment, and you and your crew are to be much congratulated, Captain. I do not believe a faster airship is to be found anywhere in the skies. I take my hat off to you, sir."

There was a bow again, and the fine bowler hat lifted a few inches. Roberts did not return the bow, and his eyes were beginning to burn with a slow fire. Wakefield seemed oblivious as he pressed forward eagerly. "My company is contracted with Smothers airships, but I must say, Captain, that we would be delighted to sign on with you..."

"No," Roberts interrupted him with a growl.

Wakefield's high brow furrowed slightly in confusion. "Captain, we are prepared to pay thirty pounds a ton if you can guarantee flight to London in ten hours or less..."

"Mr. Wakefield," Roberts cut him off harshly. "I'm not a greedy enough bastard to take food away from those who are starving to death and bring it back to a country that already produces enough of its own." There were no armed military men fending off hordes of starving Irish at this wharf, but Roberts too vividly remembered a few years ago when the people of the country had been willing to risk bullets to get their hands on anything edible. "The Corn Law may have been repealed, but there still too damned much starvation going on in this country," Roberts continued sharply. "The *Horizon*'s not going to make it worse by moving food out of Ireland. You can find yourself another airship."

Wakefield made a motion as if to protest, but Roberts put a heavy hand on the merchant's shoulder and firmly steered him off the *Horizon.* He watched narrowly as Wakefield tugged at his hat with an indignant jerk, then stalked away angrily, vanishing into the riotous sea of activity on the dock. As his unwanted visitor disappeared, Roberts felt some of the anger leave him. He hadn't been surprised at the offer: food was one of Ireland's main exports, but the thought still enraged him. True, he was essentially broke and his men hadn't been paid in a month but he hadn't sunk low enough to take on a job like *that*.

A question from Oboe redirected Roberts' attention down below deck. When he emerged several minutes later, there was another visitor standing hesitantly at the gangplank, hat clutched in his pudgy hands. "Excuse me, Captain," the visitor squeaked, and Roberts did not know if it was from nervousness or habit. "Might I have a word with you?"

Still angered by Wakefield's offer, Roberts barked out, "What?" and the man winced visibly. Roberts cleared his throat and tried again. "What can I help you with, sir?" he questioned in a calmer tone as he stepped forward to meet the newcomer.

The man's balding head just about reached Roberts' sternum, and his heavy jowls were buried in the midst of a dense forest of mutton chops. Small glasses perched on the bridge of his nose, and the eyes behind the lenses were bright. He looked to be in his late thirties, but there was a certain plumpness to his face that indicated a possible younger age. "Michael Bloomberg," a pudgy hand was extended. "Postmaster. British Royal Mail." The man's appearance and last name were vaguely Jewish, but his voice was English.

Roberts took the proffered hand and shook it, some of the dark furrows lifting from his forehead. "Pleased to meet you, Mr. Bloomberg," he said. "How can my airship be of service to you?"

Bloomberg, however, did not drop Roberts' fingers after the obligatory two shakes and continued to pump his arm with excited vigor. "The whole dock is abuzz with news about your airship, sir," Bloomberg squeaked, his voice rising in excitement. "Ten hours! What an accomplishment! Sir, I must say it is a deep honor to make your acquaintance!"

Roberts' arm was still lifting up and down without any effort whatsoever from his muscles. Tactfully, he placed his other hand on the postmaster's shoulder and steered him forward onto the *Horizon*'s deck, then withdrew his fingers from Bloomberg's grip. "Are you in need of an airship, Mr. Bloomberg?" he questioned.

Bloomberg was practically dancing next to Roberts, his rather small feet stepping lightly across the floorboard of the main deck. "Oh yes! I mean, pardon me, Captain, but I'm afraid I'm in a bit of a bother." He gave Roberts an apologetic look. "The *RMS Clementine* was due in port almost six hours ago, and there has been neither hide nor hair seen of her. She's the only RMS airship from Larne to London, and I have a ship's load of mail that needs delivering right away." Bloomberg's voice had settled a trifle and was no longer quite so high. He was still holding his hat in one hand, and now the other one swung around to grip the brim between both sets of fingers.

"Bit of a sticky wicket, I must say. The *Clementine*'s been running behind quite a bit the past few months, and the home office is in a froth. I contracted out the *Clementine* a year ago. At first, she was a fine airship but lately she simply has not been up to snuff." Bloomberg gave Roberts a bright-eyed look. "Ordinarily I'm not authorized to arrange transport on a ship that doesn't have the RMS seal, but, well..." he smiled slightly mischievously. "If this delivery can get to London by six o'clock this evening, between you and me, I don't think there will be much fuss about what it arrives on, Captain."

Bloomberg twirled his hat in his hands. "It's six tons of mail at forty pounds a ton, sir." Roberts' face was impassive but elation played a jig along his spine. The mail delivery would net more than half of what the grain and flour shipment had earned, and he would walk away from this two-day jaunt with a tidy profit. Six tons was a trifling amount, and the *Horizon* would have no problem carrying it back to London.

But Bloomberg wasn't finished. "Not knowing what other contracts you may have, sir, I'll tell you that between you and me, the Royal Mail Service is in desperate need of more airships, particularly ones who can fly as fast as your fine vessel here." Despite the fierce monopoly Sir Smothers had seized upon most air transit, the only Smothers airships to bear the Royal Mail Service prefix before their names were long-flight vessels. The Royal Mail Service preferred to contract their own private airships for domestic and European postal deliveries. Speed was of the essence for postal airships and the requirements for a Royal Mail Service seal were stringent, but Roberts knew that the *Horizon* could meet them. The pudgy, eager-eyed man at his side just might be his ticket to steady, long-term employment.

"I'd be willing to hear your offer, Mr. Bloomberg," Roberts answered, holding back his elation. "But first, how about we get this first delivery to London on time?"

"Right! Of course!" Bloomberg exclaimed, the high tones returning to his voice. "I'll return with the mail coaches and the necessary paperwork."

"The *Horizon* will be ready when you are," Roberts assured him.

"Excellent!" Bloomberg seized Roberts' hand again and pumped it vigorously several times before dropping his hat back onto his head and scampering off the airship. Roberts watched the postmaster for a few moments before turning his attention back to the *Horizon*. She was obviously eager to take to the air again, and her crew was assiduously attending to tasks prior to takeoff.

By the time the *Horizon*'s airbags were fully inflated and the ship prepped for travel, Bloomberg had returned, this time at the helm of a steam-powered automobile and with several others in a line behind him. With little thought for the people roaming the dock, Bloomberg propelled his automobile forward, leaning heavily on the horn and calling out of the window, "Make way for the Royal Mail Service if you please!"

When the line of mobile mail came to a stop, a small army of postal workers exited the vehicles and began carrying mailbags into the belly of the *Horizon*. Bloomberg was last on board, clutching a small traveling bag in one hand and an umbrella in the other. Roberts looked at him, brow furrowing. "Standard regulations, sir," the postmaster squeaked. "If a ship does not have an RMS seal, a postal official must be on board at all times to supervise."

"We're not exactly set up for passengers, Mr. Bloomberg," Roberts responded, but the man made a brisk, dismissive gesture.

"Never you mind that, Captain, just tuck me away somewhere where I won't be a bother. You'll hardly know I'm on board."

***   ***   ***   ***

"Marvelous!" Bloomberg yelped into the swift rush of air. "Simply marvelous, Captain Roberts!" The *Horizon* was racing forward at twenty-eight knots under a clear blue sky and the chronometer clocked in at a little past ten in the morning. All was status quo on board except for the presence of their enthusiastic visitor. Bloomberg was practically delirious with joy, the wind whipping his ill-fitting coat around his stocky body and the heels of his little feet constantly bouncing up and down with excitement.

The goggles on Bloomberg's face kept slipping down to his chin and nesting in the forest of his mutton chops as he gestured to them. "Custom ground," he said over the wind. "It's a bother trying to fit goggles over eyeglasses, so I had my optician grind the lenses for me." The surface of the lenses magnified Bloomberg's eyes, giving him a comical look as he swiveled his head back and forth.

"Fly often?" Roberts questioned in a bellow.

"As often as I can, Captain!" the postmaster laughed.

Bloomberg's enthusiasm was infectious and Roberts was feeling generous, so he called out over the wind, "She can do faster. Care to see?"

"Faster?" the postmaster repeated, and his bouncing increased exponentially. "Oh please, Captain, I'd love to see!"

"Then come on up here and grab hold of something, Mr. Bloomberg," Roberts called back. The man was so energetic, Roberts was half-afraid a vigorous bounce would catapult Bloomberg into a gust of wind that would blow him off the *Horizon*. Roberts had never lost a passenger and didn't relish the thought of doing so, especially when this one might just be his ticket for continued work.

Bloomberg had been standing several feet away from Roberts and at a word, he scampered happily toward the helm to peer excitedly at its controls while Roberts shouted the necessary information down to the engine room. Swiftly, the *Horizon* obeyed her captain's commands and began surging forward with increasing speed.

"Thirty-one knots! Captain, this is simply amazing!" Bloomberg shouted over the growing roar of the engines, stabbing an excited finger at the speed gauge.

"We've got more to go!" Roberts hollered, his eyes steady on the speed gauge as the needle inched forward. Finally he called into the com device, "We're at thirty-five knots and holding!" The *Horizon* was lightly loaded with just six tons of cargo and though her engines were roaring, it was clear that moving at high speeds was no challenge for her, not with so little weight to keep aloft and no winds buffeting her. As they charged forward, Bloomberg seemed nearly delirious with excitement and constantly squeaked bits of excited speech that Roberts could not decipher. He paid little attention to the postmaster's garbled attempts at communication since the *Horizon*'s ground-eating pace demanded all of his focus; Roberts could only hope that Bloomberg wouldn't attempt something foolish at this speed.

For a good twenty minutes, Roberts let the *Horizon* streak along at thirty-five knots before he finally called for a shift back down to a more leisurely twenty-five knots. Time was on their side, and there was no sense pushing her that fast for long. When the winds died down, Bloomberg shoved his goggles back on his forehead and gave Roberts a look of sheer admiration. "Incredible, Captain! This is an amazing airship, sir! Never flown on one finer!"

Pride filled Roberts as he gave a nod of thanks. "She's a good vessel," he replied with no small amount of satisfaction.

"Indeed!" The goggles came off again as Bloomberg wiped a few drops of sweat off his face, polished the lenses on his sleeve, then pulled them back over his eyes again. "I wonder, Captain..." he began hesitantly, then paused, something like a blush rising up on his face. "I wonder if you would be so kind as to...let me have a turn at the wheel?" The blush deepened. "I've had...a bit of experience."

Roberts considered it. The skies were clear without another airship in sight, and the aether couldn't have presented more idyllic conditions for an inexperienced pilot. Bloomberg was looking at him with a wistful, hopeful expression, and saying no would have been like kicking a puppy. Roberts' overweening protectiveness of his airship hated the idea of some daft landlubber at the wheel, but he knew it was in his best interest to humor Bloomberg as much as he could, especially considering what the postmaster was paying for transport. Somewhat against his better judgment, Roberts motioned his passenger over, and Bloomberg scurried to the wheel with alert adroitness.

The *Horizon* accepted the new pilot with surprising aplomb and Roberts watched narrowly while his airship continued her passage forward smoothly, although Bloomberg was scarcely tall enough to see over the wheel. His eyes danced with excitement but the man clearly had directed an airship before. His movements were smooth and confident, and the *Horizon* continued forward with scarcely a hiccup.

"I always wanted to be an airship pilot," Bloomberg said wistfully to Roberts over the rushing wind. "But, well, when I was a boy, those were the early days of flight. Only tough, strong men were accepted as airmen. It was my eyes, see? Too weak. And my lungs are bad. Father insisted I follow him into the mail service. He was a postmaster as well and never quite understood my love for the air." Bloomberg sighed in longing for what might have been, and Roberts gave him a rueful look.

"Still," Bloomberg brightened. "A postmaster's job is not that bad, especially now that airships are the main mail carriers. I regularly have chances to fly on board, and sometimes the captain lets me have a turn at the wheel." As he spoke those words, a sudden wall of wind snuck up on them and gave the *Horizon* a vigorous smacking, sending both men staggering and the airship bucking in the wind.

"Whoa! Steady there, old girl!" Bloomberg called out as Roberts moved forward to reclaim the wheel. The *Horizon*'s gondola was swaying under her envelope, but the postmaster seemed cheerfully unconcerned with this minor setback. With calmness and a surprising level of skill, Bloomberg happily manipulated the wheel to set the airship back on course.

Roberts had to give Bloomberg credit: the postmaster had nerve and stayed cool under pressure, and the *Horizon* easily settled back on course again under his guidance. If the winds increased, Roberts would insist on taking the wheel back but for now, the airship seemed perfectly happy with Bloomberg at the helm. Besides, the charts on the table were clamoring for his attention, and Roberts turned his eyes back to mapping their course. "You just keep her steady now, Mr. Bloomberg," he said genially.

"Aye, aye, Captain!" Bloomberg responded cheerfully, giving every indication that he would be happy to stand at the wheel for hours. In the face of such boundless enthusiasm, Roberts didn't have the heart to reclaim the wheel, so he let the postmaster stay in position, reflecting on the fact that Bloomberg had paid for the privilege. Granted, his abilities ended at steering, leaving Roberts to manipulate the steam divert valve, communicate with the engineers, plot their course, and perform other piloting duties. But all in all, Roberts wasn't inclined to spurn free labor when it insisted on offering itself.

They reached the Irish Sea in good time, and found that the winds over the water were stiffer. Clouds lay low and thick, holding back much of the sun, and there were subtle warnings that a storm at sea might just be on the menu for the evening. By then, it was obvious that Bloomberg's energy was beginning to wane, and he relinquished the wheel to Roberts with only the slightest sign of regret. However, once relieved of his piloting duties, the postmaster seemed strangely loath to stand down from his self-imposed position as a temporary crew member. He was soon scanning the heavens with a spyglass, relaying bits of information to Roberts with a childlike enthusiasm. His whole-hearted zest for being on board the *Horizon* was a source of quiet amusement for Roberts who found he rather enjoyed the postmaster's company.

The *Horizon* was nearly halfway across the Irish Sea when a shout from Bloomberg drew Roberts' eyes up from the network of charts and maps. There had been nothing in the sky for the *Horizon* to run into, and he had been keeping his attention away from the wheel and on the papers in front of him. "I say, Captain," Bloomberg hollered over the wind. "There's an airship dead ahead of us, and it seems to be jolly keen on coming over to say hello."

Roberts' head shot up from the charts as he rapped out, "Take the wheel, Mr. Bloomberg." The postmaster hurried forward to seize command of the helm, and Roberts' telescope was out of his pocket and scanning the growing expanse of low clouds in front of them. The lens fell upon an advancing airship that had dropped out from the cover of the clouds and was zeroing in on the *Horizon*. Ragged canvas snapped in the stiff wind and the wooden gondola was pockmarked with holes and broken wood spars. On the front of the bow, a tattered flag blew in the stiff wind, skull and crossbones on a field of black.

Airship pirates, Roberts thought grimly. The skies of Europe were well-patrolled, and any air under the control of the British crown was generally free of raiders. However, there had been more and more reports of air skirmishes, particularly over international waters, such as the *Horizon* was crossing now. Generally the Irish Sea was free of unwanted intruders, but patrolling the air was a much more difficult matter than guarding the water: airship pirates had an easier time invading and escaping than their marine counterparts and were subsequently bolder in their attacks.

The pirate airship had the *Horizon* in its sights and was bearing down quickly. Without pause, Roberts bellowed into the com device, "We have a hostile vessel approaching on the port side at eight hundred yards. Halloway, Jenkins, I want full speed *now*! We've going to outrun it!"

We'd better, Roberts added to himself, for the *Horizon* had no other defense save fleetness. As the *Lucky Lady,* she had carried two carronade cannons that spat out volleys of grapeshot when threatened, but those had been stripped from her before she had arrived at Halloway's workshop and

Roberts couldn't afford replacements. He hadn't much intended to, especially after the *Horizon*'s first test run gave ample proof that she was fast enough to outrun anything in the sky. If Roberts had kept her within England's borders, armament would have been unnecessary, and he was frankly surprised to see a pirate ship hovering over the Irish Sea. Any pirate vessel that shot down another airship so close to England would be hunted to the ends of the earth by the British Royal Air Force who took a very personal interest in any brigand vessel that operated near England's borders.

Thirty-one knots. They were blazing forward, and the advancing airship was clearly visible in the darkening skies. She was a little smaller than the *Horizon,* but abristle with both men and weaponry, two things the *Horizon* noticeably lacked. The pirate airship was a light bird, built for speed and maneuverability, and it would not easy to dodge. However, it wasn't the *Horizon,* and Roberts doubted that their enemy could top twenty-six knots. All the *Horizon* had to do was stay out of range of any shots or harpoon snares, and she had a good chance of flying away unscathed.

Bellows from the com device told Roberts that his orders were being carried out with prompt alacrity. The engines surged as more steam poured out of the boilers and shot along the network of intake values and copper tubing. Roberts poised his hand over the steam divert valve, ready to feed more energy into the engines but his attention was partially drawn to the skies around the *Horizon*. Dark growls of warning emanated faintly from the distance as the hint of storm became more insistent, and he shot a hard look at the piling clouds in the sky. Flying through a storm could easily be fatal, and with an enemy airship directly ahead, the last thing the *Horizon* needed was dangerous flying conditions.

A hem, barely audible through the rushing of wind and the yells of crew members, caught Roberts' attention. "Ahh, eh, what shall I do, Captain?" Bloomberg questioned, his magnified eyes round and nervous. Another distant rumble of thunder sounded, just audible in the noise surrounding them, and Bloomberg cringed visibly at the sound.

"Hold on to something!" Roberts ordered. "And for God's sake, stay out of the way!" Bloomberg retreated several feet and wrapped his arms around a sturdy post.

"And get down!" Roberts added sharply. "You want to be a target, man?" They were drawing closer to the other airship, and the bullets would soon be flying. He didn't need a dead passenger to add to his troubles.

Thirty-two knots. Roberts' hands clenched on the wheel, poised to jerk *Horizon's* nose up through the thick clouds and into the heavens. Air battles were lost and won by altitude, and an airship directly above another airship's envelope was a hard target to shoot. If the *Horizon* quickly kicked up enough speed, she could hopscotch over the attacking vessel and then outrun it as it turned around to pursue. However, timing was crucial: if the *Horizon* pulled up too late, it would put her in danger of a boarding harpoon and too soon would give the other airship time to climb upwards in tandem.

Thirty-four knots. The *Horizon* was rapidly approaching the point of no return, directly on course to collide with its attacker. Through the darkening air, Roberts could see men rushing about on the other vessel which was already rising up sharply. He gave the wheel a vicious jerk, sending the *Horizon*'s prow screaming up into the heavens and leaving the other vessel below as it fought to keep pace with the rapidly ascending *Horizon*.

They punched through clouds fat and heavy with rain, dampness soaking Roberts' clothing as he wrestled the wheel to keep the *Horizon*'s nose pointed upwards. The storm-darkened clouds around them threw shadows across the air and as the *Horizon* breached the cloud bank, nothing was visible except fitful sunlight. Beneath the *Horizon* was a vast expanse of sluggish clouds, but the attacking airship was somewhere nearby and would eventually find its prey. Roberts could just hear the engines of the pirate ship, louder and deeper than the *Horizon*, growling in anticipation of its quarry.

Quickly, Roberts shot a look at where Bloomberg stood, arms wrapped around the post and fear clearly present in his eyes as he nervously scanned the clouds under their feet. "Bloomberg!" Roberts bellowed, "I need you to find that damned pirate ship! It's gone aground in the clouds and could pop out anywhere!"

Bloomberg swallowed but gave Roberts an alert nod, then stumbled toward the side of the *Horizon*, spyglass opening up. He jammed the spyglass against his goggles and peered through the dark clouds, searching for their attacker as he leaned heavily across the railing. Roberts hoped that Bloomberg would not tip overboard, but he had no time to worry about passenger safety: the postmaster was going to have to watch out for himself.

Another ominous growl of distant thunder rolled, closer now and more insistent. They were nearly three thousand feet above ground and in the turmoil of the chase, the *Horizon* had veered several miles off course. Roberts fought for more air, more speed, but the *Horizon* fluttered just under thirty knots, her erratic course and the growing winds making it impossible for her to fly at her maximum speed. For several long minutes they flew unmolested, and Roberts was just beginning to think that they had lost their attacker when Bloomberg's voice captured his attention.

"Captain!" the small postmaster yelled. "I see her! To the left...I mean, port! Port! There she is!" Roberts whipped his head around and saw the dark bulk of the attacking airship burst out of the clouds a few hundred yards to the port bow and rise rapidly to level with the *Horizon*.

An explosion cut through the roaring of engines and crashes of the oncoming storm and something screamed through the air. "HARPOON!" Roberts bellowed, his lungs filling the *Horizon* with warning. She jerked, then keeled heavily to portside as a thick rope appeared across her top deck, courtesy of a boarding harpoon which had shot across her bow. It had barely missed digging into the wooden hull and instead had sailed right between the gondola and envelope, hitting nothing but empty air. Instead, it had raced forward until it had reached the end of its rope tether and then fallen, dangling from the side of the *Horizon*'s gondola as the weight of the harpoon stretched the rope across the main deck. In a moment, the pirate ship yanked the rope like a fisherman setting a fish on the hook, burying the harpoon's iron claws into the *Horizon's* wooden hull and jerking the rope taut. With the *Horizon* now snagged, the pirate airship started to haul its prey in for boarding.

Roberts' fingers froze – if he let go of the wheel to try to free the harpoon, the *Horizon* could easily flip into a tailspin, risking everyone on board. Bloomberg suddenly fell upon the rope in a frenzy of movement, hacking and slashing at the thick fibers with a knife that had suddenly appeared in his hands. With a snap of fibers, the rope broke in two, whipping through the air and freeing the *Horizon* from her tether. The harpoon was still embedded in her hull, but it was harmless now, and the *Horizon* pulled away from the pirate airship in a frantic whiplash of movement.

"Bloomberg!" Roberts bellowed. "Fine work!" His attention back on the wheel, Roberts pulled the nose again, sending the airship soaring into the heavens and higher above the cloud cover, determined to keep his airship from harm. The *Horizon* responded eagerly, as if determined to get away from her attacker. Heedless of what else might be lurking in the clouds above, Roberts pushed the *Horizon* upwards, straining to force as much speed out of her as he could until she was out of danger. For several long minutes, the *Horizon* charged upwards at a sharp angle, fighting for altitude until she topped out at four thousand feet, well above the thick layers of clouds and into stiller, calmer air with no enemy in sight.

Now presumably safe from the pirate airship, Bloomberg and Roberts continued to scan the air for a renewed assault as the *Horizon* moved forward at four thousand feet. None came, and the *Horizon* and crew settled down from the excitement and set back on course again. The airship had blown quite far off her original path, and with a deadline to make, they needed to resume their course toward London, this time with a heightened thought for security. Luckily, the *Horizon* seemed to have left the growing storm behind her. The clouds began to thin out and the weather settled down into more favorable flying conditions.

After a half-hour of racing the *Horizon* forward at thirty-three knots without further signs of an attack, Roberts eased up just slightly. Most pirates knew enough not to waste fuel trying to chase down another airship that had a clear lead, and as the minutes ticked by, he became more and more convinced that they had left their attackers far behind them. For safety's sake, Roberts kept the *Horizon* at thirty knots until she was safely over England again and back in well-patrolled skies.

Only then did he finally call the postmaster over to the helm. Bloomberg was still visibly sweating and his goggles were askew on his face as Roberts gave him a firm look, then grinned broadly.

"Fine work, Mr. Bloomberg!" he boomed, dropping a heavy hand on Bloomberg's shoulder. The diminutive postmaster nearly buckled under the gesture as Roberts continued, "We would have been on our arses without your quick response."

"Oh, that. Well..." Bloomberg looked down modestly. "Just glad to do my part, Captain," he said, a small curl of pride in his voice.

"We were damned lucky that harpoon was on a rope," Roberts rumbled. "Sometimes they're on chains. And even so, that was a thick rope." He looked down at Bloomberg narrowly. "Just what type of knife did you bring on board my airship? It cut that rope like a hot knife through butter."

"Oh, yes, um, this one here." Bloomberg fumbled in his jacket and withdrew several inches of wickedly shining steel, the naked blade honed to a razor sharpness and the wooden handle obviously well-used.

Roberts glanced at it. "You planning on gutting a cow while on board?" he intoned.

"Me? Oh no, Captain," Bloomberg blushed again. "This was passed down to me by my great-grandfather. Irish, you know. Bit of an oddity since he married into a Jewish family. He was quite the rabble-rouser, according to family lore. And, er, I had word that this knife was well-used, if you get my meaning." He tugged at his jacket lapel, revealing a flash of the sheath that was hidden inside. Bloomberg put the blade back where it had come from and smoothed his jacket over his chest with a slightly fussy air before remarking, "I got in the habit of carrying it on board when I fly for the Royal Mail Service. I've been through a skirmish or two, and I don't like to fly undefended. A good knife can always come in handy."

Roberts was still intently examining the little man before him, and his craggy face broke into a slow smile. "There's more to you than meets the eye, Mr. Bloomberg," he pronounced with some feeling, smiling to himself at the way Bloomberg's plump chest inflated as tight as the *Horizon*'s envelope. He followed the smile with a hearty slap to the postmaster's shoulder that nearly knocked the man to his plump knees.

The crew of the *Horizon* saw nothing more of the pirate airship and as afternoon grew toward evening, fatigue settled over the crew as the intensity of battle wore off. Their conflict in the sky had cost them time, and Roberts' attention was fastened on the chronometer. With some ground to make up, the *Horizon* was soon moving forward at thirty-five knots with her crew struggling against the cloying exhaustion that follows a rush of adrenaline.

They made it to Royal Mail Service dock with time to spare, approaching night beginning to throw dark shadows across London. The crew of the *Horizon* was exhausted from their work and the effort of evading battle, but Bloomberg was surprisingly trim and fresh. As the *Horizon* swung into the post service dock, he briskly took over operations, sending postal workers to unload the belly of the airship and directing mail into the proper channels. The workers obediently followed his commands, and the *Horizon* was swiftly unloaded.

At last, a bag of heavy coins was pressed into Roberts' hand, the first money the *Horizon* had received under his command. He accepted it from Bloomberg with a tired nod, and the pudgy postmaster nudged him meaningfully. "Our agreed price and a little extra," he winked confidentially.

"Consider it hazard pay and repair costs for what damage the harpoon inflicted, Captain." Roberts had paid little heed to the harpoon still embedded in the *Horizon*'s hull after a quick glance had told him that damage was minimal. The harpoon hadn't latched onto anything vital, and the *Horizon* had carried it back to London like a war trophy. Roberts thankfully accepted the extra funds and gave Bloomberg a nod of respectful gratitude.

Bloomberg winked again, then dusted his hands briskly. "Now Captain Roberts," he stated cheerfully. "How about you dock this fine bird of yours so you and I can chat about getting her a Royal Mail Service seal?"

"How about we chat about you coming on board her as a pilot?" Roberts countered and watched with a pleased smile as Bloomberg's mouth dropped open with shock.

After several seconds of gaping, Bloomberg managed to stutter out, "S...sir?" in blank confusion.

Roberts' grin deepened. "I need good men on board the *Horizon*. Any man that can handle a skirmish with a pirate ship like you did is much welcomed on board. You've got some skill as a pilot. A little training and practice and you'll be a fine addition to the *Horizon*'s crew."

"Why...Captain...I," Bloomberg fumbled, a blush filling up his cheeks. "I'm hardly a hearty air dog, not with my bad eyes and lungs," he mumbled, his plump cheeks quivering.

"The docks are filled with strong airmen that don't know their arse from a hole in the ground," Roberts stated bluntly. "I could use some men with brains and courage." While his offer to Bloomberg had been spontaneous, he had long learned to trust his gut instincts, and right now, his innards were telling him that the little postmaster would both jump at a chance to sign up on board the *Horizon* and would make an excellent addition to the crew.

"Oh...well..." Bloomberg's blush had turned his entire face red. He blinked several times and stated reluctantly, "I...well...I have my duties as postmaster."

"Mr. Bloomberg," Roberts said bluntly, "I'll be honest with you. The *Horizon*'s got no contracts and no assured work. What you just gave me was the first payment she's got with me as her captain. You'd be leaving a steady job with good pay to throw your lot in with us at no guarantee. But I can promise you this," he continued, watching Bloomberg closely, "I treat my men fairly and I won't be stingy with pay once I can afford to do so. Stick with me and work hard and we'll all share the profits together."

Bloomberg's eyes were moist behind his custom-ground lenses, and his voice had a visible tremor in it. "Captain, I...I simply do not know what to say!" he gasped out.

Roberts' brow wrinkled. "You a family man, Mr. Bloomberg?" he questioned.

"No, sadly not," Bloomberg replied, his excited, dazed expression falling. "I was engaged last year but my fiancée, well, she died of cholera six months ago." His mouth turned down sadly as Roberts nodded in sympathy. Both men were silent for a moment before Roberts spoke again.

"Think about it. I don't expect an answer now. But I have use for you, and you'd be welcome on board the *Horizon* if you want to take a chance on an old dream." He gave the little man a hearty slap and grinned. "You can leave a message at the Broken Spar if you want to find me." With another grin, he left the postmaster standing on the postal dock, his plump frame positively aquiver, and his eyes flashing with excitement.

Roberts reboarded the *Horizon*, his mind already honing in on the next set of duties. He met Oboe with a sharp nod. "We're going back to Halloway's," he ordered. "She's still got a harpoon embedded in her belly and some patching to do. And I've some payment to wring out of Goldson." With that, orders filled the airship as airbags whooshed and she began rising steadily into the evening air.

Chapter Ten

Goldson's flour-encrusted frame was waiting for Roberts when the captain of the *Horizon* strode into the mill, dodging workers and machinery. It was early morning and the sun was just waking in the sky, but the small mill was already chaotic with activity. As he threaded his way through the crowds of powdery white men and the clanging groans of engines, Roberts stubbornly held back the yawns threatening to escape his jaws. Halloway, unsurprisingly, had set to work on the *Horizon*'s damages the second they had shunted the airship into his workshop, and he had kept going long after the rest of the crew, Roberts included, had given up for the night and snatched a few hours of sleep.

The noise of the mill was like a hammer on Roberts' eardrums, and his nerves were already jumpy. Ignoring the din as best he could, he stalked into Goldson's office and dropped the paperwork on the foreman's desk with a grin, loosening a small cloud of flour that rose up like smoke.

The foreman's face creased with an astonished smile as his eyes scanned the paperwork. "You son of a gun," he pronounced with wonder. "You did it. Nine hours and forty-three minutes. Well, Captain," Goldson rose to his feet and thrust a cracked hand at Roberts who took it gladly. "I took you for a mad fool, and I'm glad to say I was wrong. Congratulations!" Goldson whistled reverently. "Our Smothers contract ship didn't show up at the mill until the day after you left, and its captain demanded thirty pounds a ton. Hell with that, I say," he grinned. "I'd be happy to contract you on, Captain, now that the damned Corn Law is finally overturned."

Goldson began ruffling through the various strata on his desk, flour wafting in the air. "We'll likely want two shipment a week. I'll sign you on at twenty pounds a ton."

"Twenty-three a ton," Roberts countered. "We had a run-in with pirates over the Irish Sea, and word is they're growing in activity. Right now, I'm running a skeleton crew and I have to think of my men." He was taking a slight risk at negotiating for a higher price, but Roberts had a strong suspicion Goldson wouldn't object too strenuously.

Goldson opened his mouth but Roberts added, "That's twenty-three a ton at a guarantee of ten hours. That's still less than what Smothers charges. It's a bargain and you know it." He voiced the sentences lightly, but with a slight smile.

The foreman frowned in thought, but he allotted only a few seconds for consideration before accepting. "All right then, Captain Roberts, you got yourself a deal," Goldson replied with the cheerful amiability of a man who knows he has rightfully lost a battle, yet still come away a winner. They shook hands on it, and Goldson continued, "You get your daft bird back here Thursday morning and I'll have a contract done up and another shipment for you."

"Agreed," Roberts replied. "Soon as you pay for this first shipment."

The foreman's smile was cheerfully crestfallen. "I was half-counting on getting a free shipment out of you, Captain," he chuckled as he moved to a small safe and began manipulating its dial.

"I wasn't," Roberts responded genially, but he meant every word.

"Have to admit, I've never been happier to pay for a shipment," Goldson continued as the safe opened with a clang, and he withdrew a sack of money. He counted out what he owed Roberts, then pushed it across the desk with a grin.

Roberts had to restrain himself from the urge to snatch. Instead, he picked up the money carefully and placed the coins reverently into a small sack. Bloomberg's payment was already gone, thanks to a month of back pay Roberts had handed over to the crew last night, and the new influx of cash was desperately needed. With that, the two men rose to their feet and shook hands. "Pleasure doing business with you, Captain Roberts," Goldson said cheerfully and walked Roberts out of the mill.

The London morning was full and strong. The streets were their normal crowded mess of people, trams, horses, muck, and the effluvia of the city, modern and medieval clashing together in a disjointed unity. A steam-powered tricycle roared through the city at breakneck speed, its driver cheerfully ignoring pedestrians, his goggles flashing in the bright light of the sun. Ahead, a large cluster of arguing people stood around the wreckage of an overturned horse carriage that had apparently run afoul of a greengrocer's stand. Scattered cabbages lay like decapitated heads across the filthy cobblestones, several of them quietly disappearing thanks to onlookers taking advantage of the shop owner's distraction. Flocks of sheep filled the air with their distressed bleats as they skittered nervously out of the way of a sleek steam-powered automobile tooting imperiously at the crowds impeding its passage. The stench of the city, both organic and chemical, was like a living wall, and Roberts stalked through it irritably, trying not to breathe too deeply. With the fresh wind of the high air still in his nostrils, it was always a shock to drop down into the fetid squalor that was much of London.

In Roberts' pocket was a list of items Halloway was currently braying for in order to further modify the *Horizon,* along with some odds and ends. There would be a much longer list in the near future; Halloway showed no hesitation about spending Roberts' money for him, especially now that the *Horizon* had started earning her keep. Roberts knew he would have to keep a tight rein on his money or Halloway would happily burn through everything the *Horizon* earned in order to keep her bedecked with the latest technological wonders.

Pleased to have some time to himself, Roberts poked around London's shops, picking up what he needed. It was nearing noon when he returned to Halloway's, his shoulders overloaded with sacks of supplies and his mind intently preoccupied. Thus, he did not mark the visitors waiting on Halloway's stoop until he was nearly on top of them.

"I say! Good day to you, sir!" a voice rang out. It belonged to a vivacious young woman with dark, curling hair and a gray skirt and jacket that gave her a businesslike air while at the same time subtly highlighting her attractiveness. At her side was a barrel-shaped man with a nose that had met at least one hard object and an expression of stone. He was holding a daguerreotype camera in his sausage-sized fingers as if it were a club. The lens of the camera trained in Roberts' direction as he approached.

Roberts gazed at the duo warily. "Can I help you, Miss?" he questioned, eying the camera with particular disdain.

"I do hope so!" the woman exclaimed briskly. "Would you be Captain Roberts of the airship *Horizon*?"

Roberts halted, the beginning of a frown waking to life on his face. "It depends on who is doing the asking, Miss," he responded carefully.

"Of course, how rude of me," the lady laughed. "I am Miss Victoria Pickens and this is my brother Jules. We're with the *London Guardian*."

Reporters? Roberts thought, his frown deepening with surprise. *Why reporters?*

As if on cue, the stony-faced man lifted the camera upwards and a light flashed. Roberts' puzzled frown deepened more; a camera took long minutes to process a picture, and a brief flash would capture nothing but a blur. Miss Pickens was speaking animatedly, drawing his attention away from the silent photographer.

“You see, sir, we are on the trail of the good airship *Horizon,*" she continued cheerfully. "London is abuzz with news that she flew to Larne in just under ten hours not two days ago. This is quite astonishing and record-setting news, Mr...Mr...” She smiled winsomely at him, and Roberts felt his mouth opening to offer his name. He closed it in time and settled for giving her a wary look.

Miss Pickens turned coy. “Oh, come now, sir, surely you can give me your name, can't you?” There was a flutter of long eyelashes and despite himself, Roberts returned her smile. She was quite astoundingly pretty and refreshingly direct, and it had been a long time since he last exchanged pleasant words with an attractive female. Two decades of toiling on board various airships peopled entirely with men had not given Roberts ample time for the fairer sex. In his experience, few women were as forward as this and those who were generally charged for the experience.

Caution was clamoring to make itself heard under the growing appreciation Roberts was developing for Miss Pickens' flashing eyes and pert nose. Grabbing interest by the throat and resolutely throttling it, he responded carefully, "I'm not at liberty to say anything, Miss, and I'd be glad to escort you elsewhere so that you may be on your way. This part of town is no place for a lady."

"Tush, tush, that is why I have Jules here!" Miss Pickens trilled merrily. "Now come, Captain Roberts, if I may call you that..." she smiled. There hadn't been time or money for Roberts to invest in a proper captain's coat and hat, but the reporter had obviously ferreted out enough information to guess that the man facing her was the one she was intent on tracking down.

Still playing dumb, Roberts pulled himself upright. "Miss, I wish you luck in whatever story you are hunting, but I'm afraid I can't be of help. Good day to you." He stepped forward to bang on Halloway's door, but Miss Pickens moved with him, placing one slender hand on the door and gazing up at him with her big brown eyes.

"Oh, don't be such a tease, Captain," she purred. "Your fine airship has just completed a historic run! Why on earth wouldn't you want the entire city, if not Europe to know? Think of what this means for technology, for air travel, for military and commerce. This is the story of the century, and you are going to stay mute about it?" Her eyes opened wider in shock. "You ought to be proud! You're a hero and the world should know..."

Roberts decided his best course of action was to ignore her, so he banged irritably on the door and growled into the com device, "It's me. Let me in." He wasn't about to mention his name nor Halloway's, less Miss Pickens draw more connections. She was still chattering away behind his back, but he let her words rush over him unheeded. It was approaching lunchtime, he was hungry, and the sleep debt was coming to collect with interest. Roberts had no time for nosy reporters, no matter how attractive.

Halloway's voice snarled over the com system. "Is that bloody woman still hanging around?"

Roberts sighed. He had half a mind to ask Miss Pickens how long she had been camped out on the doorstep, but courtesy nagged. "Just let me in," he responded wearily.

"I'll turn Mary loose if you let anyone inside with you," Halloway promised as the metal door clicked open.

Roberts kept a firm eye on Miss Pickens as he stepped forward. The woman seemed to possess the determination of a terrier, and he wouldn't put it past her to squeeze around the door and march inside the shop to see what she could discover. Blocking the entrance with his shoulders, Roberts nodded at the reporters. "Good afternoon, Ma'am, Sir," he said firmly.

"Captain! If I could just have one moment..." Miss Pickens persisted, quickly stepping forward as if looking for an opening, but Roberts disappeared into the darkness and pushed the door shut. It was closing on its own, but he helped it along with a booted foot, and it slammed shut in a most satisfying manner, closing off the two reporters from view.

Inside, Roberts gratefully dropped the sacks to the floor for William to put away. The interior of the shop was impressively lit by warm sunlight flowing in from the opened roof, and the airship was secure in her berth. The other crew members were clearly worse for a short night's sleep and only Halloway was brisk and alert. He looked up sharply as Roberts strode into the room.

"She gone?" Halloway barked by way of greeting as he tossed aside the tool in his hand.

"I left her outside," Roberts responded, gazing critically at his airship. The harpoon had bit into the gondola, but the holes were being patched up and the *Horizon* seemed none the worse for wear.

"Good," Halloway grunted. "Showed up an hour ago, hanging on the bell and wouldn't leave for nothing. I was about to turn Mary loose on her." Roberts frowned at the news and watched as Halloway strode angrily around his shop. "I can't stand these modern women," Halloway growled. "Pushy, demanding biddies, the lot of them."

Roberts knew that his old friend couldn't stand people in general, but he guessed that there were deeper concerns on the inventor's mind. His suspicions proved true when Halloway barked out sarcastically, "Any other guests we can expect the pleasure of receiving?"

Roberts paused for a few moments before responding carefully, "Not that I know of." He did not relish the idea of the *Horizon* splashed across the next morning's newspapers. While extra attention would garner more work opportunities, it would also generate a slew of unwanted attention, which would grow exponentially more unwanted when it reached the ear of Sir Smothers. Smothers had made a name for himself by ruthlessly exterminating competition, and Roberts had already been blacklisted by the powerful tycoon. The news about the *Horizon* would just add fuel to the raging inferno.

How Miss Pickens and her recalcitrant brother had found Halloway's shop was another troubling question. Halloway treasured his anonymity, and the arrival of reporters on his doorstep did not bode well for his continued reclusiveness. With all Halloway had done to assist with the *Horizon*'s rebuild, he didn't need to earn the ire of Sir Smothers for his efforts. Roberts owed it to Halloway to guard his old friend from any repercussions from the Smothers empire.

Halloway's voice broke in on Roberts' thoughts, directing him towards other matters. "She should be back into shape after another day or two," the inventor grunted. Roberts turned his attention back to the *Horizon*, uneasily hoping that he had seen the last of the reporters.

*** *** *** ***

The newspaper landed in front of Roberts, its headlines screaming in bold letters, "AIRSHIP BREAKS FLIGHT RECORD!" Seeing the headline, Roberts hissed several long, heartfelt words under his breath and seized the paper, his eyes blazing across the page and gobbling up words by the second.

"*History was made four days ago when the airship* Horizon, *captained by Gavin Roberts, flew from London to Larne, Ireland in an unbelievable ten-hour journey. Several witnesses at the Larne port stated that...*"

Dammit, Roberts thought with rising fury, too intent on the article to pay much heed to Carter who was facing him with a scowl of worry, his arms crossed and his mouth tight. The bosun had returned from an early morning errand with a newspaper under his arm, which he had presented to his captain without comment.

"*...to achieve that unprecedented flight time would require a flying speed of at least thirty-three knots per hour, five hours faster than the current world record held by...*"

Dammit, dammit, dammit, Roberts growled to himself as the story unfurled before his eyes, especially when he saw the prominent picture gracing the article: that was unmistakably him in front of Halloway's door, loaded down with sacks and scowling unpleasantly. He must have been mistaken about the camera; apparently it was some new-fangled device that was able to take a picture in a single, brief snap. The caption beneath his image stated, "*Captain Roberts refused to give any information, stating that...*"

Roberts stared at the words, logic trying to override the blazing trail of rage etching itself across his brain. *How they hell did they...?* he started to question before common sense kicked in. He had signed his name and the *Horizon*'s as well to several sets of paperwork, and documents were easy to trace. Bloomberg had been bubbling with praise about the *Horizon*'s swiftness, and it would only take the wrong word in the right ear to send rumors raging through London. Thanks to their celebration at the Broken Spar a week past, Roberts knew there were rumors about the mystery airship which had streaked across the sky in an unprecedented blaze of speed. The picture in front of him was crisp and clear, and it would not have been too difficult for the reporters to put a name to a face: there were plenty of airmen in London who knew Roberts by sight and could confirm that the image was his likeness. A skilled journalist could easily connect the dots for a well-supported story, like the one facing Roberts at that moment.

After leaving the reporters outside the previous day, Roberts had shrugged off the unwanted visitors and turned his mind to other matters. There were over fifty newspapers hawked daily throughout London, and the *London Guardian* was one of the smaller publications. Professional women reporters were as scarce as snake feathers, and Roberts had maintained little worry that anything he had said or denied would end up in print.

Apparently I was mistaken, he thought, exhaling a long stream of controlled air from his lungs. He knew that the oversight would cost him dearly. Dreading the thought of continuing, he kept trawling the article.

"*The airship* Horizon *was previously part of Sir Cornelius Smothers' short-flight air fleet under the name of the* Lucky Lady. *After a boiler explosion on May 8th tragically killed Albert Smothers, captain of the vessel, the airship was recently transferred to the command of her first mate, Gavin Roberts. What arrangements were made between Sir Smothers and Captain Roberts are unknown...*"

Roberts' face momentarily whitened under his tanned complexion. "You blasted fool," he said hollowly as if Miss Pickens could hear him. "You don't know what the hell you just did..."

"An anonymous airman reported that he was a crew member on board the lift ship Hercules *which transported the* Lucky Lady *off the Smothers wharf and removed her to an undisclosed location, rumored to be the workshop of the famous inventor Jacob Halloway..."*

Groaning slightly, Roberts shifted his eyes to the gaunt back of Halloway who was, as usual, hunched over a workbench, intent on a grubby set of diagrams. As much as

Roberts hated to see his name in the news, he knew Halloway would be ten times as furious. With another groan, he resolutely turned back to the article to see what further inky catastrophes awaited him there.

The article wound on, most unfortunately true to the core and full of an abundance of names and facts that indicated the writer of the article, none other than Victoria Pickens, had the nose of a bloodhound and the self-preservation instinct of a baked potato. Given the nature of the article, Roberts surmised that the *London Guardian* had either not sought Sir Smothers' permission before publishing or had blithely ignored all his threats of legal action should the article make it to print. Sir Smothers tolerated no smear against his empire or family, and the article in Roberts' hands was full of all sorts of juicy details that would send London abuzz and cause deep embarrassment for the entire Smothers family.

Although the *London Guardian* did not carry a lot of clout, Roberts knew that there was absolutely no possible way the article would escape Sir Smothers' attention for long. Thousands of families across London depended on the Smothers empire to put food on their tables, but the hard-nosed tyrant was not well-liked and a story like this would spread through the city faster than a cholera outbreak. If Smothers hadn't seen the article yet, he would catch wind of it very soon. And then all hell would break loose.

Finally done with the incriminating article, Roberts marched over to where Halloway sat hunched over his work bench and wordlessly shoved the paper under his nose. Halloway looked momentarily irritated, then froze, his eyes scanning the page. “What...the...*hell*?” he snarled and shot to his feet, his skinny frame unfolding like an umbrella. Turning violently on Roberts, the inventor spat out, “Did you do this...?"

“I said nothing to her,” Roberts growled. “Not even my name. She's obviously got a knack for finding information, and there's been enough witnesses on the air and ground for her to find what she wants.”

Halloway was practically shaking with fury, but Roberts' mind was twitching too fast to let anger seize control. “We need to get out of London, and fast,” he said heavily. “A couple months or so and things will calm down a bit, but for now it'll be too hot around here for my tastes.” He shot Halloway a firm look. “That means you too.”

Halloway stiffened. “Don't be an idiot, Roberts, I'm not leaving London...”

"You are," Roberts said with rising heat. "Don't be a bloody fool, Halloway. Smothers has been stealing your inventions for years and he knows your skills. When this article hits his nose, he'll know that you've not only managed to coax forty knots out of an airship but it's the dammed *Lucky Lady* under a different name. He'll make you an offer to work for him where he can control every blasted move you make, and it won't be one you can turn down."

Halloway shot Roberts a narrowed eye, and Roberts returned the expression furiously. "And you can call me every nasty name you want, Jacob, I know it was me that dragged you into this mess. But Smothers is going to drop like a ton of bricks on everyone he thinks is involved in this, including you. We're all best off out of England until the old bugger's had a chance to cool down. Smothers will do damage control as best he can, but his dirty laundry just got aired all over London. He'll be on the hunt for those responsible."

By now, heads were popping up, the crew alert to the burgeoning crisis. Glancing at them, Roberts barked loudly, "Fall in!" There was a hasty stampede as the crew assembled in order, rank and file, and gazed at their captain anxiously.

Facing them, Roberts drew his shoulders up and rumbled, "Men, I'll pull no punches with you. We're all in deep shite." He threw the newspaper down on the floor. "Thanks to an overly enthusiastic reporter, news of our ten-hour journey to Ireland is now widely known, as well as the boiler explosion that killed Captain Albert. All of London now knows what Smothers has been trying hard to keep quiet."

He let the words sink in, then continued, "We'd best find friendlier skies elsewhere until the Smothers empire calms down a bit, and that won't be for awhile."

He stared each crew member in the eye. "Thus being the case, I won't hold it against any man who decides to try his luck elsewhere. You all know that my name and the *Horizon* herself have a black mark against them. It would have been hard going before these damned reporters came sniffing around, and it's going to be a hell of a lot harder now. I won't look poorly on any man who wants to leave."

The crew was silent, eyes forward, and Roberts strode the rank, looking to see who was still with him. Carter and Oboe were both bachelors, and Jenkins had been a married man up until last year when his wife had run off with a butcher and taken their two children with her. That left Farrington who had a wife and son back in Clovelly and a second child due in two months. When the airship had flown as the *Lucky Lady*, Farrington had been able to go home at least every two weeks, but as the *Horizon*, she would keep the quartermaster away from his family for months on end. If anyone was to give up on the *Horizon*, Roberts guessed it would be Farrington.

Stepping closer to the quartermaster, Roberts said quietly, "Mr. Farrington, you have a family to think about."

"Not leaving, sir!" Farrington snapped out crisply and formally, meeting his captain's eyes levelly.

Roberts gave him a long look, then nodded, "You're welcome on board." As he spoke, a whiff of something fetid caught his nose. Airmen were not known for being the most hygienic of men; bathing was difficult on an airship since water was heavy and every ounce was first reserved for the boiler. Halloway had a negligence toward washing which bordered on deliberate avoidance, and his facilities were not well-equipped for ablutions. That didn't explain the sickening reek of spoiled meat that floated over the regular odors of stale sweat, grime, and engine grease, and Roberts had an odd feeling that he had smelled the scent before.

Frowning, he stepped away from Farrington and continued down the line to where William stood, gritting his teeth and doing his best to look taller. Roberts thought about bending down to level with the boy but decided it would be demeaning. Instead, he faced the young lad and said with some tactfulness, "William, we're going to be ranging far from England for long months. Your granny and aunt..."

"Permission to stay on board, sir!" William squeaked in a high-pitched voice. The boy's back was ramrod-straight, and Roberts could see that there were tears threatening to spill down his face.

Roberts looked the young steward over. "Alright," he said at last. "You're becoming a man now and a man makes his own decisions."

"Thank you, sir!" Williams said, this time not so high.

Roberts nodded and continued his way down the line until his inspection was complete and he had new orders to disperse. “We need more crew members," he announced. "I'll be out looking for new men to hire. The rest of you, get the *Horizon* repaired and back on her feet." He spoke the words with a confidence he did not feel. With the reputation the *Horizon* was rapidly gaining for herself and her captain, few airmen of any skill would be tempted by a position on board. Roberts had given his crew the back pay he owned them with a little more added in, but he couldn't afford to be overly generous and the wages he had to offer were below what a good airman would make on a Smothers' airship. With the *Horizon* leaving the safety of England's shores, she needed a full crew to tend her. Somehow, her captain would have to find enough men to keep her in the air.

Roberts continued, "We're leaving town soon, and don't be surprised if we have to do so in a hurry. I'm not ordering that you all stay indoors, but it's not going to be friendly out on the streets, and you are all best off keeping your noses inside until we leave.” The men took the news grimly, but there was no surprise on their faces: they knew the situation was precarious at best. When Roberts snapped a dismissal, they turned back to their work, but not before he intoned darkly, "Mr. Farrington, you're with me.”

The quartermaster stopped, his spine drawing up like a bowstring tightening under pressure. Wordlessly, he followed his captain off into a more secluded area of the shop where light poured from a half-opened skylight. Roberts looked the quartermaster over for a few moments, then commanded, “Show me your arm." Farrington reluctantly extended a limb but Roberts shook his head darkly. “The other one,” he corrected sharply. With extreme reluctance, Farrington extended his right arm and watched tightly as Roberts pulled up the sleeve to reveal dirty bandages and a stench like decayed meat rising up to meet his nose.

Farrington visibly stiffened as Roberts unwound the bandages, the scowl deepening on his forehead and turning to shock as he uncovered spots of sickly green, oozing flesh on Farrington's upper bicep. The bright sun clearly displayed the patches of rotting tissue, painful and infectious across the shiny pink scars of his original steam burns.

“When did this happen?” Roberts demanded.

Farrington wouldn't meet his eye. “It's not as bad as it looks, Captain."

“Like hell it isn't!” Roberts barked. “Your arm was nearly healed last time I checked your wounds, man. Why the blazes didn't you report this?”

Farrington's jaw tightened as he muttered something. Roberts bellowed, “Speak up!”

“Tore a scar open on a nail a few weeks ago,” Farrington said with more volume. “I didn't have any of the ointment left.”

"So you just left it like this?" Roberts said incredulously. "You damned idiot, you could very well lose this arm."

Farrington's expression was fixed. He said nothing as Roberts glared fiercely at him. "Take your shirt off. *Now.*" Farrington reluctantly complied, and Roberts scanned his torso critically. The rest of the burns had left behind pink, healthy scar tissue with no sign of infection, but the sickly green patches on the bicep of his damaged arm were vivid. It was abundantly clear that without prompt medical attention, Farrington was in grave danger of losing his arm. Now that Roberts thought about it, he realized that the quartermaster had been uncharacteristically withdrawn the last week or two, even avoiding Carter, and his seemingly unconquerable good humor had been noticeably absent.

Roberts glared icily at his quartermaster and thundered, "Let me reiterate, Mr. Farrington, that you are a crew member on my airship flying under my command. If any one of my crew is ill or injured, it is your responsibility to report it and my responsibility to see it corrected. Have I made myself clear?"

"Yes, Captain," Farrington mumbled.

Roberts' furious stare did not lessen as he ordered, "You're relieved of duty until I get Harding back here to take a look at your arm." Farrington moved as if to protest, but backed down under Roberts' fury. With a curt word of dismissal, Roberts stalked away from the quartermaster, anger burning hot in his belly.

He found Oboe and stated, "I'm leaving things in your hands. I have a surgeon to hunt down and new crew members to hire." Without another word, Roberts undid the locks on the front door and thundered out into the street.

The day had gone from bad to terrible with an option on catastrophic when several minutes of angry tramping were interrupted by a familiar and much unwelcomed voice.

"Captain Roberts! Captain, if I could just ask you a few questions!"

Like a snake, Roberts whipped around to see Victoria Pickens hurrying toward him, Jules behind her like some sort of living siege weapon. "Captain!" she gasped as she minced nimbly across the dirty cobblestones, her dainty boots adroitly avoiding the muck of the street. Giving Roberts a dazzling smile, she said, "How fortuitous that I ran into you!"

Roberts gave her a look that would have cut diamonds. A lifetime of cultural demands that he treat women with respect was brawling furiously with a very human desire to wring Miss Pickens' lovely, lily white neck. Even the curve of her full lips and enticing flash of her brilliant eyes did nothing to cool his ire.

As graceful as a deer, Miss Pickens skipped her way to Roberts, fetchingly breathless, and situated herself just a few inches from his glowering frame. A white lace glove was placed lightly on his rigid arm as Miss Pickens' brilliant brown eyes gazed up at him appealingly. "Now, Captain," she cooed, "Won't you...?"

Roberts cut her off bluntly. "Have you any idea what you have just done, Miss Pickens?"

The lacy glove fluttered in front of her face. "Captain, you simply could not expect a story like this to stay silent," Miss Pickens smiled. "A historic flight! A dashing race against time! The mysterious death of an heir! This is something all of England, no, I correct myself, all of the world needs to know! This is..."

"Something that just put you, me, and a number of people I am responsible for in grave danger, Miss Pickens," Roberts growled ominously.

"Grave danger? Come now, Captain," Miss Pickens trilled a light laugh, but Roberts caught the faintest breath of fear hiding under the pretty words and cheerful bravado. He had met one or two women like her before, smart enough to realize that a lovely face coupled with a cunning brain was a force few men could withstand. However, Roberts was growing steadily more furious with the reporter's cheerful refusal to heed his words.

Squaring his shoulders and ignoring the looming wall that was Jules, Roberts towered over Miss Pickens' head and growled, "I'll have you know, Miss Pickens, that I wasn't anywhere near a favorite of Sir Smothers, for reasons I will not tell you lest you take it into your pretty head to write more. Your article has just guaranteed that Smothers will go after me and anyone under my command until he's crushed us. Because of you, I am now forced to take my airship and my crew out of London and I don't know when we can safely return, if ever."

Miss Pickens was visibly wilting under Roberts' proclamations, and he could see the beginning tendrils of doubt creeping up on her face. But he wasn't finished. "There's public interest, Miss Pickens, and then there's frank stupidity, and the problem with frank stupidity is that it tends to get people killed. And one of these people just might be you."

Miss Pickens' brown eyes widened and she let loose a laugh, confident yet touched with a trace of nervousness. "Me? Oh, Captain, surely you exaggerate."

"I'm not exaggerating, Miss Pickens," Roberts corrected her. "Before this day is over, you'll be lucky if the *London Guardian* is still in existence, much less if you still have a job and any sort of reputation in this city." Miss Pickens looked suddenly crestfallen and for one moment, Roberts almost felt sorry for her. There were very few women who held professional positions anywhere in the country, and Miss Pickens must have clawed her way up from the very bottom one painful rung at a time. She probably had seen the story of the century and the chance to make her career. What she would very likely end up with was a firm kick to her attractive backside to the street and a host of other newspapers who would sooner hire a baboon over her.

Miss Pickens drew herself upwards as much as her height and Roberts' iron stare would allow. "This is a historic story that the public deserves to know..." she began again.

Roberts cut her off. "At the cost of men's lives, Miss Pickens?" he demanded bluntly. "I'm speaking true when I say that your neck and mine are at risk here. I know Smothers. He won't stop until he gets his revenge. I doubt you set out to get blood on your hands, but it may end up that way. If I were a heartless man, I'd say no more but I consider myself one of honor and I'll give you a piece of advice, Miss Pickens." He leaned down to look the reporter in the eye, inches from her face. "Leave town. Now. Not to be dramatic, but there's a storm coming and you'll be in the dead center of it. And no one survives a storm when it's Smothers making it rain."

Miss Pickens blinked her long lashes, and Roberts could see a faint glow of moisture appear on her smooth forehead. Without a word, he turned his back to her and stalked away, losing himself in the crowd and leaving the reporter and her silent bodyguard behind.

Chapter Eleven

The Broken Spar was half-full with a motley assortment of airmen, most hunched over their drinks and a few snoring in their seats. As Roberts shoved back the door and stomped inside the bar, eyes swung his way to inspect the newcomer and darkened in recognition. A palpable frisson of tension shot through the room as most of the men carefully turned back to their drinks, studiously ignoring the captain of the *Horizon*. He crossed the room towards the bar where Tom was wiping a tankard clean.

A copy of the *London Guardian* was resting on the bar. Roberts' black and white picture scowled up at the living version as he glanced down at the article and frowned angrily. It had been a long walk over to the Broken Spar and he had taken it in a ground-eating stride that cooled his fury to a low simmer, logic wrestling the controls back from blind rage. Sitting heavily on a bar stool, Roberts planted an elbow firmly on the newspaper and turned to the barman, jerking his chin by way of greeting.

Tom nodded in return, but warily, and he quickly bent to set the tankard down on a low shelf, not meeting Roberts' eyes. “Morning, Captain," he said distantly. "What are you drinking today, sir?”

Roberts caught the formality of the landlord's voice, and his frown deepened. Tom was a gruff soul, markedly lacking in the convivial charm one expected of a tavern owner, and he didn't often stand on courtesy. Behind him, Roberts could hear the sound of chairs scraping and feet moving; he didn't need to turn around to see that the bar was quietly emptying, save for a few souls here and there.

Tom turned around and caught Roberts' expression, then shrugged his thick shoulders. "Can't be helped much, Gavin," he said, dropping the formality with his voice. "Most of the men, well," he shrugged again, "It's their jobs, not to mention their arses, on the line if anyone sees them talking with you." He waved vaguely in the direction of the newspaper under Roberts' elbow. "Miserable old bugger's hopping mad about this and you know Smothers. When he gets mad, God help the poor fool who gets in his way." A third shrug, and Tom was reaching for a tankard. Filling it, he pushed the container toward Roberts. "On the house, Captain," he said. A grin broke over his thickly-jowled face. "Here's to bothering a rich, arrogant old sod who deserves it."

Roberts allowed himself a small smile of triumph and took the tankard without a word, nodding at Tom. The barman returned to his industrious tankard wiping while Roberts sat a moment in thought, swilling down the rough, sharp beer. Finally he broke the silence. "I need some more men, Tom."

The barkeeper whistled discouragingly between his teeth. "I hate to break it to you, Gavin, but your airship and your name have been blackballed here to Scotland and back. The only airmen you are going to find are crazy mothers or pirates or both."

"I just may need crazy mothers or pirates," Roberts grunted back.

Tom sniffed. "What can you pay?"

"Not much," Roberts responded with another grunt. "Five pounds a week to start."

Tom wiped a nearly invisible spill off the rough wooden counter. "Not good odds, Captain. Not good at all."

Roberts finished the last of the beer and thumped the tankard down on the counter. "Just keep an eye out for any decent airmen in need of a job, will you?"

Tom sniffed audibly. "What kind of men and how many?" he questioned.

"About six," Roberts responded. "A pilot, maybe two. Couple of able airmen. Catwalk man or two. At least one assistant engineer." He was already rising to his feet, knowing that there was little more he could accomplish inside the Broken Spar's dubious hospitality.

Tom gave him a complicated look. "I'll see what I can do," he said, but there was little hope in his voice.

Roberts nodded. "I'll be back soon," he pronounced. "I've got to go track down Harding." With that, he stalked out of the Broken Spar and back into the crowd-choked streets. The tavern was relatively close to the Smothers wharf, and Roberts spotted several airmen he knew as he pushed his way through the crowds. They all studiously avoided him as he passed by as if being in Roberts' general vicinity was hazardous.

Harding's small, dingy office was squashed between an insalubrious greengrocer and a pawnshop, and the surgeon was in residence when Roberts banged on the door and walked in without waiting for an answer. "Good morning to you, Captain Roberts," Harding said, his eyes on a thick medical tome as the irate captain stomped up to his desk. "And tell me, whose ire will we be incurring this afternoon?"

Roberts ignored the comment but noted the newspaper sitting on the cluttered desk, his portrait glaring up at him. He glared back at his image, then rumbled irritably to Harding, "I've got a crew member that seems to think hiding an armful of gangrene is the best way to cure it."

"Oh dear, what did that idiot Farrington get up to again?" Harding questioned sardonically.

"Tore a scar open on a nail, so he told me," Roberts responded. "It's bad and it smells terrible. He needs a working arm, not a stump. Can you heal it?"

"Sounds like a job for the leeches," the surgeon replied. "They're devilishly wriggly creatures, but they've saved more than one limb from the chop." Harding moved to a series of drawers and began shoveling equipment inside his worn doctor's bag. Roberts watched him measuringly. Halloway had not let off insisting that the *Horizon* would fly internationally, and with the wrath of the Smothers empire riding on her bow, the airship and crew needed to put several countries between them and England. A doctor on board was vital for long-distance flights, and by the time Harding finished his packing and reached for his hat, Roberts had made up his mind.

The two strode out into the streets. Roberts again saw familiar eyes that slid off his, landed briefly on Harding's, then dropped studiously to the ground. Harding recognized this too, and after a few minutes he commented, "Not exactly popular in this town, are we, Captain Roberts?"

"You saw the article," Roberts grunted.

"Yes, I must say that I read it with a rather refreshing interest," Harding responded almost gaily. "Splendid to see the old tyrant brought down a peg or two. Well done, Captain."

"It wasn't my intent," Roberts growled. "A pair of reporters showed up on the doorstep. I didn't say anything, but they managed to ferret out enough information for the article."

"Ah, well, the *London Guardian* is a relatively new paper with what I may call a more modern approach to news reporting," Harding stated lightly. "Their editor and owner seem to believe that it is important to present the news unvarnished, not after it has been heavily colored and edited by the powers that be."

"They sound like men after your own heart, John," Roberts snorted, biting back a smile.

"Thank you, Captain," Harding responded. "I consider that a compliment."

This time, Roberts did smile. "Well, how about this for a compliment? Why don't you come on board the *Horizon* for a spell? I'm in need of a good surgeon."

Harding paused and looked at Roberts critically. "Not planning on making an international flight in that little bird of yours, are you, Captain?" he questioned. "If I'm not very much mistaken, she is short-flight only."

"You might be surprised," Roberts said evenly.

Harding stayed paused for a moment, then took a step forward. "And what remunerations can I expect?" he questioned suspiciously.

"Five pounds a week to start, a hammock in a crowded bunk, a skeleton crew so you'll have your turn on the airbags when needed, long hours, and meals made by a steward who can barely boil water," Roberts responded bluntly.

"Oh dear, how can I possibly resist?" Harding drawled with cool sarcasm.

"I forgot to mention the half-mad cocaine addict in the boiler room who's the only thing keeping the whole damned ship afloat. I need him weaned off the white powder as soon as you can manage it," Roberts added as an afterthought, trying to slow his footsteps to match the surgeon's pace. Harding was lugging a heavy medical bag, and his sagging frame was starting to puff with exertion.

"You really know how to drive a bargain, Captain Roberts, that you do," the surgeon remarked, switching his bag to the other hand.

Roberts nodded, "On the plus side, you'll be leaving this Godforsaken town behind you for a while and getting some fresh air under your feet. It comes time you've had enough of flying, then there's plenty of towns who would welcome a talented surgeon and where Smothers isn't poking his nose into your business."

Harding's face twisted thoughtfully as he considered the proposition. Roberts continued, "You and I both have no good name to carry here in London and most of England, and there comes a time where a man has to try his luck elsewhere," he said practically. "A fresh start could do you some good, John. I could use you."

Harding was silent, but Roberts could see that the surgeon was considering the offer carefully. The pair said nothing for a few minutes as they strode through London's crowded streets, each man consumed with his own thoughts. Finally, Harding sniffed loudly. "First, let's see this gangrenous quartermaster of yours," he stated decisively. "Then we can talk further about this little proposition."

Roberts nodded in agreement and nothing more was said until they reached the street where Halloway's shop was located, Roberts watching carefully lest he be besieged by further inquisitive reporters. However, there was no sight of Miss Pickens or anyone else with a camera, a notebook, and a suicidal wish to scrawl further exposé on the Smothers empire.

Inside, Roberts left Harding to scowl and chastise Farrington in a corner. He waded through the mess of activity inside the airship to find Halloway swearing fluently at the boiler. The shop was the normal riot of wood planks, spilled liquids, and assorted bits of metal, and the August sun was beating down on the building, making everyone irritable. Being irritable was Halloway's default state of being, but he seemed particularly testy at that moment in time, most likely due to Miss Pickens' incriminating article.

"Problem, Halloway?" Roberts questioned as he reached the inventor.

Halloway impatiently threw a coil of wire down on the floor. "Yes, but nothing you'd understand. You're in the way," he complained as he shoved past Roberts to unearth a wrench from a pile of tools. Lifting it, he stated tersely, "We'll need to take her out soon for a test flight. I recalibrated the engines, but I won't know if everything's right until I see her fly."

Roberts nodded. "We'll take her out this evening. I'm spending the afternoon looking for new crew members."

"Preferably a decent engineer," Halloway barked. "Jenkins can't do everything, not if you're going to be flying day and night."

"That's where you come in," Roberts responded, gearing up for the fight he knew was forthcoming.

Halloway dropped the wrench and thundered angrily back to the pile for another tool. "Who says I'm flying with you?" he spat out.

"Well, you're not staying in London," Roberts pronounced with finality. "It's too damned dangerous after that article. The best thing you can do is put as much distance between you and Smothers as possible. Things will calm down eventually, but for now we're all hightailing it out of town until the worst blows over." Roberts was generously stretching the truth: he highly doubted if London would ever be hospitable again for anyone remotely connected to the *Horizon*, but he knew the bare truth would only incite Halloway into a froth of anger that would render him unfit for anything.

"Besides," Roberts continued. "Your name made it into the paper, and rumor is going to spread. You really want hordes of people showing up on your doorstep?" Impending doom from Smothers wouldn't be enough to break through Halloway's stubbornness, Roberts knew. Threatening the inventor with an onslaught of unwanted visitors would likely be the only way Halloway would agree to abandon London.

Halloway's lips tightened. He jerked the wrench he was holding viciously, and Roberts smiled thinly. It was the closest the inventor would get to admitting he had lost an argument, and Roberts took it as a victory, then frowned in thought. Halloway's workshop was stacked to the rafters with all manner of items, and while most of it was junk awaiting rebirth as some clever invention, the building was heavily scattered with blueprints, schematics, working mechanisms, and completed inventions such as the mecha. Left unguarded for months, Halloway's shop was guaranteed to be raided by enterprising looters, and the consequences could be disastrous. Like it or not, Halloway was going to have to identify his most valuable handiwork, and Roberts would need to figure out a way of transporting it to a secure location. However, Halloway would happily drag every single rusted cog and piece of bent wire with him if he could, and keeping his baggage to a minimum would not be an easy task.

Choosing not to share these thoughts, Roberts turned back to the crew to check that everyone was staying on task and continuing their repair work on the *Horizon*. Despite the heat and the growing tenseness of the situation, the crew members were promptly carrying out their duties under Oboe's watchful eye. Harding was still busy at work on Farrington's arm, and Halloway, despite his obvious anger, was industrious to the point of frenzy. Satisfied that everything was in order,

Roberts headed for the door again. It was time to return to the Broken Spar and start his hunt for new crew members.

There was a familiar, eager face waiting nervously at the bar, and Roberts was not entirely surprised to see none other than a transformed Bloomberg. The dark blue, ill-fitting suit had disappeared to be replaced by a shabby pair of trousers, a tattered shirt with the sleeves rolled up, and a square of cloth tied around his head in a vaguely nautical manner. The diminutive postmaster had forgone his spectacles for his goggles, and in the darkness of the bar, his magnified eyes were uncannily frog-like. The mutton chops had disappeared under the wrath of an inexpertly wielded razor, and dark stubble clung to the man's cheeks. When viewed at a distance and in bad lighting, Bloomberg could pass for a tolerable airman. The image was somewhat diminished by a furled umbrella and a fussy-looking traveling case carefully placed on the bar stool at his elbow.

The entire tableau nearly made Roberts laugh, but he stifled his mirth and moved forward to meet the postmaster, or more properly, former postmaster. When he spotted Roberts, Bloomberg eagerly bobbed off his stool and bounced across the room. "Captain Roberts!" Bloomberg puffed out breathlessly, holding out his slightly trembling hand. Roberts took it, noticing the softness of the proffered palm, and smiled to himself. *A few weeks on board the Horizon, and you'll have hands like an old saddle,* he silently promised as Bloomberg tried to match Roberts' grip strength.

"Captain, I..." Bloomberg stammered, then pulled his shoulders up as high as they would go and managed a tolerably crisp salute. "All ready to fly, sir!" he squeaked out.

Roberts gave him a long look. "Seen the paper this morning?" he questioned.

"Why, yes, Captain!" Bloomberg's voice was bright. "Fine article, sir, fine article. Does you and the *Horizon* credit. And," he winked conspiratorially at Roberts, "does a certain Sir Smothers no credit whatsoever, I'm glad to say."

Roberts watched him critically, then spoke, "You do realize that my name and my airship have a bad reputation in this town. You sure you still want to fly with us? It will be hard going and light wallets and..."

"Yes, Captain, I am sure," Bloomberg responded firmly. "Why, I've never been more sure of anything in my life." His smile stretched even further across his face. "I've done what my father asked of me and followed him into the postal business. He was proud as anything when I attained a postmaster position four years ago, and he went to his grave in peace last year, God rest his soul. I don't think Father wouldn't mind much if I followed an old dream, sir, and even if he did, Captain, well..." A wisp of impudence sailed across Bloomberg's face, "he's not around to object!"

Roberts laughed, but Bloomberg wasn't finished. Firmly, he continued, "I'm not much bothered by what that old Sir Smothers thinks about the *Horizon* and her crew, sir. I'll gladly shake hands with the captain of the *Horizon* if he still has a place on board for me."

Roberts' bark of laughter reverberated to the ceiling, and he slapped Bloomberg on the back. "I do, by Jove, I do, Pilot Bloomberg!" It would take some serious training before Bloomberg was flying the *Horizon* with the skill needed to keep her on course, but Roberts knew that the plump, bespectacled man in front of him had what it took to become an excellent pilot. *One down,* he thought to himself, feeling a bloom of hope lifting away some of the dark worry that had become an almost permanent companion.

As if on cue, the door to the Broken Spar swung open and the thumping swish of a construct leg signaled the entrance of another person. Roberts turned to see four men step into the bar, sight him across the dark room, and make toward him purposefully, three of them trailing obediently behind the tallest of their group. The leader sported a battered construct arm that stuck out of his left sleeve, and his right trouser leg ended with a metal peg that stomped heavily on the filthy floor. He was youngish, his unshaven face grinning in that special bright way that suggests the smiler is overly confident, half-mad or both.

The other three consisted of a thin, balding fellow with a limp and an enormous nose like the prow of a ship; a short, stocky man sporting a wild tangle of grizzled beard and exceedingly luxurious eyebrows under which two tiny eyes gleamed brightly; and a scarecrow of a man whose overlarge feet, head, and hands were almost comically out of place on his thin frame. Unlike their leader, these three were solemn-faced and waited quietly behind the metal-limbed man, whose glassy smile had yet to leave his face.

With a clang of metal and the whooshing hiss of poorly sprung pistons, the man presented himself in front of Roberts and whipped off a good-humored salute. "Greetings, sir! Would you be Captain Roberts of the *Horizon*?" he inquired heartily, his resonant voice filling the room.

"I am," Roberts acknowledged evenly, assessing the quartet carefully.

"Pleasure to meet you, sir," the man said. "Name's Barking Jack. Not what my momma named me, but it's what I answer to." He waved a hand at the trio behind him. "The fellow with the nose would be Sparrowman, Long Tom's the one with hands like shovels, and this short fellow here is Big Tom." The men nodded as their names were mentioned but said nothing; Barking Jack was clearly running the show.

"My fine companions and I heard that you were in need of some men on the good airship *Horizon*," Barking Jack continued, his grin deepening. “Truth was, we heard about it before you thought to ask, Captain."

Roberts was surprised at the statement but he kept his face impassive, waiting for the next words. Barking Jack had the look of a man who enjoyed an audience and had a tale to tell that he was in no hurry to finish.

Barking Jack looked pleased with himself. "I heard of your ship nigh on a week past, Captain, right here in this bar. Word had it there was a blazing fast bird in the sky that outstripped an airship owned by Sir Smothers. Well, that gentleman carries a fine reputation for being a ruthless bastard, so I kept my ears open for more news." He tapped the side of his nose significantly. "A little bird told me that I'd be hearing of this airship again, and this time with a name for her."

"Well, wouldn't you know it?" Barking Jack continued confidently despite Roberts' deadpan expression. "Not seven days went by but there was word in this morning's newspaper about the airship *Horizon* and her ten-hour flight to Larne."

Gesturing to Big Tom, he continued. “Big Tom here is what you might call the secretary of our crew. Knows his letters, he does, enough to read that fine article in this morning's paper to the rest of us. I said to myself, 'Barking Jack, here's a captain that will shortly be finding himself in need of men crazy as he is.' And I say crazy with the most sincere of complements, Captain.”

The construct hand twitched as if moved by some internal flux or madness from its owner because Barking Jack's eyes were growing brighter. “Only a crazy son of a mother would risk the wrath of Sir Smothers. A man like you, Captain, I take my hat off to. 'Barking Jack', I said to myself, 'there's the type of man for you to serve under.' So here I am with my crew, Captain. We'd be glad to join a crazy man if he'll have us.”

Barking Jack tapped himself on the chest. “I'm a pilot, sir, born with a wheel in my hand!”

He moved a finger to the man with the enormous nose. “Sparrowman here can fix any engine you set him to and he's a blessed man, he is. Survived two falls from an airship and all he had to show for it was a twisted leg! That's why we call him Sparrowman, sir, he must have wings that brought him back down to the ground."

The thin man was pointed out next. “Long Tom's the finest catwalk man you'll find in Europe. Not one much for cold, but he'll handle whatever heat and steam you throw at him. You can guarantee nary a leak in your airbags when Long Tom's on the catwalk.”

The shortest man of the quartet was introduced last. “Big Tom's our Jack-of-all-trades airman,” Barking Jack continued. “From her bowsprit to her tiller, he knows an airship like the back of his hand. Big Tom here is steady as she goes and reliable as a compass.”

Roberts measured the crew carefully. Barking Jack had the swaggering confidence often found in men who spent their days trusting their luck and their lives to a network of steam-filled canvas balloons hovering hundreds of feet above ground. The four had the weather-beaten, worn look of workers accustomed to long hours slaving under the sun, and all but Barking Jack carried old steam burn scars. Of the four, only Barking Jack had spoken, and Roberts wondered if the other three were capable of speech. However, he was in no position to be choosy. Four seemingly able-bodied airmen had presented themselves for hire, unfazed by the *Horizon*'s standing with the Smothers empire and nary a word about wages or flight destinations. There was work in London for skilled airmen, but the four had deliberately chosen the *Horizon* over more lucrative positions elsewhere.

These thoughts flashed quickly through Roberts' mind as four pairs of eyes gazed at him expectantly. Finally, he nodded. "Well, gentleman, we'll try you out and see what the *Horizon* makes of you." The four men looked capable and experienced, but he wanted to see them in action before he made his decision. Although his current hiring options were severely limited, it was dangerous have unskilled or untrustworthy men on board. The four could help take the *Horizon* on a test flight while Roberts observed them and made up his mind.

Barking Jack's smile revealed two gleaming rows of teeth, a gold one flashing in the upper deck, and there was a tint of mischief in his eyes. "Much thanks, Captain," he replied.

During the interchange, Bloomberg sat quietly at Roberts' side, and with a gesture, Roberts introduced him to the newcomers. "This is Michael Bloomberg, our other pilot. He freed the *Horizon* from a pirate harpoon snare over the Irish Sea a few days past, and he's the most murderous former postmaster you'll find roaming the skies."

Bloomberg's chest swelled visibly under the complement, and he practically levitated off the bar stool. The four men assessed him measuredly, taking in the pale skin, soft hands, and overly plump frame of one who spends his days indoors. Next to them, the once-postmaster looked cosseted and weak, and Roberts suspected that Bloomberg was due some hazing from the rest of the crew to test his mettle. There was no room for weakness on an airship, and a man who couldn't fulfill his duties would find little sympathy.

Roberts decided that this wasn't the time to inform Barking Jack that part of his duties would be helping Bloomberg get up to scratch in his piloting skills. Instead, he slid off the stool and nodded at Tom before turning to his five new crew members. “Fall in,” he commanded. “We're returning to the airship.”

Chapter Twelve

There were some murmurs of discontent from the new crew when they first clapped eyes on Oboe. Most airmen didn't mind serving next to non-European crew members but often drew the line at being commanded by one. In response, Oboe merely peered down at the new crew members from his vantage point of more than six feet and smiled in a way which promised creative and all-encompassing misery to anyone who showed disrespect. This quelled any lingering complaints, and Roberts quickly dispensed introductions and orders.

"We're taking her out for a quick run," he announced. "Full bags out in two hours." With that, he deliberately stood back to see how Barking Jack's crew would step into their positions. An airship demanded highly skilled crew members to keep her aloft, and the four new men would have to prove their worth if they wanted permanent positions on board. The *Horizon* was in dire need of all the hands she could get, but incompetent or lazy airmen represented the highest risk factor on an airship, and the human error rate for crashes was consistently high.

Roberts was pleased to see his new crew members quickly set to work with practiced smoothness and integrate easily into the older crew. Halloway's shop was soon abuzz with bodies moving expertly and swiftly as the men prepped the *Horizon* for liftoff.

Bloomberg was an entirely different story. Although he was eager to take on his share of the work, his softer hands gave evidence of only nodding acquaintance with manual labor. Luckily, Roberts had an answer for that: his first mate. After some basic instructions, Roberts happily dumped Bloomberg on Oboe's hands and turned his attention to other matters, leaving the new pilot to discover just how badly out of condition he was and how much he had to learn.

Activity burst forth as the *Horizon* was carefully raised to the opened ceiling in preparation for departure, the shouts of men and the squealing of gears filling the air. While her airbags inflated, Roberts ordered Barking Jack to the helm. "We'll hoist her to the roof and take off from there. Take the wheel and let's see your piloting skills." The man grinned and grasped the wheel, metal and flesh fingers wrapping around the sun-bleached wood as Roberts eyed him. Construct arms, unless well-made, were not known for their finesse, and he wondered how carefully Barking Jack would be able to manipulate the wheel. "She's a sensitive little thing," he warned Barking Jack sternly. "I'll have no ham-fisted manhandling of her."

"Worry you not, Captain," the pilot responded. "I'll stroke her like a kitten."

"Good," Roberts grunted. The novelty of owning his own airship was still too fresh for him to like anyone's hands on the wheel except his own, but with more crew members to supervise, it was time to turn the helm over to someone else. Barking Jack radiated confidence, and although Roberts knew he would be watching his new pilot like a hawk for the next several runs, he had a strong feeling that Barking Jack would rise to the challenge.

The activity increased to a fever pitch as the *Horizon* drew closer to takeoff. Halloway was cursing fluidly in the boiler room, Jenkins at his side and Sparrowman bearing up under their frenzied commands. Long Tom was stalking the catwalks inside the envelope with Carter and Oboe, checking carefully for leaks. Farrington, a fresh bandage around his arm, was relaying information to Big Tom and barking orders to a harried Bloomberg, all the while avoiding his captain's eye. Roberts had almost left Farrington behind at the shop to rest but with five new crew members to supervise, he needed people on board he could trust, injured or not.

Harding was standing off to the side, well away from most of the bustle, and observing the proceedings with a wary eye. Roberts shot him a look and called out, "Having second thoughts, are you?" over the babble of voices.

"Certainly not!" Harding barked back, but there was a decidedly green tinge to his face. Earlier in the day, he had reluctantly confessed to Roberts that he had never set foot on an airship. Roberts had insisted that Harding accompany them for the evening flight. He didn't need another chronically airsick crew member on board; Captain Albert's repeated bouts of nausea had been quite enough to manage. As *Horizon* began rising into the slack of her ropes and bobbing a bit in enthusiasm, Harding clung grimly to her side, belligerent determination written on his face.

Finally, Carter bellowed out, "All ready, Captain!"

Nodding, Roberts commanded, "Untie! We're casting off!" A chorus of responses chimed the crew's obedience as last-minute preparations were completed and the airship continued to rise slowly. She bucked and swayed a little under Barking Jack's hands, but the man merely chuckled and whistled merrily as he directed the *Horizon* upwards to cruising height. She was a bit shaky as she leveled off, and Roberts watched Barking Jack carefully as the new pilot delicately steered the airship forwards, already getting a feel for her moods and whims. Once she topped out at a cruising altitude of five hundred feet, she calmed down and primly sailed forward, obedient to Barking Jack's directions.

The sun was beginning to settle down for the evening and the winds were still as the *Horizon* sailed through the air, London's vastness spread out under her hull. Roberts ordered Barking Jack to direct the airship toward the northern edge of the city, hoping to keep away from any airship bearing Smothers' crest. Since there wasn't much lift to be found in the warm summer air, traffic over London was light, which suited

Roberts just fine. He could see a few vessels to the south, and there were two airships a fair piece behind the *Horizon* and going in her direction, but they were keeping their distance. Roberts didn't pay them much mind.

Barking Jack was careful to keep the *Horizon* under fifteen knots and above three hundred feet as they crossed London, and Roberts was pleased to see his new pilot stringently obeying flight regulations. There had been a sharp increase in national air flight rules during the past few years after an airship collision over London two years ago had left all fifty-seven crew members on both airships and eleven people on the ground dead. The disaster had swiftly pushed forward several new fight laws, and London's skies were now heavily regulated. Any airship breaking regulation would be swiftly subject to harsh penalties, and its captain risked destroying his career. With enough troubles already on his plate, Roberts wasn't about to tempt fate by taking liberties with the law. The last thing he needed was for Her Royal Majesty's Air Force to take a deep, personal interest in the *Horizon*.

As the *Horizon* sailed forward, the sounds of Halloway shouting in the boiler room increased exponentially: he was apparently keeping Jenkins and Sparrowman on the hop, but Roberts also detected a slight change in the engines. By the level of Halloway's bellows, Roberts surmised that the recalibrations had not gone off quite as well as intended, but he wasn't worried. The only thing to fear from Halloway's tinkering was that he never knew when to leave well enough alone. A mechanical problem had yet to defeat him.

The *Horizon* was leaving plumes of steam behind her but no smoke, thanks to the anthracite fueling the boiler. Airships needed constant cleaning and painting to counteract the incessant damage and filth of bituminous coal smoke, but anthracite burned cleanly and was virtually smokeless. That and the wonderful efficiency Halloway's boiler and engines were pulling out of the new fuel source had quickly overcome Roberts' initial dislike of using expensive anthracite over standard bituminous. The thought of coal sent him reaching for the com device, and he yelled down at the boiler room, “How's she running for fuel?”

“Eating too damned much of it,” Halloway bellowed back. "We keep shoveling it in by the scoop, and she keeps demanding more."

"What's wrong?" Roberts questioned.

"Not sure," Halloway responded, but his voice was relatively genial. "Keep your shirt on, Gavin. I'll find out why.”

“Take your time,” Roberts sounded back, not terribly concerned. The *Horizon* was chugging along gamely without any apparent effort, and they had just left the outskirts of London behind them. Barking Jack was still whistling cheerfully at the wheel, and the other men were busy with their work, with Oboe's critical eye carefully monitoring the new crew members. Bloomberg was still determinedly struggling to match pace with the rest of the crew, and Harding, ashen-faced, was managing to retain both his composure and the last meal he had eaten. For the moment, all was peacefully productive on board the *Horizon* and even the minor engine problem below couldn't disrupt morale.

Roberts glanced idly over the top deck, enjoying the fact that for this moment in time, there wasn't much for him to do. He was aware that the two distant airships had followed them out of London and were still sailing, apparently benignly, behind the *Horizon.* His eyes kept flicking over to them, but neither showed any sign that they were spoiling to start a fight or do anything other than simply fly in the same general direction as the *Horizon. Just going our way, that's all,* Roberts thought but he could not shake a nagging feeling that something was about to go terribly wrong. The brilliant sun was a fireball of orange to portside and the English countryside was under their gondola, all a peaceful sight to an airman. Still, the hairs on the back of Roberts' neck prickled with a strange alarm as the minutes rolled past.

Such thoughts were foolish, he knew that. No airship captain with a grain of sense would take it into his head to attack another airship with London just a few miles behind them. The two ships were clearly not pirate vessels: any brigand airship entering London airspace was begging to be shot out of the skies. Even so, Roberts could not push those worries out of his head, and finally he moved to the com device. "Oboe, report to the helm," he commanded, his eyes not leaving the two airships. They were closer now, he was sure of it. As he waited impatiently for his first mate to materialize, both airships suddenly kicked into high gear in an impressive burst of speed, their prows pointed at the *Horizon.*

"Captain!" Barking Jack called out sharply, his cheerful expression twisted with surprise.

"I see them," Roberts replied in measured, controlled tones. He wasn't sure what the two airships wanted, but he didn't intend to stick around to find out. Bellowing into the com device, Roberts barked out, "We have two approaching airships at six o'clock! They don't look like hostiles but I want every man alert! Prepare for possible enemy action!"

In a few seconds, it became glaringly apparent that evasive maneuvers were needed and quickly. Cannons appeared on board the other two airships and swung around to aim directly at the *Horizon* as both vessels honed in on their target, smoke pouring from their boilers like lava from a volcano. When Roberts saw the muzzles pointing at his airship, he had a moment of peeved incredulousness. *I don't believe it,* he growled to himself. *We're going to get bloody shot out of the sky ten miles from London and by English airships.*

He had little time to ponder the blasted unfairness of the situation; with no cannons on board the *Horizon,* they needed to get her out of firing range and fast. "Enemy approaching!" Roberts barked out briskly, keeping his voice level as if having to dodge cannon fire several miles out of London was a routine occurrence. "Every man to his station! Halloway, Jenkins, give me everything you've got! We've got to outrun them!"

"Barking Jack!" Roberts bellowed, whipping around to face his new pilot who gave him a brisk nod. "Let's see how good you are at dodging cannon fire!" Barking Jack expertly spun the wheel, sending the gondola listing out to the side and tipping the decks severely. "Hold tight and stay in the ship!" Roberts bellowed to all who could hear him as his men scrambled to obey orders. Behind the *Horizon,* the pursuing vessels also banked sharply and were veering to intercept their prey.

Shouts poured along the *Horizon* as crew members yelled information and orders at each other. Through the ensuing thunder of voices, the engines sounded a high, worried squeal that raked its sharp fingers along Roberts' spine. He knew the *Horizon* was in trouble and as he fought his way to the helm, he could feel his airship faltering in the sky.

"Speed! What have we got for speed, Barking Jack?" Roberts demanded when he reached the wheel.

"Twenty-five knots, Captain!" the pilot called back. His face was tight with restrained anger, but his manner was cool, each movement controlled and purposeful.

"Not good enough! Divert more steam to the engines!"

"Did so, sir! I need more!"

Roberts half-ran, half-stumbled to the com device and yelled into it, "Halloway! Jenkins! Give it all you got! *Now*!"

"Tell that to this damned bird of yours!" Halloway screamed back, his voice nearly drowned by the clang of malfunctioning engines. "She's fighting me every step of the way and a blasted valve just shot loose! We're doing an emergency patch job, and you're not getting more steam until we fix it!"

Snakelike, Roberts' head whipped back to the speed gauge. The *Horizon* was fluttering between twenty-four and twenty-six knots, not nearly fast enough to outrun her enemies. The two vessels behind them were gaining fast. In a few moments, the *Horizon* would be within cannon range.

Roberts jerked his spyglass out and jammed it against his eye, scanning the oncoming airships for clues to their intentions. They were lightweight escort ships, ostensibly military but most likely connected to the Smothers empire. The indomitable tycoon was friends with every admiral and commander that ruled the air, and he had plenty of favors to cash in from various parties. Smothers had doubtlessly found a few sympathetic ears with enough power to order, if not an attack, at least a harassment on the *Horizon* and enough clout to keep the incident from going public.

Uniforms moved on the two oncoming airships, and weapons were being flourished with deadly intent. Roberts paused and weighed the situation carefully. From all appearances, it looked as if the two airships were poised to blow the *Horizon* from the skies, but he knew that even the vast authority of Sir Smothers didn't extend that far. Friend of the queen or no, the tycoon would have some explaining to do if word reached Her Majesty that he had ordered a peaceful merchant airship fired upon ten miles from London.

Oboe was suddenly at his captain's elbow, stoic as always, and Roberts passed him the spyglass. Peering through it, Oboe raised one eyebrow slightly. "Two military airships?" he questioned.

Roberts scoffed audibly. "Two ships deep in the pocket of Smothers."

"But for what reason?" Oboe questioned, then amended his statement. "Other that he has essentially declared you his mortal enemy, Captain."

"It's Smothers," Roberts snapped. "He's got too much money to need a reason; he only needs an excuse." Jamming the telescope back into his pocket, he hurried back to the com device and yelled into it, "Halloway, you better have some good news. We've got two airships on our arses, and they've got cannons pointed at us!"

"He's not going to shoot us out of the sky, you idiot!" Halloway barked back. "Even Smothers isn't that mad!"

Glancing back at the rapidly approaching airships, Roberts called into the device, "I wouldn't half bet on that, not while our feet are still off the ground. I'm not keeping us around long enough to find out if you're right."

"Just shut up and... Wait, no! Don't...*stop*!" Halloway's voice trailed off as his attention was diverted elsewhere. Several loud clanging sounds echoed from the device, then the *Horizon*'s engines whined loudly. Roberts' eyes jerked over to the speed device and saw the needle falter, then twitch down to twenty-two knots.

"Twenty-two knots!" Roberts thundered into the com device. "Halloway, whatever the problem is, fix it *now* and get us back up to speed!"

"We're trying, Captain!" Jenkins' voice was one angry, exasperated shout. Roberts let loose a frustrated growl and turned his attention back to the oncoming airships. They were practically riding the *Horizon*'s stern, and he could see them clearly, particularly the cannon muzzles pointed directly at their target. Short-flight, light, and agile, the military vessels were built to attack anything that threatened slower merchant airships. With the *Horizon* floundering helplessly in the sky, she was a regrettably easy target. Roberts watched in grim impotence as the approaching airships closed the distance and reached his little bird which was fighting valiantly in the air. *Well, what are you planning on doing next?* he thought, almost in irritation. *Your move.*

The two airships split formation and took sides, each zooming past the *Horizon* just a few feet from her envelope, almost squeezing it between their gondolas. Roberts could see faces on board looking down at him as, just as quickly, the airships broke and veered off, banking sharply for another run.

As they turned in almost mirror-perfect unity, Oboe observed their tight maneuver. "They're trying to intimidate us, Captain," he commented solemnly.

Roberts attempted a stab at humor. "Is it working?"

Oboe's mouth split to reveal a flash of gleaming teeth. "No, sir," he responded calmly.

Roberts' eyes did not leave the other airships as they wheeled around sharply. Faster and closer the second time now, they soared past the *Horizon*, one on each side as before, almost kissing her envelope with their wooden gondolas, then wheeled again. Roberts watched. Somehow he knew they would make three turns, and they did, the third time actually brushing the *Horizon*'s envelope and almost snagging it.

After the third pass, the airships wheeled sharply and sailed away, plumes of smoke streaking across the red-tinted sky. Roberts could hear mocking cries rising on the wind. He glared murderously after the vessels as they turned their noses back toward London.

On board the *Horizon*, the frantic activity began to calm down as the crew realized that the danger had passed and no serious harm had been inflicted. However, everyone on board looked unnerved and orderly discipline threatened to break down by the second.

Crew members began moving Roberts' way, but Carter beat them all, his eyes blazing with fury. "Captain!" he barked out, "What the...?"

"They were just trying to rattle us, Carter," Roberts cut him off, forcing his voice to answer calmly and firmly stamping down the boiling rage that threatened to spill over his controlled exterior. "I suspect Smothers wanted to send us a little message, namely that we are no longer welcome in this airspace and it's in our best interest to leave town."

"We should report those ships, sir!" Farrington spat out angrily as he shoved his way forward.

Roberts shook his head. "Think anyone would listen to us? Also, what evidence do we have?" The two airships had done their work well: the *Horizon* had nary a scratch and no damage had been inflicted. No authority figure would believe any complaint Roberts or anyone else on the *Horizon* raised, and doing so would only make the situation worse.

"What do we do now, sir?" William's tremulous query broke through the rising babble of voices. The practicality of his question redirected some of the mindless anger threatening to engulf the crew.

Roberts considered the question carefully. It was no idle threat that had been sent their way, and the message had been clear. London was no longer safe for the *Horizon* or anyone attached to her. Their best option was to turn tail and leave the city, but with a blown valve, the *Horizon* needed repair work before she was at her full strength. Halloway needed to clear his shop of anything that shouldn't fall into the wrong hands, Harding likely had other medical supplies at his office he needed, and there were scarcely any provisions on board. Going back was hazardous, but so was leaving town on a poorly functioning airship.

After a few moments of consideration while eyes watched him carefully, Roberts hurriedly made up his mind. "We're heading to Knockdowns," he announced sharply.

Knockdowns air wharf was at the opposite end of London from Smothers' domain, and its small number of rickety berths were primarily occupied by the rough, dangerous, and desperate. Docking at Knockdowns was risky, but it had the advantage of being a place that Smothers airships never visited. The *Horizon* would hopefully escape scrutiny there. Her crew could spend an uneasy night at Knockdowns keeping a vigilant watch for any potential saboteurs while they made repairs to the *Horizon* and finished last-minute tasks, then leave before dawn rose.

Wary and with a goodly amount of reluctance, the crew brought the *Horizon* back into London's airspace, every eye carefully scanning the heavens for a renewed attack. Thankfully, the darkening skies held few other airships, and Knockdowns was nearly deserted when the *Horizon* touched down on a rickety berth. Roberts saw no other souls on the wharf for almost a half hour before the wharf master, a rough-looking fellow of advancing years, shambled carelessly up to the airship to collect a docking fee.

Roberts dropped more than the demanded amount into the wharf master's filthy palm and said shortly, "You look like a man who knows when to hold his tongue. My crew needs some time to tend to our ship with no questions asked." He didn't expect further inquiries: airship captains chose Knockdowns precisely because the wharf's regular clientele usually meted out swift repercussions for unwelcomed inquisitiveness.

The wharf master shrugged, magnificently uninterested. "You and everybody else. Suit yourself, Captain," he growled. With that he left, disappearing into the murky shadows as Roberts turned his attention back to the *Horizon*. Halloway was causing no small amount of fuss, barking orders and dispensing free criticism to anyone within eye contact. As he made his way toward the recalcitrant engineer, Roberts was already plotting out the next few hours. Although Halloway's services were direly needed on board, someone had to clean out his shop before Smothers beat him to the task.

Approaching Halloway, Roberts clamped a hand down on the engineer's shoulder and hauled him away from a small but resentful knot of crew members. "You and I are going back to your shop, Halloway," Roberts pronounced bluntly as he towed the inventor along with him. "We're leaving town as soon as we can, and you'd best grab anything back home you don't want falling into the wrong hands."

Halloway shook off Roberts' hand, his natural disinclination toward physical contact objecting to the gesture. "Who said I'm going anywhere with you?" he snapped peevishly, his mouth tight.

With one quick snatch, Roberts grabbed Halloway's shirt and pulled his face forward several inches. "*God dammit,* Halloway," he growled in a deep, barely controlled voice. His patience had reached its limits and Halloway had gotten on his last nerve. "You're in this as deep as I am, but you're on *my* bloody ship, and I damned well am giving the orders around here!" he barked irately.

A shove and Halloway was staggering backwards, his emaciated frame scrabbling to regain his balance before he collapsed to the deck. Roberts advanced, grimly pleased to see

Halloway too shocked to object, the inventor's ingrained mulishness abandoning him as he stared at Roberts with trepidation. Towering over the recumbent Halloway, Roberts snapped, "You and I are leaving *now* to go back to your shop, then all of us are getting out of London. I don't want to hear another damned word from you unless it's 'Yes, Captain'."

With that, he stepped directly over Halloway, purposefully giving him a kick in the process and well aware that Halloway was long overdue for any number of kickings. The engineer's brilliance was overshadowed only by his complete intractability and marked lack of social skills. However, since Halloway was going to be a member of the crew for the foreseeable future, he was going to have to learn to obey orders and like it, particularly in times like this when stubbornness could get everyone on board killed. With the lives and well-being of twelve men in his hands, Roberts wasn't going to tolerate any insubordination. He was done making allowances for Halloway's overweening eccentricity.

The rest of the crew, sensing a storm of authoritative fury was about to break loose, scattered at Roberts' approach, adroitly scuttling off to whatever tasks needed completing. Only Oboe remained, impassively watching his captain as Roberts stalked forward, out for blood and taking no nonsense. More harshly than he meant, he barked at his first mate, "You and Halloway and I are going back to his shop. He's got to clean out the place. There's too much there that I don't want others getting their hands on."

Oboe nodded solemnly, then stated quietly, "That may be dangerous, Captain."

"I know," Roberts said shortly. "We'll get in and out and make it fast." However, he knew in his boots that cleaning out Halloway's shop of everything that shouldn't stay behind would be no easy matter. The premises were littered valuable items, a lot of it heavy machinery that was too big for the *Horizon* to carry. They could at least take Halloway's schematics and blueprints, although the inventor stored most of his plans inside his head. The rest they would simply have to leave behind in unfounded hopes that inquisitive minds wouldn't strip Halloway's shop of anything promising.

Across the deck of the *Horizon*, Roberts caught Barking Jack watching him intently. With a scowl, he stomped towards the new pilot. "You and your crew are free to leave," Roberts stated bluntly. "You've all seen what the *Horizon* is up against. I need men to crew her but she's as good as crashed if I can't trust the men running her."

Barking Jack paused, and for a moment his face held nothing but sober consideration. Then his bright, glassy grin broke forward, chasing all seriousness from his expression. "I told you, Captain, you'll be needing some crazy mothers on board your ship here, yes I did," he replied almost jovially, but his light tones were girded with steel. "We'll not be daunted by the likes of that great bastard Smothers," Barking Jack added.

"While I have a distinct feeling I will regret this decision," Harding's sardonic voice followed Barking Jack's words, "someone has to look after Farrington's arm or remove it if the gangrene spreads." The surgeon bore a look of weary resignation as he clumped forward to stand at Roberts' side. More quietly, he added, "I don't think anyone on board has a mind to abandon the *Horizon*, Gavin. I'd concentrate on getting your men out of London in one piece."

As neatly as that, it was settled. There wasn't much time to waste. With a few barked volleys, Roberts dispensed orders to the crew. Jenkins and Sparrowman were set to work on the blown valve, which they could easily set to rights without Halloway's assistance. Harding left the *Horizon* with Barking Jack, both bound for the surgeon's office to pick up his equipment and personal items. The rest of the crew were given strict instructions regarding security on board. There were no guards at Knockdowns, and any captain careless about his airship's safety was asking for it to be raided or stolen. The type of airmen who regularly peopled Knockdowns would think nothing of bashing another man's brains out for a few farthings, and Roberts made a point of drilling this into everyone's head.

Roberts left his crew with a final instruction: if the three men were not back at the *Horizon* by dawn, the remaining crew was to abandon ship and leave town. Roberts knew that if he was apprehended by Smothers, retaining possession of the *Horizon* would be the last of his worries. He wasn't going to risk his crew by insisting they wait at the airship for too long, lest they also fall into Smothers' hands.

Knockdowns was in a crime-riddled part of town, but two large men with a third man in their midst would make potential attackers rethink a robbery. As an extra precaution, Roberts had two revolvers conspicuously displayed in his belt, and the slow-burning anger emanating off him in waves was a further deterrent to any would-be mugger. Part of him would have welcomed the chance to exchange a few blows, but no one potential punching bags offered themselves and the three men made their way through the dark London streets unmolested. Halloway was uncharacteristically silent, meekly following Roberts' lead, and he said nothing until the men halted at the filthy street leading to his shop.

The long cobblestone passageway was dark and silent, and the lone gas lamp burning fitfully in the night illuminated little but shadows. The moon gave faint definition to the factories edging the street, and Halloway's shop was vaguely distinguishable amidst the other buildings, mainly because small flickers of light were emanating from its heavily-shuttered windows. Roberts' eyes narrowed at the sight, coolly noting the scattered beams flickering through cracks in the shutters. Someone was inside and, by the pattern of movement, it was more than just one person.

Halloway inhaled sharply. "How the hell did they get inside my shop?" he demanded, stepping forward indignantly.

Roberts restrained him. "*Easy,*" he growled. "We don't know how many of them are in there."

"Well, there bloody well won't be any of them left, not when Mary gets through with them!" Halloway snarled, pushing against Roberts' hand.

"*Easy*!" Roberts snapped. "We can't go rushing in blind, not until we know how many there are."

Halloway paused, his face twisting with the effort of holding back his impulse to blatantly ignore Roberts' edict, but he restrained himself with uncharacteristic quietness. Oboe stood watchful, every muscle stilled yet poised for action. For the moment, there was only the sound of three sets of lungs breathing carefully. Roberts' mind raced, ideas churning violently, weighing options. There could be a handful of intruders, or dozens. That they had breached Halloway's complex defense system and found their way inside was particularly troubling. Leaving the scene and returning promptly to the *Horizon* was clearly the most prudent of actions, but both Roberts and Oboe had survived numerous scuffles before and were not men to back down from a needed fight. Halloway had likely never experienced combat, but there were plenty of potential weapons inside his shop that only he could make full and creative use of in their defense.

A subtle movement at his elbow, and Roberts looked up to see Oboe's eyes gleaming with a strange light. Halloway was near manic with anger and mad, burning energy and Roberts could feel cold fire stoking to life in his belly, goading him forward as his mind formulated a plan of attack.

***　　　***　　　***　　　***

A few bright lanterns threw long fingers of light across Halloway's chaotic shop, illuminating the figures of men moving about. With hurried movements, they freely rummaged through the shaky piles of mechanisms and grubby stacks of paper. They looked up sharply when Roberts strode boldly through the mess and into a pool of light, visible and seemingly at ease. "Evening, gentleman," he said pleasantly.

A collective hiss swept the room and hands began reaching for various weapons. Alarm turned to surprise, then calculation, when they realized only one man was facing them. As they eyed Roberts, one or two faces began to twist in evil amusement. Coolly, he examined the room, taking in everything at a quick glance. Nine men faced him, and noises to his right told him that at least one more was somewhere in the building.

"Well, well, if it isn't the famous Captain Roberts," the biggest of the intruders sneered. Roberts eyed him levelly. He knew the face, and some fragment of memory unearthed a name: Hiram Tobben, one of Smothers' hired thugs kept around to do his dirty work. Roberts was frankly surprised that Smothers had sent out grunts to do the work of intellectuals; it would take well-trained minds to sift through Halloway's mess and pick out the important bits. Perhaps they were only here to secure the premises until the *Horizon* was well out of London, and Smothers' best minds were free to cherry-pick Halloway's shop for what they wanted. Another distinct possibility was that the thugs were there solely to beat a solid message into any member of the *Horizon*'s crew foolish enough to return to base.

Whatever their mission, Roberts had no intention of allowing it, but with nine opponents moving his way, the situation was turning dire. As the first of the men stepped toward him, Roberts' ears cocked to catch any sound of Oboe and Halloway inside the shop. They needed time, and he had to stall as long as he could, even as the men began closing in on him. Doing his best to remain nonchalant, Roberts reached for a cigar that had been nesting in his breast pocket for weeks. Time and movement had warped the cigar into a dried, squashed tube, but he lit it anyway, taking his time and watching out of the corner of his eyes as the men sized him up.

"Sir Smothers is not a happy man right now," Tobben commented, a grin on his face. He was closest to Roberts and plainly the ringleader of the motley crew. Roberts didn't move, lazy smoke drifting off the end of the cigar as Tobben reached inside his coat and withdrew a set of knuckle dusters which he slid onto his fingers with some theatrical care. The other men began reaching for clubs and other blunt objects, and the definitive way they handled their weapons bespoke of their ability to cause pain. *So that's how it's going to be,* Roberts thought with a sniff. Smothers' justice was quick and brutal and while he might not stoop to outright murder, there were so many ways to make a man prefer a quick death to the alternative. The two revolvers in Roberts' belt clamored for attention, but he resisted the urge to draw them. Smothers' men would be armed with more than clubs, and an aimed gun leaves a man with few options at his disposal.

"Smothers may not be happy, but this is London. Here we've got laws against breaking and entering," Roberts said evenly. "You gents are trespassing on private property." He took a puff on the cigar as his ears strained urgently for information concerning Halloway and Oboe's whereabouts. He was rapidly running out of time, and the intruders were closing in fast.

Tobben's snort echoed ominously. "What, you gonna stop us, Roberts?" he drawled. The other eight men eyed Roberts with malicious glee, clubs and fists at the ready.

The groaning thump of something heavy broke through the tense air. Heads jerked to attention as one ponderous footfall followed another. With an ominous squeal of gears, Mary thundered into the light, directly behind Roberts. He didn't move as the automaton lurched forward, blocking the narrow passage to the door with her metal frame. Halloway was at the controls, hidden behind the mecha's steel-plated torso and prepared to turn his creation loose on the intruders.

Something buzzed like a hornet's nest and Oboe appeared at the other end of the room, arms cradling a long metal shaft whose pronged end crackled with a strange energy. Roberts had seen the device before; it was some rudimentary weapon that Halloway had cobbled together purely as an intellectual exercise and then abandoned for other pursuits. As a rule, weapons weren't something Halloway paid much heed to, and there was no telling if the device in Oboe's hands would fire, falter, or explode if pressed into combat. Nevertheless, the energy sparking from its business end promised all matter of interesting pain, and Oboe held it at the ready, poised to ram it into the nearest available target.

With a shout, two more men came roaring out of the shadowy recesses of Halloway's shop, bringing the total number of intruders to eleven. Despite their numbers, Smothers' men were hemmed in, caught between the automaton blocking the door and Oboe's odd weapon at the rear. Roberts surveyed the motley crew, smoke trailing off the end of his mangled cigar while they sized up Mary and Oboe, weighing the merits of combat verses retreat. The faint hissing of Mary's pistons were the only sound in the tense air.

"You boys have about five seconds to scarper," Roberts said, his pleasant tones darkening to harshness. More than one man looked perfectly willing to do so, but their leader sneered and took two menacing steps forward, daring Roberts to throw the first punch.

"You and what army, Roberts?" Tobben spat derisively. "Oh, looky, you've got a fancy metal toy." His voice rose in derision. "Why, we're all just pissing our boots in fear." The mecha was an impressive sight, but currently her metal limbs were stationary. The men darted a look at Halloway, working out the connection between the inventor and the machine and realizing that taking out Halloway would render the automaton useless. For all her strength, Mary was relatively slow, and a man with good reflexes and enough courage could get past her defenses and target Halloway. Their leader's boldness was putting heart in the intruders and they were starting to press their way forward, eyes sharpening with the onset of battle.

"*I said leave.*" Roberts' voice would have cut steel, but the men were advancing, a few nervously but others brazenly, emboldened by their numbers. Halloway's hands were busy at the controls and Mary stirred, one massive arm reaching forward with an ominous creak of gears. The intruders froze, bravado deflating under the sight of self-propelled metal moving their way, and one took a quick step backwards out of healthy regard for his own skin. Something groaned deep in the automaton's innards and with a screech, she froze in place, arm outstretched. Halloway cursed fluently as he wrestled the recalcitrant levers to force the automaton back to life.

"Get 'em, boys!" Tobben bellowed. As one, the eleven men roared forward, fists and assorted weapons at the ready. The fastest one reached Roberts who ducked at the last second. A clenched hand punched through the air and almost made contact with his nose. A second punch followed a heartbeat later, and this one Roberts managed to block before returning it with one of his own. His hard fist met the thug's jaw halfway and laid him out cold on the ground.

A thunderous voice bellowing an unknown language cut through the yells of battle as Oboe stormed into the knot of intruders, weapon primed. There was a crackle of pent-up energy and one of the intruders twitched violently as Oboe rammed the tip of the rod directly into his back and pulled the trigger. The man fell to the ground in a tangle of convulsing limbs, and four of his mates rushed forward, bent on getting the weapon out of Oboe's hands. Gracefully, Oboe twisted and spun while the weapon buzzed alarmingly, spitting out sparks. He managed to connect with another opponent, but his weapon's energy seemed to be draining because the man collapsed to his knees, stunned but not immobilized. The other three went for Oboe's weapon, trying to wrestle it out of his hands as he struggled to retain mastery of it.

Roberts, meanwhile, was lashing out with both fists and feet at any opponent who presented himself. He was dimly aware of Halloway's frantic cursing as the inventor struggled to wake the automaton back to life. Mary jerked and her metal arm swung through the air again. Seeing an opportunity, Roberts grabbed an intruder and whipped him around directly into the path of the automaton's arm. The man hit the metal limb with a heart-rending crunch, then slithered soundlessly to the floor. Mary's movements were erratic but she was moving again, and other intruders were closing in, warily searching for safe passage around a ton of mobile metal to Halloway.

Instinct warned Roberts a fraction of a second too late as pain exploded in his midsection, the blow almost collapsing his abdomen wall. As he staggered backwards, his cigar flew from his mouth and fell on a jumbled pile of oozing metal tins and battered barrels that leaked oils and lubricants. There was a loud "whump" as assorted flammable liquids caught the embers of the cigar and enthusiastically ignited, sending green-tinted flames licking greedily up into the air.

In an instant, the men turned their attention from the rousing fight to the climbing tower of flames which was quickly racing toward the roof. In the sudden chaos and alarm,

Roberts' quick assessment told him that five men were down and the remaining six were rapidly dissolving into panic. Tobben was bellowing scattered orders over the confused din, and three of his men raced to a narrow trough of dank water in the corner. With hurried, barely controlled movements, the men ferried buckets to the blazing tower of flames but the liquid only seemed to enrage the inferno. Roberts knew that fighting chemical fires with water was pointless at best, dangerous at worst, and the thugs clearly reached the same conclusion when their emptied buckets produced no results but increased flames.

Like a tsunami rolling toward an island, the flames raced through the building, eagerly gobbling up everything burnable. Halloway's premises were rich with spilled oil puddles and barrels of assorted flammables, and the fire grew by the second. As panic spread, Halloway abruptly abandoned Mary and raced for his workbench, hurriedly grabbing up piles of disorganized papers scattered across it. With that, Roberts knew that the building was doomed. Halloway had clearly given up all hope of quenching the flames and was simply trying to save what he could. Flames licked up the rafters, spreading eagerly throughout the cavernous workshop and racing toward the heavy door. In a few minutes, everyone inside would be trapped. It was time to move; every second counted in the hot, dangerous air.

With the automaton now minus her controller, the still-conscious thugs took to their heels and went charging around Mary toward the door, fleeing the billowing clouds of dark smoke. Five of them jerked back the heavy door and raced into the dark night, leaving the burning building in their wake. Tobben spotted Halloway's movements and bore down on him, knowing that whatever Halloway grabbed would be most valuable. The building was clearly doomed, but the thug's leader seemed determined to come away from the fiasco with at least some spoils of battle.

Roberts intercepted Tobben, shielding Halloway with his sturdy frame, his hands itching to draw his revolvers. The interloper grunted and whipped out several inches of gleaming steel, its edge reflecting the shimmering fire. As the knife streaked through the air, Roberts redirected his attacker's arm and clamped both hands down on the knife's handle to wrestle it loose. His opponent was prodigiously strong and the two men grappled fiercely for control of the blade, muscle matching muscle, grunts filling the hot air as flames crackled ominously around them and smoke clogged the air. Tobben was slowly overpowering Roberts. He felt the blade digging down, cutting into his arm as blood and pain blossomed on his skin. He saw an opening, and one well-placed knee connected solidly with Tobben's groin, dropping him in a clump of twitching agony and leaving Roberts in possession of the knife.

Panting, Roberts whipped around to survey the battle. It was over: six intruders were down and the rest had fled the building. Halloway raced across his shop, feverishly gathering up what he most valued in a desperate attempt to save some of his life's work from perishing in the flames. Oboe came roaring out of the raging inferno like some battle god of ancient times, his strange weapon still sparking erratically in his hands. His right arm was dripping blood, but his eyes burned bright with combat as he barreled towards his captain.

Roberts barked at him over the snapping roar of flames building by the minute, "OBOE! WE'VE GOT TO GET EVERYONE OUT!" The floor was littered with unconscious bodies. By all rights, they should have stayed there. The intruders had invaded Halloway's shop and vastly outnumbered Roberts' band, and he was under no compulsion to save them. He knew, though, without a snippet of doubt, that if any of Smothers' men died that night, there was no place distant enough for the *Horizon* to flee that she could ever be safe again. Burning was a terrible death and despite his fury, Roberts wasn't going to leave six unconscious men to die.

Without another word, Roberts and Oboe hastily picked up two of the downed intruders and began dragging them toward the door, adrenaline lending them strength. They lumbered across the crowded work floor, maneuvering the slumbering fighters to the door whose metal components were already growing warm to the touch. Flames were curling closer to the portal, and Roberts' lungs were heaving from breathing in the acrid, smoky air. The five who had fled the building had slammed the door behind them, and Halloway's intricate locking system had sealed the portal. Roberts' fingers flew across the door's latches, cursing Halloway's inventiveness and ineffective security measures as he feverishly undid the locks.

The door finally swung open into the dark night. He and Oboe pulled the two injured fighters clear of the burning building and put them down on the dirty cobblestones, then reentered the inferno for the others. Inside, a man was crawling on all fours, and he did not resist as Roberts pulled him upright and hauled him toward the door. Oboe seized a fourth man who was beginning to stir to life and lifted him bodily onto his shoulder, carrying him to safety out. This left two more men, Halloway, and very little time left. Flames were burning through the roof and from the sounds of it, the building's structural integrity had already been breached.

"HALLOWAY!" Roberts yelled as he and Oboe pushed back inside the building and made for the last two fallen enemies. "WE'VE GOT TO GET OUT NOW!" The air was choked with smoke, the situation perilous. Oboe bent and with graceful strength scooped a fifth man onto his shoulder and rose. The man dangled from Oboe's back while Roberts struggled with Tobben. The man was enormous, and Roberts felt like he was dragging a dead cow as he hoisted Tobben by his shoulders and dragged him from the building, shouting for Halloway with every step he took.

Barely had he cleared the building with the unconscious Tobben than Roberts heard the heart-sickening sound of fire-weakened timbers collapsing to earth as the building began to cave in, trapping Halloway inside. He swore frantically and dropped Tobben, bellowing Halloway's name as he raced toward the door.

"Captain!" Oboe restrained him. "No! It's too late."

Roberts fought against Oboe, desperate to get back inside. "HALLOWAY'S IN THERE!" he bellowed.

"No, Captain! Don't!" Oboe shouted but Roberts, drunk on adrenaline and desperation, threw off Oboe's restraint with a violent twist of his arms and raced directly inside the building. Inside was a hellish riot of light and searing heat, the air poisonous and painful to breathe. He pulled his shirt collar over his mouth to stave off the worst of the smoke as he pushed his way forward. There was nothing to see but flames and dark objects barring Roberts' way. He struggled to move deeper into the inferno, calling for Halloway, fighting the instinct to flee, desperately pushing away despair and panic as the searing heat pressed down on him like a vise.

You are going to die here, you fool, a voice in his head growled, reality blurring before his eyes as his ears roared with the sound of flames and impending doom. But there was a rhythmic sound rising above the advancing flames and the thudding sound of wood crashing to the earth. As in a dream, Roberts turned his head to see Mary stepping ponderously forward. She was pushing aside piles of hot tin and flaming wooden beams, something cradled in her metal arms.

"Halloway!" Roberts yelled, his voice rasping in his throat and his mind nearly drunk on the poisonous air. Stumbling forward, he fought his way across the floor to Halloway. The mecha kept moving forward, never stopping as Roberts reached her and tugged Halloway from her metal fingers. She neither resisted nor stopped, and Roberts forced his exhausted legs to move with the automaton. He lifted Halloway from her grasp with arms as limp as a deflated airbag and nearly doubled under the weight.

Halloway's emaciated frame sagged against Roberts as he stumbled toward the door, flames roaring around him and his vision narrowing to a tunnel, the exit dancing miles in the distance across a vast chasm. His knees buckled, weakness trembling in his legs as he willed himself forward, pushing desperately for one last burst of energy.

Hands were on him, lifting him up, steering him forward out of hell and toward the blessed street. Roberts gasped in great lungfuls of air and he staggered forward, dimly aware of Oboe at his left side, bolstering him up and guiding him out of the inferno to safety. With the last dredges of his strength, Roberts staggered out of the building with Halloway in his arms, Oboe keeping him upright until they collapsed onto the filthy cobblestones, coughing and retching in relief.

Roberts gasped painfully for air, never more thankful to be alive despite the beginning overtures of assorted injuries warming up their voices in complaint. Blood was running down his face and right arm and a cavalcade of burns were starting to blaze with pain. Oboe had lost some braids to the flames and blood was dripping down his arm, but he was alert and his eyes still blazed with the heat of battle. Halloway was unconscious, but his skinny chest was rising and falling in shallow breaths.

Noise was starting to approach. The roaring fire had caught the attention of others who were surging forward to lend their assistance. A fire in London could spread with wicked force, and reinforcements were arriving to ensure that no other buildings were affected. Through the haze of pain and shock, Roberts was dimly aware that he and his men needed to get clear of the area before questions started flying.

But first. Willing himself to his feet, Roberts shakily pulled himself erect and staggered toward Tobben, who was struggling to rise up to a sitting position. Roberts helped by reaching down, grabbing the man's shirt, and jerking him forward. "Tell Smothers what happened here," Roberts rasped, smoke still heavy in his lungs. "Tell him I could have left his men to die, but I didn't. I won't be so merciful next time."

Tobben's face was flushed with heat and his eyes were rimmed with fear as Roberts growled more deeply, "You tell that son of a bitch Smothers that we had an agreement, he and I, and no one else. If he ever threatens my men again, I'll let all of England know what a backstabbing, ruthless bastard he is."

Roberts threw Tobben aside but kept his eyes fixed on him. "Whatever vendetta he's got against me, he's to leave my crew alone. That's final. You tell him that to his face."

With that, he turned back to his men, every muscle screaming in protest. Oboe was reaching for Halloway to lift him up, but Roberts stopped him. He didn't trust anyone but himself to carry his old friend. Although his arms trembled, Roberts welcomed every ounce of Halloway's weight as a penance for the burning building that had been his fault and his alone. Bringing the *Horizon* to Halloway's doorstep had placed his old friend under the wrath of Smothers, and the aftermath of that decision was currently a violent mass of orange flames licking up into the dark night.

The roof to Halloway's workshop was caving in by the second as the fire consumed everything inside, eating away every timber and shingle and burning Halloway's life work to ashes. Roberts had seen enough fires to know that the brilliant flames would warp and melt the piles of metal, engines, and inventions crowding Halloway's building, leaving behind misshapen lumps. Even Mary would be a blob of melted gears and burnt wires, annihilation her reward for bearing her creator to safety. There was one small comfort and that was Smothers would find little of value once the flames died. However, such knowledge would be pitiful solace for Halloway when he awoke.

Roberts paused for one moment, eyes on the burning building, then set his jaw determinedly. Footsteps were nearing and people were racing forward to provide assistance, but with a burning building and several unconscious men at his feet, he was in no mood for questions. As one, he and Oboe disappeared quietly into the dark shadows, Halloway unconscious in Roberts' arms and their feet carrying them back to Knockdowns where the *Horizon* awaited.

Before the flames of Halloway's shop had begun to lessen, the *Horizon* was already bearing her crew away from London, the light of the moon shining on her canvas envelope and the roar of her engines gliding on the warm summer air, trailing plumes of steam and heat behind her.

Author's Note

This is the beginning of a series of what might be deemed "historical steampunk fiction": a merger of reality and fantasy, the probable with the wildly impossible, the mundane and the fantastical. The plot of this series was born out of some research rabbit trail I had wandered down awhile ago, something to do with shipping practices in the 19th century. The more I dug into the past, the more a host of interesting historical tidbits begged for attention: Corn Laws, cholera plagues, the Crimean War, dirigibles, the East India Trade Company. In the midst of this pleasant muddle of history, the *Horizon* rose to life, closely followed by Captain Roberts and trailed by a cavalcade of ideas that grew from one book to a trilogy to a series.

I was introduced to steampunk several years ago and have happily delved into a number of excellent books written in the steampunk genre. As I read and explored, I observed that the realm of steampunk is one heavily fueled by marvelous technology, all Tesla coils, sprockets, and wire circuitry, yet generally hazy on the specifics of how all this technical wizardry functions. What I have endeavored to do in my own writing is build a tale within the framework of reasonable scientific probability and create a steampunk setting where technology is less prevalent and more realistic. I have labored to provide somewhat of a theoretical basis for the operations of the *Horizon* and the other technological elements that make an appearance and have considered such issues as weight ratios, fuel consumption, and thermodynamics.

Even with this approach, a generous "suspension of disbelief" is still needed, particularly when it comes to the *Horizon* herself. A steam-powered airship is a thing of fantasy, and an aircraft built to the specifications of the *Horizon*, wooden hull and steam-filled airbags, would be lucky to get a few feet off the ground, much less transport twenty tons of cargo across the sea.

However, if useful airships had been available to Victorian England, those vessels would have filled the sky. London in the 19th century was the shipping center of the world, culminating in the economic super boom of 1872-1873, and the year this story unfolds (1854) was a peak shipping year in England. Had airships existed, they would have been a tremendous boon to transportation, neatly overstepping problems such as bad roads, mountains, impassible rivers, and other hazards to ground transportation. For this series, I have envisioned a 19th century world where airships and marine ships work in tandem to capitalize off each other's particular strengths. This partnership will be more fully explored in the next book and will play an important role throughout the series.

A great deal of both questions and research on my part has gone into this book, as well as many obvious technological and historical errors. Although I make absolutely no claim to engineering prowess, I am surrounded by those who do possess such knowledge and have been gracious enough to lend me their expertise. Such scientific accuracy as exists in this book, I owe to far superior minds than mine. The mistakes and obvious oversights are mine and mine alone. For these, I cheerfully offer up the explanation that this entire series is a merry romp of make-believe, history, and reality, and I humbly ask the reader to graciously overlook any laughable flaws have made in explaining how all this steampunk technology has come to pass.

About the Author

Melissa Ann Conroy is an Omaha, Nebraska native who has dabbled with words since birth. She earned a Master's in English literature (including a brief stint at Oxford), did freelance writing, and taught college-level writing courses for several years before finally getting serious about this whole "write a book" idea. *Steam on the Horizon* is her first novel.

Follow Melissa on

www.melissaannconroy.com

www.facebook.com/steamygirlpublishing